Franny wanted to lift her gaze and see his face. She kept staring into her coffee mug. "Yes, but did you bring jeans with you?"

"If you're willing to let me help with those bulls, you'll find out, won't you?" The warmth. The tease. The magnetism.

She closed her eyes. "You make me afraid." Afraid she'd find out too many other things about Shane Monroe and fall for him.

"I scare you?"

She opened her eyes and met his gaze, firmly, the way a woman with responsibilities would. "Because you aren't a cowboy. Because you don't aspire to the ranch life. And because you aren't going to stay in Second Chance."

"Meaning these long glances we exchange aren't predictive of a future together."

"Yes." Her pulse raced. She couldn't believe she'd told him that nothing was going to happen between them. Nothing *could* happen between them...

Dear Reader,

Harlan Monroe left a small town in Idaho to his twelve grandchildren. What did Second Chance mean to Harlan? Why did he leave it to his grandchildren? His adult heirs are going to find out. And while they're at it, they'll get a second chance at love.

Family dynamics fascinate me. Why are some brothers bossy and others laid-back? Why do some cousins get in your business and others just enjoy the occasional visit at the holidays? Shane Monroe falls into the bossy get-in-your-business camp. Got a problem? He can fix it. He's a great guy to have around when the going gets rough. And the going is definitely rough for rancher Franny Clark. This widowed single mom has a lot on her plate, including feral cattle and the fate of the family ranch. How in the world can a former CEO help her?

As with all the Monroe romances, there's a little laughter to go along with the journey to a happily-ever-after. I hope you come to love The Mountain Monroes as much as I do. Each book is connected but also stands alone.

Happy reading!

Melinda

HEARTWARMING

Lassoed by the Would-Be Rancher

USA TODAY Bestselling Author

Melinda Curtis

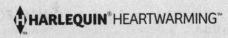

Recycling programs
for this product may
not exist in your area.

ISBN-13: 978-1-335-88953-9

Lassoed by the Would-Be Rancher

Copyright © 2020 by Melinda Wooten

This edition published by arrangement with Harlequin Books S.A.

For questions and comments about the quality of this book, please contact us at CustomerService@Harlequin.com.

Printed in U.S.A.

www.Harlequin.com

Prior to writing romance, award-winning *USA TODAY* bestselling author **Melinda Curtis** was a junior manager for a Fortune 500 company, which meant when she flew on the private jet she was relegated to the jump seat—otherwise known as the potty. After grabbing her pen (and a parachute) she made the jump to full-time writer. Melinda recently came to grips with the fact that she's an empty nester and a grandma, concepts easier to grasp than her former life jet-setting on a potty. Exciting news! Her Harlequin Heartwarming book *Dandelion Wishes* will soon be a TV movie!

Brenda Novak says *Season of Change* "found a place on my keeper shelf."

Jayne Ann Krentz says *Fool For Love* is "wonderfully entertaining."

Sheila Roberts says *Can't Hurry Love* is "a page turner filled with wit and charm."

Books by Melinda Curtis

Harlequin Heartwarming

The Mountain Monroes

Kissed by the Country Doc
Snowed in with the Single Dad
Rescued by the Perfect Cowboy

Return of the Blackwell Brothers

The Rancher's Redemption

Visit the Author Profile page
at Harlequin.com for more titles.

THE MOUNTAIN MONROES FAMILY TREE

Harlan Monroe (deceased)

- **Darrell Monroe (Oil/Finance)**
  - Holden Monroe
  - Bo Monroe
  - Kendall Monroe
- **Carlisle Monroe (Hotels/Entertainment)**
  - Shane Monroe (twin)
  - Sophie Monroe (twin)
  - Camden Monroe
- **Ian Monroe (Yacht Building)**
  - Bryce Monroe (twin, deceased)
  - Bentley Monroe (twin)
  - Olivia Monroe
- **Lincoln Monroe (Filmmaking)**
  - Jonah Monroe
  - Laurel Monroe (twin)
  - Ashley Monroe (twin)

PROLOGUE

WHEN FRANNY BOUCHARD was ten, there were three things she loved completely.

Sunny, her horse, who was the best cutting horse her father had ever trained, plus the most beautiful creature on the planet.

Kyle Clark, who was two years older than she was and had come over to her family's ranch the previous spring to help move cattle from the winter grazing pastures to the ranch proper. She'd beat him at the county-fair roping competition, and he'd bought her and his sister, Emily, ice cream to celebrate. He hadn't cared that he'd been beaten by a girl. Franny was going to marry that boy one day.

And stories. Franny loved stories. Scary stories, stories about aliens, westerns, Nancy Drew mysteries. Whatever books she could get her hands on, she read. And when she'd been allowed to go on her first cattle drive, she'd been ecstatic to learn that at night the adults sat around the campfire and told tales.

One particular night, Gertie Clark had promised to tell a story about Merciless Mike Moody, who was Second Chance, Idaho's very own bandit.

Franny shrugged deeper into her jacket, shivering more from excitement than the high mountain cold. Dinner had been eaten. Horses taken care of. The cattle were mostly quiet. The Clarks and the Bouchards gathered around the large fire beneath a blanket of bright stars.

"Granny Gertie." Emily sat next to Franny on a log. "Do we have to hear about Merciless Mike again?" She turned to Franny, rolling her eyes. "She tells that one all the time at home."

"But I never get to hear it," Franny said quickly. Well, except for the few times she'd spent the night at Emily's house. But that wasn't the same as hearing a story of the Old West while camping out on the high plains.

"It's got to be Merciless Mike." Gertie sat in her husband's lap. She may have been a grandmother, but she wasn't shy about public displays of affection. "You can't come out along the stage route and not talk about the brassiest bandit in the Idaho Territory."

"You can talk all you want," Franny's

father said, giving Franny a stern look. "Just remember it's a myth."

Gertie and Percy laughed. Those two laughed a lot.

And then Gertie got down to business, turning to Kyle and the two girls. "Some say Mike Moody grew up back east, a dandy of sorts. Others, like me, believe he was raised on a farm outside of Boise, dirt-poor and envious of anyone better off than he was." Gertie's shoulder-length gray hair gleamed silvery red in the firelight. "When Mike was about Kyle's age, his parents decided he'd had enough schooling and told him he'd be working the farmstead full-time."

Franny spared a glance to her father, who was drinking a beer and staring into the fire. As an only child, she'd been told the Silver Spur would be hers one day. Some days she felt as if her father expected her to take over the ranch sooner rather than later. Just this morning, he'd made her rope strays instead of letting her horse Sunny funnel them back to the herd. Last week she'd had to go along with her dad while he mended fences, which would have been fine if he was a talker or a storyteller, like Gertie Clark.

"And then Mike got in over his head and

pulled the trigger." While Franny's thoughts had wandered, Gertie's tale had progressed from Mike leaving the farm to him becoming an outlaw. "And he ran to this valley. Made himself a hideout in the mountains, where he could see the law, a passing stage or pony-express rider."

"A smart man would've changed his name," Franny's dad grumbled, pulling the brim of his sensible straw hat low.

Percy grinned. His white hair was as long as Gertie's and looked like a waterfall beneath his tall black cowboy hat. "Being good at one thing doesn't necessarily mean you'll be smart in *all* things."

"Tell that to your millionaire Monroe friend," Franny's father grumbled. "Mark my words. Harlan Monroe will do something he regrets someday."

"He already has." For once, Percy was dead serious.

"The cattle-drive campfire is for story-telling, not kibitzing." Gertie got up and went to sit next to the kids on the log. "There's something to be said for admitting who you are to the world, be it with your name or your actions." She pulled in a deep breath and shook herself, as if needing to shake off the bad. "Where was I? Oh, yes… They said Merciless Mike had one of the fastest horses in the Idaho Territory. He'd hold up the stage or rob a poor unsuspecting settler on their way out west and be gone before they drew bead on him with a rifle."

"That's fast," Kyle whispered.

"Sunny is that fast," Franny whispered back to him across Emily. It wasn't exactly the truth. Sunny was sure-footed when it came to outmaneuvering cattle, but not fast on the straightaway.

Emily and Kyle laughed, but didn't argue.

And neither did Gertie. "But ol' Mike got cocky. He didn't get discouraged from robbing the stage when they added more protection or when he knew there was a posse traveling through the area in the hopes of catching him. He pressed his luck instead and robbed one stage too many as the good guys were closing in."

"I like this part." Kyle tipped back his straw cowboy hat.

Emily snickered. "Only because our great-great-great-something grandfather got stabbed when Merciless Mike's horse threw a shoe."

"Can I tell the part about Old Jeb Clark?"

Gertie asked her grandchildren. "Without interruption?"

"Yes, Granny," the children said, including Franny.

"Fine." Gertie nodded and tossed her silvery red hair. "Merciless Mike's horse threw a shoe in the chase. So, he crept into town and asked the blacksmith—"

"Old Jeb," Emily said.

"—to shoe his horse quickly. But Old Jeb was busy, and he knew who Mike was, so he stalled."

"And then they got into it." Kyle grinned.

"They got into a fight and Old Jeb was stabbed." Gertie leaned in close, as if this was the most important part. "Which would have meant the end of the Clarks in Second Chance if not for having a doctor in town."

"Or if the posse hadn't ridden up before Merciless Mike could finish him off." Kyle grinned again. He could be a little bit bloodthirsty.

"Pfft." Gertie shook a finger at Kyle. "When you have grandkids, you can tell the story any way you want, young man." But she said it with a smile. "The posse came thundering into town, just like Kyle said. They picked up his trail heading into the mountains.

And then—" she spread her thin arms wide, pressing the kids back as if bringing them out of harm's way "—there was an earthquake."

Franny shivered. She'd never felt the earth move.

"Boulders tumbled down the mountain from high above. Boulders the size of bulls." Gertie's eyes widened and her voice dropped to a whisper barely heard above the crackle of the fire. "Those stones knocked over trees and bounced off other boulders on their way downhill. Their collisions sounded louder than gunshots. And when the shaking and the rolling stopped, a riderless horse raced past the posse toward town. It was Merciless Mike's horse. They found what was left of the bandit beneath a boulder. But they never found the gold he'd stolen."

"Because it's a myth," Franny's dad grumbled.

Gertie and Percy just laughed.

CHAPTER ONE

THE WEDDING WAS OVER. The cake eaten. The bridal bouquet tossed, and the garter snapped to a thin crowd of eligible bachelors.

Shane Monroe sat on the steps of the hundred-year-old church in Second Chance, Idaho, and waited for the revelry to end and the family drama to begin.

His sister, Sophie, the bride, danced with her newly minted husband, Zeke, looking happy. Blissful, even.

The reception was being held in a wildflower-filled meadow next to the white clapboard church. Across a narrow ribbon of rural highway, the Salmon River barreled past at its high-water mark from snow melt and spring rain. Beyond that, the Colter Valley stretched toward the mighty Sawtooth Mountains, their peaks still blanketed with snow even though it was April.

The day was clear. The sky blue. Sophie's four-year-old twin boys from her first marriage ran through the crowd playing tag with the three Clark kids. Cousin Laurel sat in a folding chair, hands circling her baby bump as she talked to Ella, Cousin Bryce's widow. It was a beautiful day for a wedding. A beautiful day to be surrounded by family you loved and trusted.

Sophie, Laurel, Ella. They were the family Shane loved and trusted. They believed in him.

And the rest?

His father and three uncles were grouped near the back corner of the church meadow, expressions of displeasure on their faces. They didn't approve of Sophie marrying a penniless cowboy and moving to Second Chance. Shane's Grandpa Harlan had left his four sons millions. There was only one condition to their inheritance—they'd had to fire their children, all of whom had been working for the Monroe Holding Corporation in some capacity. Tough love, they guessed. Regardless, it had felt like a coup.

Fired. You might just as well say failed...

Bitterness scaled Shane's throat. He'd tried so hard the past few years to make his father proud, to garner the respect of his uncles, to be the Monroe among the third generation who would ascend to the throne. He'd run the Monroes' chain of luxury hotels in Las Vegas. He'd been respected. His ideas embraced. He'd put family profits above time with family. And for what? To be fired so his father and uncles could inherit everything? To be humiliated in the global hospitality industry?

And by his grandfather, of all people. The man who'd taken him in and given him a chance when his father no longer would. That's what Grandpa Harlan's last wishes were? For his children to fire his grandchildren?

Shane passed his thumb over the narrow scar on his chin.

Today, he was unemployed, living off his savings and serving as an honorary council member in Second Chance. Why? Because the only thing Harlan Monroe had left his dozen grandchildren was the small town. That's right. A town. And the town was in need of saving.

"I never have to worry about your dedication to family," Grandpa Harlan had told Shane when he was a teenager. The older man's faded gaze had strayed to the oldest of his grandchildren—Holden. "You were taught that power and wealth comes hand in hand with responsibility, and that you have a duty to uphold your heritage."

What good did that do Shane? It was a curse, this need to be responsible. To live up to some unwritten code about protecting the Monroe family name, not to mention his grandfather's reputation.

On the far side of the cake table, Cousin Holden held court with Shane's brother and other cousins, planning a coup of their own. They wanted to challenge Grandpa Harlan's will and regain their leadership positions within the Monroe conglomerate, to take down their fathers and uncles a peg on the power-and-wealth scale. But to do so they'd have to prove Grandpa Harlan wasn't in a fit mental state when he'd written his will.

They wanted to besmirch the reputation of one of the wealthiest and one of the most compassionate men in America, a man Shane had idolized, a man who'd ultimately betrayed him.

And now the only thing standing in their way was Shane.

FRANNY CLARK STOOD on the edge of the crowd at Zeke's wedding reception and tried to remain calm.

Breathe in. Breathe out. Focus on the good things.

Sunshine. Her children's laughter. The happy bride and groom.

Panic crept past calm, and made Franny feel brittle.

"Who was on the phone?" Emily, Franny's sister-in-law, didn't take her eyes off the cluster of Monroe men and women on the other side of the cake table.

Men of a certain age were hard to come by in Second Chance, and Emily, being of a certain age, was on the lookout to be part of a matched set.

Franny could've told Emily not to set her sights on those Monroe men. They were here today, but would be gone tomorrow. Except for one…

Her gaze strayed to Shane Monroe. He sat on the church steps in a suit that probably cost more than the price of a straw of Buttercup's bull semen. He had wavy brown hair in a corporate haircut and studied his estranged family like a cowboy sized up a bull he'd drawn for a rodeo competition.

Shane had been in town for more than three months, doing Granny only knew what.

He wasn't dancing. At least, he wasn't dancing today. And certainly not with Franny.

He spared her a glance, one that lingered and made Franny feel...*not* like a widowed mother of three. He stared as if he considered her worthy to have a discussion with, worthy to spend time with, worthy to—

Shane looked away.

"Franny?" Emily prompted. "The call?"

"Oh." Franny tried to sound nonchalant, as if the fate of the Bucking Bull didn't hinge on that call. "It was Bradley Holliday." The rodeo-stock contractor they sold most of their trained bucking bulls to. "He claims our bulls last season weren't *rank* enough."

Rank was achieved by being near impossible for cowboys to ride for eight seconds.

When Franny's husband, Kyle, had died two years ago, the Bucking Bull Ranch still had a reputation for providing athletic, beefy bulls with a killer instinct. It was why folks like Bradley Holliday paid top dollar for their stock and why breeders from around the world paid top dollar for their bull semen.

Or they used to.

A breeze swirled around Franny.

"We'll be fine." Emily held the bouquet she'd caught in one hand and her skirt in the other. She wore a simple yellow sundress. Her brown hair floated freely down her back. "I'm sure when we round up the main herd there'll be a straggler to bring some excitement to the mix."

By straggler, Emily meant one of the feral bulls that roamed the slopes above the Bucking Bull.

There'd been no stragglers for two years.

"Bradley wants to visit in two weeks and ride our bulls himself." Franny's sensible white flats pinched her feet.

Bradley would come with a posse of cowboys. He'd see the truth—their stock wasn't as dangerous as it used to be. He'd leave without anything. And he'd tell others. Then the second mortgage and the taxes would go unpaid.

How long could the Bucking Bull survive without the lucrative rodeo contracts and sperm sales? Franny felt the weight of generations of Clarks press down on her shoulders.

"But…" Emily's jaw dropped as the objects of her regard, the visiting Monroes, shifted like a mesmerizing school of brightly colored fish. "Zeke is going on his honeymoon." Her speech slowed. "And I'll be working in town the next few weeks. There's no one to help you round up and train stock for Bradley. Put him off."

Like she hadn't tried? "It's the only day he can come."

Franny considered reminding her sister-in-law what was at stake. But Emily had decided that nearly thirty was over the hill and her best chance to meet a man was to work in town, at least part-time. Sophie Monroe had fueled Emily's dream by hiring Emily to run her oddity shop while she was on her honeymoon with Zeke, their one paid ranch hand.

"I can manage without you." Franny tried to sound confident and cheerful. "I just need to find a cowhand to help me get the cattle to the lower pastures. And a couple of brave souls to ride bulls." Because bulls without a hatred of humans had to be trained to buck to put on a good show at the rodeo.

But feral bulls…

Feral bulls were a danger to cowboys on or off their backs.

Kyle had casually told her two years ago, "There are a couple of stray heifers who got through a break in the fence. I can bring them down myself." He'd tried to reassure Franny, making it sound as if he was only driving into town to pick up a gallon of milk, not riding the western border of their property, where a herd of feral cattle roamed, watched over by a wily bull with sharp horns and a sharper temper.

A quick hug. A peck on the cheek. And that's the last time she'd seen him alive.

And now if she wanted to save the ranch, Franny needed to venture up the western slopes in search of fresh stock. Rank stock. Feral stock.

Fear darkened the edges of her vision, threatening her calm.

She'd been raised to be fearless, but dark woods and killer bulls had chipped away at her courage.

Emily gasped, drawing Franny's attention back to blue skies and wedding laughter. "This is my chance." Meaning the Monroe debate on the other side of the cake table was over. She turned to Franny, holding the white-rose bouquet and quivering like a Labrador about to receive a command to fetch. "How do I look?"

"Beautiful." Too good for the likes of those rich city boys. Franny smoothed Emily's brown hair and gave her an encouraging smile. She'd often wished that her sister-in-law would find the love she yearned for.

Emily marched across the field like she wore jeans and cowboy boots and they were calling her number for the barrel-racing competition. Her target? A burly, tanned Monroe. The one who hadn't worn a suit and tie to the festivities today. He'd slid the white lace wedding garter he'd caught around his forearm.

"Be smart, Franny." Granny Gertie sat in a chair, her walker nearby. She'd been sidelined by a stroke last Christmas and was still struggling to regain full speech and mobility. Unlike Emily, she'd listened to Franny's phone call. "You know you can't do this alone."

Franny grabbed hold of her grandmother-in-law's right hand. "I know."

"We'll find a way." Gertie's grip was strong. "To keep going." Decades ago, Gertie had married into the Clark family, same as Franny. Gertie and her husband, Percy, had run the ranch, same as Franny and Kyle. Only the older couple had done a better job of it. "You stay safe."

Safe? Franny had been playing it safe ever since Kyle's death, when she'd taken over the ranch. And look where that had gotten the ranch. Sales of bull semen were down, prices for Buttercup's straw negotiable. They were at risk of losing their prestige and price point for two- and three-year-old bulls. And now, the fate of the ranch hung in the balance.

I can't play it safe.

The pretty flowers. The blue sky. The sound of laughter.

It all melted away.

Words caught in Franny's throat, trapped by fear and loss. She had to swallow twice before she could say, "I have to go up there." Before Zeke returned. Before Bradley arrived. "I'll find someone to help me."

Gertie's bony fingers dug into Franny's flesh. "There's a Monroe. He could go with you." She pointed to Shane. "Take him."

"He's not a cowboy, Gertie." Up until a few months ago, Shane was the kind of man who'd only existed in magazine ads for Franny. He was pretty to look at and as far as she could tell not good for much else.

But kissing. He'd be a good kisser.

That was loneliness, talking out of turn.

"Put Shane on a horse." Granny's eyes were bright. She knew what was at stake. "Monroes learn quick, especially from pretty cowgirls. And there's safety in numbers."

"Numbers higher than two." Franny would find cowboys hungry for a challenge or with nothing to lose. "I'll call around."

Although... April was a busy time for cowboys—calving, branding, mending fences, entering or attending spring rodeos. This time of year, skilled cowboys looking for work were scarce.

Two weeks.

That was all the time she had to capture at least one killer bull and make him workable on the circuit.

"You need someone to have your back." Gertie's eyes slanted sorrowfully. "Like Shane." Her expression softened into an uneven smile. "I bet he can dance, too, like my Percy."

Franny couldn't remember the last time she'd danced. "Save your Monroe match-making for Emily."

Her sister-in-law was on the other side of the cake table talking to the burly Monroe. Her smile was brighter than a newly minted penny. And his smile... His smile was indulgent, because...

He was humoring Emily.

Emily, who could ride any horse of any temperament.

Emily, who could referee any argument Franny's boys had.

Emily, who'd held Franny when they'd found Kyle's body.

Anger jutted Franny's jaw. That muscle-bound Monroe didn't appreciate what was standing right in front of him.

Worse, a few feet behind Mr. Muscles, a redheaded, goateed Monroe studied the pair, curiosity in his gaze.

Did the bearded redhead think Emily wasn't good enough for Mr. Muscles?

Franny wanted to stomp over there and tell those two men what a wonderful woman Emily was.

"Shane can help you." Gertie pointed to the lone Monroe again, drawing his attention this time.

Shane gave Franny a look, one that said, "Why do you look so interesting to me?"

Yes, his look was a question. Because there was no way a worldly man like Shane Monroe would find a small-town rancher interesting.

"No." Franny shook her head. Shane didn't know her. And contrary to what Granny thought, he couldn't help around the ranch. He couldn't ride a bull. And she was certain he couldn't help her capture feral stock, either.

Shane Monroe was a city slicker. She recognized the high-quality leather of his shoes and the glint in his brown eyes that said he'd left a trail of broken hearts in his wake. Never mind the thick brown hair with the unruly curl that tempted fingers. Never mind that he looked deep into her eyes, or how he carried himself that said he could handle anything.

No one can handle anything.

Franny's little boys—Davey, Charlie and Adam—collapsed on the grass around her.

"Mom." Davey was nine and the leader of the pack. He had his father's sturdy frame and can-do attitude. A birth defect had left him with only a right hand, but he wasn't going to let the lack of a left slow him down. "There's no more cake. Can we go now?"

"Yeah, can we?" Charlie was seven, with wild brown hair and wild-eyed ideas. When he wasn't doing something foolish, he followed Davey's every lead. "There are cookies at home."

"No more sweets." Add cooking vegetables for dinner to Franny's list of things to do before bedtime. Her bedtime, that is.

"Cookies!" Granny Gertie raised her right hand and then held it toward Charlie for a fist bump and a series of handshakes, accompanied by fireworks sound effects. Despite the stroke, the old dame had game.

Five-year-old Adam grabbed the hem of Franny's green dress and pulled himself to his feet. He clung to her legs with his skinny arms. Of all her children, he was the most like Franny—loving, plucky, yet small. "I'm tired." And dirty. His face needed a good washing. He wiped his nose on her hem.

In no mood to scold, Franny swung Adam into her arms. Only then did she realize he'd wet his pants. She didn't have dry ones with them.

"Don't tell," Adam whispered in her ear.

She patted his little back. There wasn't much she could do. As soon as they got into the truck, his older brothers would know and tease him mercilessly.

The gentle breeze turned into a tug of wind. Franny's skirt billowed, stretching to show the smudges from Adam's dirty hands, face and shoes.

"Time to go," she said, before the visiting Monroes turned their judgmental eyes her way.

"Franny." Zeke, a tall, ginger-haired cowboy, approached with his bride alongside him so fast that her red glasses slid down her nose. "I'm sorry to leave you in a lurch."

Zeke had no idea the lurch Franny was in. Her shoes pinched the back of her heels, forcing her to shift her stance, searching for relief.

Zeke might postpone his honeymoon if she asked. It was on the tip of her tongue to do so, but pride kept her silent. Clarks didn't quit and they didn't beg, either.

Lovestruck Zeke gave his bride a slow grin before returning his attention to Franny. "We wanted to get married right away and get past the honeymoon."

Get past *the honeymoon?*

He referred to honeymoons as if they were a chore.

Franny forced herself to smile, to pat Adam's back, to acknowledge the warmth of the sun on her face. To remember the good things—a time when she could sit and watch sunsets, when she had a hand to hold and a pair of steady brown eyes to gaze into, a partner to share problems with, to dream with.

Franny hugged Adam tighter, wet pants and all.

I'm not envious.

Or lonely.

Or in wretched denial of said envy and loneliness.

"Don't go it alone," Zeke continued as his bride was greeted by one of her Monroe cousins. "I made Shane promise to check up on you."

Shane? Shane Monroe?

Franny dug her sore heel in the dirt as she tried to backpedal. "That wasn't necessary."

"Franny." Zeke's eyebrows dropped. "Shane can help on the ranch. He used to play lacrosse. He's tougher than he looks."

"But he's not a cowboy." Therefore, her unwanted appreciation of his good looks was even more unwelcome.

"He can ride." Sophie swiveled around as she juggled two conversations at once. "He tried out for the polo team at school."

"Your school had a polo team?" Davey stared up at Sophie in wonder. "We don't even have a football team. Or a stadium. Or even a school."

Because Second Chance was in a remote mountain location. The kids were all homeschooled via the county's independent-study program. Luckily, the county coordinator lived in town.

"Things are different here, for sure." Franny tried to smile while simultaneously performing a mental inventory of the contents of her freezer. Did she have anything to cook for dinner? Did she need to pick something up at the general store before heading back to the ranch?

What else could she distract herself with so as not to think about Shane, feral bulls and financial ruin?

The Monroe in question stood, looking polished and professional. If he'd ever regularly ridden a horse, there were no traces left. No slight bow to his legs from hours spent in the saddle. No callouses on his hands, one of which she'd shaken when he'd visited the ranch last month. No lines emanating from his eyes from hours spent in the sun.

I'd have to be pretty desperate to ask him for help catching feral stock.

"I want you to promise me you'll ask Shane if you need help," Zeke said with a straight face. "I know how you get. You take on too much by yourself, just like Kyle." He lowered his voice. "Especially now that Emily's covering for Sophie."

Franny mumbled something, but made no promises.

"I'll help Mom while you're gone." Davey got to his feet.

"I'm sure you will." Zeke smiled kindly at her son. "And if you need an extra…"

Hand.

Davey was missing one and could be sensitive about it.

The cake in Franny's stomach did a slow churn. She forgot about rich, handsome single men and prepared to protect her firstborn.

She shouldn't have worried.

Zeke was good. He didn't so much as glance at Davey's left wrist as he pivoted in his reply. "Davey, if you need an extra someone, you call Shane."

"We'll be fine," Franny stated matter-of-factly, determined to be brave.

Kyle had been brave. But being brave hadn't been enough to keep him safe in the mountains.

Fear threatened to rise up and knock Franny backward again. But it could just have been another stiff mountain breeze.

She pressed a kiss to Adam's forehead. He nestled his head beneath her chin.

She couldn't call Shane for help.

The kind of help she needed…could get a man killed.

CHAPTER TWO

"MAKE THIS QUICK, SHANE." Holden and his collection of disloyal family members clustered about in the common room of the Lodgepole Inn, the only hotel in Second Chance. "Most of us are headed to the airport tonight to catch our flights."

They were essentially dismissing Grandpa Harlan, Shane and Second Chance.

"When you're at rock bottom, there's no place to go but up," Grandpa Harlan had once told Shane. "You just have to find your footing."

"Sure. I'll make this fast and painless." Shane had been sitting on the hearth next to the big stone fireplace and its modest fire. He drew a deep breath and set his feet firmly on the floor's wide wooden planks. "Grandpa Harlan left us the town where he was born. His family's been here for generations. They were the town's founders. They were fur traders and cabin builders. There's history here. Family history."

"There's Monroe history in Hollywood." That was Cousin Jonah. Up until the reading of the will, he'd written scripts for Monroe Studios.

"And in Texas." That was Cousin Bo. Up until the coup, he'd worked on the family's oil rigs.

"Not to mention Vegas." Shane's brother, Cam, stood apart from the bunch wearing a white shirt that looked more like a chef's jacket.

Shane held up an open hand, a peaceful gesture to make them pause. "Let's revisit the facts. Grandpa Harlan loved us." Cut off financially or not, Shane refused to believe otherwise.

"He loved us enough to disown us," Cousin Holden grumbled.

"Yes, he did." If Shane was going to win over the family, he had to face every argument Holden put up. "But he didn't do it on a whim. And he wasn't ill or confused. Grandpa Harlan wrote his last will and testament over a decade ago." As expected, Shane's announcement brought a hush to the room. "That's right. Let me refresh your memory. Twenty years ago, Grandpa Harlan was taking us to Yellowstone and county fairs for amusement rides and cotton candy. Ten years ago, he was taking us on tours of family companies outside our own individual family branches." Because his four sons, who'd each run a branch of the family business, didn't encourage cross-pollination. "You can't prove he wasn't of sound mind when he wrote the will. He knew exactly what he was doing."

Silence.

"Which was what?" Holden was the first to recover, to slice the quiet with his sharp tone.

Laurel stood, one hand cradling the babies she carried in her belly, her gaze on her twin sister across the room. "Grandpa Harlan wanted us to discover what's important to *us*, and not to settle for what's important to the Monroe Holding Corporation."

Sophie had been standing at the check-in desk with Zeke, new wedding ring glinting on her finger. She joined Laurel. "Grandpa Harlan wanted each of us to think about the unfinished business we had with him and to make peace."

Holden scowled at Shane, waiting for him to add something.

But it was Ella who spoke next. She was

only a Monroe by marriage, but as Bryce's widow and her daughter's guardian, she had a say. "Harlan wanted us to remember the importance of family."

Holden didn't deign to look at her. He checked his watch instead. "Get to the point, Shane."

Shane nodded, holding back a lecture about the nature of family heritage and legacy. It would be breath wasted on his unfeeling cousin. "On the day Grandpa Harlan's will was read, six of us decided to challenge the will and six decided to come to Second Chance and honor his wishes." He gave hard looks to the two who'd bailed on that promise—Cousin Jonah and Shane's brother, Camden. "Now there are eight of you wanting to contest the will. How will it look if all twelve of us aren't united?"

"How does it look that our own fathers fired us?" Holden countered. He'd been a Wall Street honcho before Harlan's death, managing millions for the family. Like Shane, his image and prestige were everything to him. Like Shane, he'd been positioning himself to ascend to the throne. Unlike Shane, he wanted to use the courts to take down the man who'd built it.

Shane kept his cool. "If you contest the

will, Holden, you'll need medical records and testimonials. You'll need to prove Grandpa Harlan wasn't thinking right a decade ago." *Thank you, Mitch, the Lodgepole Inn's manager and one of Shane's new inner circle in Second Chance, for that information.* "And the four of us will testify against you."

The eight family members willing to shred Grandpa Harlan's reputation to gain a share of his wealth fidgeted. They knew the press would have a field day with it. *With them.* It was probably the only reason they'd kept quiet so long.

"What are you proposing?" Holden demanded.

Shane made sure his feet were firmly planted. "I'm suggesting you respect Grandpa Harlan's last wishes. This town is like everything else the old man purchased. An investment. Bought low. And what we need is to shine it up to make it pay." Shane glanced at his allies—Laurel, Ella, Sophie. He hadn't told them what he was going to say next. "You come here and contribute something to this town. And after that, on the anniversary of Grandpa Harlan's death, if you *all* still want to challenge the will, we'll stand with you."

Ella gasped.

Laurel sat back down.

Sophie adjusted her glasses to glare at him.

"And just what are we supposed to contribute?" Holden asked in a sour voice.

Shane looked at each of the eight in turn. "If you think on it long enough, you'll figure it out."

When the eight dissenters had filed out the door, Laurel grabbed Shane's arm. "What are you doing?"

"He's gambling," Sophie said flatly, still glaring.

"But..." Ella looked like she might cry. *"Why?"*

"Other than the fact that I'm from Vegas?" Shane shifted his feet and ran a hand through his hair. "Because I have a hunch."

"I HEAR YOU had a war council."

The familiar baritone had Shane turning abruptly on the Lodgepole Inn's back porch.

A thousand retorts came to mind at the sight of the man emerging from the shadows, but the singular word that made it from Shane's mouth was *"Dad."*

"Fantastic view here." His old man settled his elbows on the porch railing, as comfortable in his fine wool suit in the Idaho mountains as if he was standing in the boardroom in Las Vegas. "Thousands of stars in the sky. Moonlit meadow. Sawtooth Mountains silhouetted in the distance and…I smell money."

Shane sucked in cold, sharp air. "You would, seeing as how you inherited millions."

And disinherited me.

Despite Shane playing this meeting time and again in his head, he didn't sound much more composed than an angry teenager, the one who'd been torn between the taciturn man who'd fathered him and the loving grandfather who'd brought out the best in him.

"People…" Dad cleared his throat. "People we know would pay through the nose for a piece of property up here. Fresh air. Pristine vistas. I'm assuming you're planning to parcel and develop the land."

The cold in Shane's throat and lungs spread to his fingers and toes. If his grandfather would have wanted to tear down Second Chance—his hometown—and rebuild, he'd have done so ten years ago, when he'd bought it.

"This valley could be very lucrative for development given the right direction," Shane's father continued. "Have you considered a small airfield in that meadow across the river?"

"Have you?" There it was again. That bitter resentment. Shane pressed his lips together.

"Of course you have." Dad chuckled. "You never met a loose end you didn't tie up or a stray cat you couldn't find a home for. You're more like my father than I am. Used to make me jealous."

Inwardly, Shane reeled. From the cold. From the shock of his father's admission. He gripped the railing.

A coyote yipped in the distance, its call answered by the rest of the pack.

"Coyotes howl and gripe until they out their nervous prey," Grandpa Harlan had once said as he sat at a Utah campfire surrounded by his twelve grandchildren. "It's when they're silent that you've got to worry."

Shane's father had been silent after Grandpa Harlan died. He was yipping now, trying to throw Shane off balance.

And succeeding.

"Not that my coldheartedness couldn't use a dose of compassion now and then," Shane's father said. "A man with your experience and skill set won't be satisfied hanging around this one-horse town." Dad tapped his palm on the porch railing like he used to dismissively pat Shane on the head when he was a boy. "Make me an offer after January first, Shane. It should take you about that long to come to your senses." He disappeared into the night.

Was he implying...?

Did this mean...?

Shane sucked in cold mountain air until his lungs were burning.

He doesn't think I can turn things around here.

Shane heard a car start and drive away, listened to the ensuing silence.

He thinks the soul of Second Chance is for sale. Shane shook his head. *Never.* The coyotes had gone quiet. The silence...

It made Shane wonder...

What game was being played? Was Shane one of the pack? Or prey to be gutted?

Along with Second Chance.

FRANNY WAS UP before dawn.

Feeding livestock. Mucking stalls. Moving fast to keep warm. Juggling her to-do list in her head, which was better than thinking about Monroe men or bulls, branded or otherwise.

The heater in the chicken coop was on the

fritz. She tightened the electrical connections to get it running and then stopped at Buttercup's enclosure to stare into his rheumy old eyes.

"You made it through the winter, old man. You can make it through another spring and summer." Or at least the next two weeks. The Bucking Bull's fortunes rode on Buttercup's back until she captured another fierce bull.

Buttercup, once known as the baddest bull on the northwest rodeo circuit, snorted his amusement. Buttercup, once part of the feral herd to the west, turned his back on her. Years on the rodeo circuit had broken him, made him soft.

A horse nickered in a nearby stall. Danger, the once-headstrong black gelding Franny used to ride on the rodeo circuit, whinnied impatiently. Years of semiretirement had undermined his spirit, made him soft.

Franny used to ride Danger without concern for angry, charging stock. She used to stand in the saddle during a gallop and throw a lariat over a racing bull's head. Back in the day—before kids—she'd thought she'd been invincible.

Years at the Bucking Bull have made me soft. Franny buried the thought. She wasn't soft.

She was smart. Smart didn't quit. Smart found solutions. Smart won the race.

All I need now are the smarts to kick in.

When Franny returned to the house with the morning's bad news—no eggs because of too-cold chickens—coffee was brewing, and bacon was sizzling in the pan.

Granny Gertie sat at the kitchen table setting up the Scrabble board. It was Sunday. The family played games on Sunday and listened to Gertie tell stories from the old days just as she used to on cattle drives all those years ago. Well, not exactly the same. She didn't laugh as much and there were gaps in her storytelling.

"Okay, then. Bacon and biscuits, it is." Emily stirred the biscuit batter like she was at the rodeo tying a calf's legs together with a short pigging string. A wayward dollop flew into the frying pan. She fished it out and gave Franny a sheepish look. "I'm thinking about my new job. This is the right thing, isn't it? Me working in town? You here alone?"

"I'll be fine." She'd do what needed to be done for two weeks. Responsibility had a way of wrestling fear to the ground. And she wanted Emily to be happy.

"Franny won't be fine." Gertie scowled,

rubbing her forehead. "Why go fishing for a man in a dry watering hole?"

Emily hissed, sizzling louder than the bacon. "You caught Grandpa Percy when you worked in town." She flung batter into muffin tins.

"Ladies…" Franny tried to calm them. They'd been at each other since the New Year.

"There were men in town to catch back then," Gertie huffed at Emily. "What are you going to do with a man just passing through? What are we going to do when you move?"

"You'll have Zeke." Emily shoved the biscuits in the oven and slammed the door closed. "And the little man." Which is what she called Davey.

As was usual, Gertie wasn't letting off Emily easily. "If you wanted to leave the ranch, you should have done so when you were—"

"*Younger.*" Emily's voice was harder than a layer of thick ice on the ranch pond. "You've made that clear many times."

"Ladies, please," Franny begged.

"There is much to be gained by staying on the ranch." This was one of Gertie's favorite refrains. She had something in her hand beneath the table and was working it nervously, like an artist molding clay.

"Much to be gained? Like Merciless Mike's cash box?" Emily rolled her eyes, but came over to hug Gertie in the first sign of a truce Franny had seen in months. "Granny, I'm not ten anymore. I want to chase a man, not a myth about lost gold."

"I never said Merciless Mike's story was a myth." Gertie blinked rapidly, patting Emily's hand with her pale one. "If you want to chase someone, stay local. Pauline Willette's nephew's grandson is single. He has acne scars, but he's got a job repairing the ski lifts in Aspen every winter."

"Not interested." Emily returned to the bacon with a double eye-roll.

"What about Uncle Ogden's second cousin, Samuel?" Gertie was tenacious. "He works in road maintenance for the state."

"Ew." Emily lined a plate with paper towels and transferred a strip of bacon to it. "Let's not fish in the relatives pond. And please don't say beggars can't be choosers."

Gertie pressed her lips together and huffed. "When you harvest so late in the season, you can't bank on the frog prince."

Franny and Emily laughed.

"I'm trying to say that the Bucking Bull can draw more men to you than working in town." Gertie fisted whatever she'd been holding in her right hand.

"Percy and Kyle would let her go her own way." Having broken ranks with her father to follow her heart, Franny didn't want to judge Emily.

"Percy and Kyle." Gertie's brow furrowed.

Upstairs, Davey was getting his younger brothers out of bed. Their feet didn't pitter-patter. They pounded their heels into the floorboards. Bolt, the family's old, black Labrador, was curled up in a ball in front of the fireplace, eyes open, looking toward the stairs. One of Adam's chores was to feed the dog.

"I don't have to be at the trading post until Tuesday." Emily put the biscuits in the oven. "We can move cattle today and tomorrow."

Because Emily's offer was so generous and unexpected, given her desire to put distance between herself and the ranch, Franny nearly overfilled her coffee cup in her rush to thank her.

"And who knows?" Emily took more bacon from the pan. "Maybe we'll net a couple of feral stragglers."

"Who knows," Franny murmured, not putting any store in luck.

Granny Gertie put more tiles on the Scrabble board.

"Getting ready for a game with the boys?" Franny drifted over to see what the elderly dear was doing.

Gertie turned the board, so Franny could see.

LET MONROE HELP

Elderly dear, my eye.

Emily leaned over the counter to look. She gave Franny a puzzled glance. "Let Monroe help? Are you referring to Shane, Granny?"

"I am." The old woman's pointed chin went up.

Emily laughed and returned to the stove. "Glad to see I'm not the only target in the room."

"We've already talked about this." Franny gathered the tiles into a jumbled pile, thinking about Shane and exchanged glances that made her pulse race in a way it hadn't since she was in her twenties and drawn to any risky adventure. She didn't have time for adventure or a man, much less a Monroe. "If you're going to wish me a man, wish me a cowboy with plenty of experience with cattle."

Boyish feet pounded down the stairs.

Franny boxed up the Scrabble game to free up space for hungry boys at the table. "I don't need a matchmaker."

"That's right." Emily chuckled. "You could always settle for Pauline Willette's nephew's grandson."

The boys ran toward the kitchen table.

Franny huffed. "I need cowboys and—"

"I'm a cowboy," Adam insisted from beside her, patting Bolt's broad forehead.

"You're too little to be a cowboy," Charlie teased, standing on his toes to look at Emily's bacon. "You're hobbit-sized."

"Cowboys come in small sizes, don't they, Mom?" Adam's lower lip trembled.

"Cowboys come in all sizes," Franny reassured him. "Besides, you'll grow." She paused, struck by the image of her three sons, grown and riding through the woods in the Clark tradition, seeking their fortunes and killer bulls. Was that what she wanted for them? She was no longer sure.

"When's breakfast?" Davey leaned on the kitchen table, not committing to a chair.

"Another fifteen minutes." Emily returned her attention to the bacon.

"Can we play a game?" Davey very carefully did not look at the Scrabble box in Franny's hands. He wanted to play a video game. Last summer, he'd gone to a camp with other children who were missing appendages or limbs. He'd come home with a special controller that adapted to his limitation of only having one hand. It kept him ahead of Charlie in skill level and enamored of video games.

"You can't play now," Franny told him, raising her voice above her children's ensuing protests. "I know you haven't made your beds or brushed your hair or—" she ruffled Charlie's scruffy locks "—brought down your dirty laundry. Now scoot."

They ran back upstairs, just not as quickly as they'd come down.

"Used to be the Clarks turned to the Bouchards and Monroes for help." Gertie looked just as somber as her words. "You still could."

"You know how Shane could help?" Franny's patience was wearing thin. "He could invest in our ranch." They could hire an extra hand, someone with experience capturing feral stock. They could pay off the first mortgage, and the second she'd taken out for the ranch's roof, the cover for the arena Kyle insisted they build and Davey's special summer camp.

"No selling," Gertie said firmly.

"I'm not abandoning you," Emily declared, although the opposite felt more like the truth, especially when she no longer met Franny's gaze. "Once I'm married, things will be different."

Franny's eyebrows went up. "Even if you snag a Monroe?"

To that, Emily remained silent.

CHAPTER THREE

BIRDS SANG EXUBERANTLY in the trees bordering the upper pasture, oblivious to the grumble of thunder above the dark, cloud-covered mountain slope.

Emily and Franny rode toward a cluster of cattle that were lingering half-in and half-out of the trees.

"When was the last time you rode the fence line?" Franny asked, eyeing the field.

"Last December. With Zeke." Emily was a good cowhand. If ownership was earned by ability to work with their stock rather than financial investment, she'd be running the place. "Do you remember when we were kids and we rode everywhere?" Emily wore a cowboy hat and jean jacket, just as adorable now as she'd been when they were younger and both vying for rodeo-queen titles. "We overnighted at the scout camp by the lake."

"That was a lifetime ago." Back when she'd felt invincible. Since her marriage, she'd limited her physical work on the ranch to a minimum—first because she was pregnant, then because she had babies to care for. Kyle's passing only added to her reasons. Franny's ponytail looped and twisted about her neck the same way fear looped and twisted inside of her.

There'd been a forest fire in the mountains to the northwest last summer. So this year, the feral herd would most likely be looking for food in the lower pastures that bordered their property. Franny kept her eyes on the tree line, pulling the brim of her cowboy hat lower to shade her eyes.

"We used to be giddy to see a bull on the wild side of the fence line." Emily sighed as if missing the good old days.

Franny was no longer giddy at the prospect of seeing a wild thing. Wild things killed. She counted the cattle in front of them. "I only see about twenty head."

"I see some faces in the tree line. We need to sweep through the woods."

Franny's lungs felt leaden. She needed to look for good things. Safe things. Blue sky. Wildflowers.

Clouds were thickening above them. In the pasture, cattle had trampled the wildflowers.

"We'll stay within sight of the main herd," Emily reassured her.

"We'll be fine." Franny gave a tight nod, listening to birdsong and the gentle lowing of cattle. The birds were her early warning system. When they went quiet…

Her gaze darted from one shadow in the trees to the next.

Their horses were used to working with cattle. Heads held high, a spring to their step, ears alert to sudden noise. They were ready.

Franny patted Danger's dark neck. They entered the woods behind the herd, both vigilant. They rode twenty, forty, fifty yards into the trees, swinging around the backside of the cattle. Pulse pounding, Franny noticed her palms were slick with sweat. But why? The birds kept singing.

Because I'm soft.

By unspoken agreement, Emily trotted ahead while Franny continued to push deeper in the trees.

Young bulls and heifers raised their heads upon her and Danger's approach, meandering around trees to rejoin the rest of the herd in the open pasture. Registered tags hung from their ears. The cattle they were rounding up were mostly two- and three-year-olds. They'd been dehorned, a sign they were domesticated stock.

A few months after Kyle died, she'd been out riding fence when a bull on federal land charged at her. Luckily, the beast had only glanced the post that separated them with his beefy shoulder, more intent on reaching across the barbed wire with his head and long horns. He'd disappeared into the trees, but Franny had been shaken and galloped back to the ranch.

Franny blew out a breath. That was in the past.

And then she realized the birds had stopped singing.

Something huffed to Franny's left, deeper in the trees. A hoof pounded the ground.

Franny pulled Danger to a halt. They both turned to look.

A large bull with long horns stared at them from fifty feet away. He made the aging Buttercup look like one of the yearlings. His head was up. His dark eyes alert. His nostrils drinking in air.

Franny nearly cried out.

"No big deal," Kyle had told Franny once as they'd rounded up strays in the high country and been faced by a similar, though smaller bull. "It's all pretend. We pretend it's no big deal and eventually he'll pretend we aren't worth his time."

No big deal.

No big deal?

Franny was having trouble believing that right now. And breathing. She was having trouble breathing.

If Franny was worth his time, the bull would charge only a few feet. Just enough to let her know he considered this his turf. If he viewed Franny as a threat, he'd charge full speed and barrel down upon her and Danger, intent on *defending* his turf.

No big deal. Kyle's words echoed in her head.

Was this the bull that had taken Kyle from her?

No big deal.

Unable to win the staring game, Franny looked away, urging Danger forward.

She tried to remain calm even with her warring emotions. Grief, fear, anger. Anger at Kyle for believing he was invincible.

No big deal.

She couldn't look back. She didn't dare.

But she could think.

There must be a fence down. There could

be others from the feral herd in the trees, on their land, in their pasture. If she mended the fence quickly, they might collect some stragglers and sell them. Not the large, glaring bull because he was too experienced in maintaining his freedom, maybe even fighting for it. But perhaps others. Franny's hopes began to rise.

Careful.

Hope was nearly as scary as that bull. She didn't turn and look back at the beast. She couldn't, afraid for her safety, afraid she'd scare the bull away. Afraid he'd take other ferals with him.

But she could listen.

Not with ears swiveled back like Danger. But she could listen for thundering hooves or birdsong.

She heard neither. She heard nothing beyond Danger's muffled hooves on soft earth.

And Emily… She was nowhere to be seen.

Blood roared in her ears. Where was Emily?

Unable to take rein in her fear anymore, Franny let Danger break into a trot.

"Emily?" They were still in the trees and suddenly Franny needed to be in the open. "Emily!"

Danger lurched away from a bush, as skittish as Franny, who nearly fell out of the saddle.

"Emily?"

"Here." Her sister-in-law emerged safe and sound from the trees behind several head of cattle.

Franny paused in the open field, turning Danger to face the woods when everything inside of her was urging her to race back to the ranch, to unlock the cabinet with Kyle's gun and return here with it fully loaded. She'd show that filet mignon just what a big deal was. Except...

That bull was exactly what Bradley Holliday was looking for.

That bull could save the ranch.

CHAPTER FOUR

THERE WAS ONE thing Shane missed about the large metropolitan area of Las Vegas.

Privacy.

"Congratulations," Ivy said when Shane entered the Bent Nickel Diner with his two nephews. She set the coffeepot to brew. "I hear Sophie's twins were accepted into prekindergarten. They start today."

Alex and Andy gasped. And then turned as one and ran to the back of the diner, where the teacher who ran independent studies in Second Chance held court.

Shane paused near the front door, having come in for a town-council meeting. "Is there such a thing as prekindergarten in the public-school independent-study program?" The boys were in his care while Sophie was on her honeymoon. She'd said nothing about this. "And does it involve much homework?" He'd promised the boys he'd take them to visit their ponies this week.

"In my day, you brought the teacher an apple and she excused you from homework." Roy, the town handyman, scratched his thinning white hair and shook his head. "You came empty-handed."

Ivy and Shane exchanged glances and shrugs. Roy had the power to stall a conversation with his observations and recollections.

"Well, when Nick was pre-K—" Ivy headed for the kitchen, tucking her brown hair behind her ears "—he had worksheets with pattern identification, number-and-letter practice and simple algebra."

"Algebra? That does it." Shane sat down at the counter, nodding to Mitch, the mayor, who sat with his daughter in a nearby booth. "I'm canceling my sister's honeymoon."

The diner was beginning to fill up. Shane knew everyone there apart from a man, a seasoned cowboy, who was his father's age and sitting alone in a nearby booth, and the two ladies in the next booth over. He'd made it his business to meet everyone in town. The man wore a neat long-sleeved plaid shirt, jeans and cowboy boots, and a frown that discouraged conversation. The women were middle-aged, their haircuts and clothing prim and uninspired. He peered out the window and found what he was looking for. A beat-up truck with an Idaho plate, most likely belonging to the cowboy, and a blue sedan with Montana plates. Both parties were most likely just passing through.

"Uncle Shane." Andy ran up to him with a black crayon, a worksheet and a tear in his eye. "I got in trouble at school."

"How could that be? You've been in pre-K less than five minutes."

Pouting, Andy climbed in his lap and whispered, "I copied off Alex's paper."

"Now that you're in school," Shane whispered back, "you probably shouldn't do that anymore." Andy was smart—smart enough to let his brother do the work if he could get away with it.

"But we're twins." Andy curled over the counter in his precry position. "We do everything the same."

"Eli." Ivy caught the teacher's attention and pointed to Andy.

"On it," Eli said, leaning down to speak to Alex.

"Hey, hey." Frowning at Ivy, Shane rotated his nephew sideways in his lap for some privacy. "Being a twin is awesome. You have a built-in best friend for life." Shane was a twin himself. "But when you get to school you can't do everything together anymore."

"Nothing but recess." Roy sat next to Shane. "Recess is a team sport."

"Recess isn't…" Shane sighed. Arguments with Roy were often a lost cause. "Never mind."

In his lap, Andy was as bent as a fisherman's pole when he'd hooked a big one. Shane rubbed his back, rocked him from side to side and ordered him a hot chocolate.

Alex appeared next to them, brown cowlick at attention. He hugged his brother. "Come back to school, Andy. I fixed it for you."

Andy slid out of his lap with a sniff, gathered his crayon and paper, and followed his brother.

The old cowboy he didn't know made a scoffing noise and drank deeply from his coffee cup.

Roy pointed to him with his thumb. "Ignore Rich. Widower. He's a glass-half-empty man."

Good advice. Shane got up and poured himself a cup of coffee from the community pot, leaving a few bucks in the jar.

The door opened and the three Clark boys raced inside, backpacks bouncing off their shoulders. They were followed by their mother, Franny Clark. To Shane, Franny was like the mountains—cool and beautiful, tough yet engaging to look at. Her gaze stuck on Shane a few moments too long before she joined the lone cowboy in the booth.

That was the thing between Shane and Franny. They looked at each other. But Shane was determined looks were the limit of their relationship. Things were complicated enough in town for Shane without adding a romance to the mix. Besides, he was a temporary resident and she had deep roots.

"Thanks for coming into town to meet me, Dad." Franny waved off Ivy's offer to make her breakfast.

"You're late, Francis," her father said, without any of the fondness Shane had expected.

Roy sighed, as if he'd heard this exchange before and didn't approve. "We'll have our town-council meeting as soon as Mack gets here."

For once, Shane didn't mind Mackenzie being late for a meeting. He wanted to hear more between Franny and her father. After all, he'd promised to watch out for her while Zeke was gone.

"I need to bring in some stock." Franny cut right to the chase. "I was wondering if you and some of your hands could help out. I'm short-staffed until Zeke gets back."

Her father studied her, poker-faced. "Stock or ferals?"

Franny didn't squirm so much as sink down in her seat. *"Dad."*

Shane willed her to stand up for herself. She crossed her arms instead.

Rich shook his head. "I taught you to run a ranch, to build a breeding program, not to cut corners like the Clarks."

Oh, I bet Christmas is a barrel of laughs with this guy.

"I'm not breeding bulls for the quality of their filet mignon, Dad." There was a hint of spirit in Franny's statement, but it was diluted by her gaze constantly drifting toward her boys. She should have had eyes on her opponent.

"The quality of your filet mignon was obvious the last time you invited your mother and me to dinner." Her father stood. "I told you when you bought that place with Kyle and decided to sell that feral bull's seed... You're on your own." He walked out.

Franny stared at the empty seat across from her. The urge to comfort her was strong.

True, Shane had promised Zeke he'd watch

out for Franny, but he wasn't wading into family waters without being asked.

Mackenzie scurried in, long brown braid swinging. "Sorry I'm late. Can we sit by the door? I couldn't find anyone to watch the store." She plopped down in the front booth.

Roy, Mitch and Shane went over to sit with her. Ivy served the two women from Montana their breakfasts and then joined them.

Head high, expression grim, Franny left, conveniently timing her exit to coincide with her father driving away in his truck. Against his better judgment, Shane made a mental note to ask about the man later. For now, he had a responsibility to the town.

"What's on the agenda?" Shane asked since the town council didn't operate according to *Robert's Rules of Order*. There was no paper trail. No motions made or seconded. No minutes recorded. And no set meeting dates. This session had been called half an hour ago.

"We received a preliminary ruling on historic buildings in town." Mitch shuffled papers. As a former lawyer, he was good with official documents.

"And?" Shane supported Mitch's preservation effort. It would help him honor his grandfather's wishes by blocking the dissenting eight. But Mitch's delivery needed work.

"I don't want anyone to get upset." Mitch tried to soften the blow, but as usual he went about it all wrong, leading with the bad news. "They've ruled Ivy's diner and Mack's store-slash-garage don't qualify for historic protections."

"Really?" Ivy glanced around the diner with a frown. "Everyone has always been fond of the Bent Nickel."

"It's not a popularity contest." Shane tried to keep the snark out of his voice, but based on Mitch's frown, he hadn't succeeded. "Let me rephrase. We're talking about import in history, not emotional connection."

Ivy shrugged, unconvinced.

"I guess I should cancel plans for all that souvenir merchandise I ordered depicting my business," Mack griped. She should have been a Monroe. She had drive.

"Did they give a reason for rejecting Ivy and Mack?" Roy asked before Shane could nail down Mitch on how many buildings were still under consideration.

"They didn't reject *me*." Mack was petite, but she had a big sense of humor, earning her a smile from Shane. "Let's not make this personal, Roy."

"Mack and Ivy's structures have been altered too much." Mitch set down his papers, looking demoralized. "The Lodgepole Inn made it to the next round of consideration." Mitch tried not to look happy, but how could he not when his home was still in the running? "The trading post, mercantile and blacksmith shop made the cut, too. Plus the church, the old schoolhouse and—"

"What about my place?" Roy twitched. "Other than electricity and plumbing, my cabin is just the way it was a hundred years ago."

"Your cabin made the cut," Mitch reassured him.

"Winner!" Roy pumped his scarecrow arms in the air.

The schoolkids all laughed.

"Why do I sense a *but* coming?" Shane asked.

"Because there is one." Mitch nodded, still looking grim. "This isn't the final decision. Most other places that have achieved historical significance aren't towns where people still live and work. Also, those towns have proven to have been important in the history of the state. Mining towns, mostly. I've never heard of anyone mining gold or silver in this valley."

"Second Chance was important to the state," Roy said defensively.

Shane angled in his chair to face him. "How so?"

"We're the birthplace of Harlan Monroe."

That earned the old man head shakes from the rest of the town council.

Shane tried to think like a history-loving bureaucrat. "So, we need to prove something important happened here. What about that Merciless Mike Moody legend Egbert is so enthralled with? He had a reputation for robbing stagecoaches and his loot was never found." Personally, Shane believed his grandfather had found the stolen gold and used it for a stake in an oil field in Texas.

No one said anything, which was the problem Shane ran into when someone knew something. But as part of their low-cost lease deals with Harlan, they'd all signed one-year nondisclosure agreements with his estate.

"Aren't you always talking about details and logistics?" Mack watched a car pass by on the highway. "Wouldn't we need to find Merciless Mike's hideout?"

"Well..." Mitch sounded stilted and lawyerly. "He stabbed Old Jeb Clark in the smithy. And that building made the historical-committee cut."

"If we go that route, I could sell popguns and rubber knives." Mack was always ready for a new economic opportunity.

"Please don't." Ivy rolled her eyes. "The last thing my boys need are more weapons. I vote no on Merciless Mike."

"I was thinking about selling to tourists." Mack's grin contradicted her words. "I vote maybe."

"Every time you put something new in your store window, you know my boys are after me for it." Ivy no longer cared about votes or Merciless Mike. "They hounded me for a new sled this year when you got them in."

"There's always next year, too," Mack murmured with a calculating smile.

"The *Farmers' Almanac* says we'll get more snow next year." Roy looked pleased with himself to be able to share this information. "Growing boys can always use a new sled."

"Stay on point." Shane washed a hand over his face. "We can't just cross our fingers and hope for historical significance." If there was anything he hated, it was meetings that went around in circles. "We have to load the deck. Add some razzle-dazzle. Make it sexy." Get something moving so Shane could feel like he was making a difference here. "Who wants to help me organize a fair celebrating Second Chance's Old West days?"

In business school, they'd taught Shane to pause after presenting a big idea and read the room. Shane paused, looking at each council member in turn. The read was grim.

"There's not much in Second Chance to dazzle with," Mitch deadpanned.

"This isn't Las Vegas." Roy had taken offense. He straightened more rigidly than a five-star general. "Next thing you know, you'll be asking Ivy and Mack to wear skimpy bathing suits and fancy headdresses for those festivals you're always proposing."

Ivy's brow furrowed. "I'm out on all counts."

Shane turned to Mack, who grimaced. "I have too much on my plate right now. I don't have time to load your deck, Shane. Sorry."

"Or we could dig around for another idea." Shane sat back in his chair. "One that proves the importance of the town in the state's history."

They groaned and Shane tightened his grip on his patience.

"Next item on the agenda," Ivy said, to change the subject, and fixed Shane with a firm stare. "How's that search for the town doctor going?"

Shane suppressed a groan of his own. He'd been very close to getting a doctor to accept the position. Twice. You'd think with all his hiring experience he could have found someone to agree to the job in the two months he'd been looking, although he might have fared better if Cousin Holden hadn't decided to try and date Dr. Carlisle. "Can't I pass the ball back to Mitch?" He'd started the search in the first place.

Mitch shook his head. "My fiancée's having twins."

"The last doctor we almost hired—" Ivy's gaze caught on the out-of-town ladies, who were digging in their purses "—said the clinic was extremely out-of-date. Shouldn't we modernize it?"

Shane waited a beat for someone to volunteer to take on that responsibility. "And I suppose you want the Monroes to pay for it."

They all nodded.

"It is your town, after all." Ivy slid out of the booth, her attention tuned to her customers.

"Perfect." Mitch made note of it. "Assignment for Shane."

"What about the history assignment?" Shane got to his feet. As usual, he'd come up against a wall, given what he, versus the council, considered a priority.

Just like Franny Clark had come up against a wall with her father.

"That boy back there is missing a hand." One of the women from Montana craned her neck, peering toward the children. She hurried over for a better look at Davey Clark.

Stranger danger.

Without thinking twice, Shane followed the nosy woman.

"You poor dear." The woman stopped next to Davey. "What else is wrong with you?" And then she reached for him.

"Okay, that's enough." Shane had so much experience with drunks and disorderly guests in Vegas that he didn't hesitate to jump in. Besides, he'd met Davey a time or two and really liked the kid. He gently pried the woman's fingers free from Davey's shoulder and marched her back to her table. "Haven't you heard? Touching someone else's child is a crime."

"I can help." The woman's expression was sincere. "If you'd only let me. I once knew a boy who—"

"Permission denied," Shane said firmly.

"I'm going to have to ask you to leave." Ivy's face was ashen. Shane knew that wasn't the norm. Ivy was almost always smiling. She enjoyed having the children attend school in her diner, where she could keep her eye on her own two kids.

The woman's mouth gaped open. "But—but—"

"No buts," Shane said before the woman could form what was certain to be a lengthy story. "Or we'll have to contact the authorities."

A few awkward minutes later and the two women were gone.

"This is why I don't want the town to grow." Ivy's voice was rock-hard, but her face looked like she was about to break down in tears.

Shane sympathized. "You need to put up a sign back there. Private Party or Reserved Section." Or Keep Out. Shane was going to have to find a place for the schoolkids to meet that was safe and Ivy-approved. His list of fixes and repairs was constantly growing. Too bad all that refurbishing wasn't going to translate into substantial change.

Feeling like someone had sat on his chest, Shane walked back to Davey, who was listening to his teacher, Eli. "Can I talk to Davey alone for a second?" Shane was also experienced in comforting employees who'd been mistreated by hotel guests. He drew Davey into a booth and sat down next to him. "Well, that sucked."

Davey had his left wrist tucked into his side. His face was scrunched, as if he was trying not to cry.

Two boys on the brink of tears in one morning? This was not the way Shane had seen his day going.

"She meant well," Shane began diplomatically. "I mean, she wanted to help you, but she went about it all wrong. Knowing the right way to handle things, which men like you and I are aware of, can make all the difference to a person."

Davey slid Shane a sideways glance, facial scrunch loosening. "Yeah?"

"Have you met my cousin Laurel?"

Davey shook his head.

"My cousin Laurel is an identical twin." He nudged Davey with his arm. "Twins run in the

Monroe family. Anyway, she looks exactly like her sister, who started acting on TV when she was five or six. People would come up to Laurel and insist she was her sister, Ashley. It was the most annoying thing I ever saw."

Davey nodded blankly.

"Now, Laurel… She could have dressed in camouflage and tried to fade into the background. But she didn't. She wore bright, shiny colors. She decided if she was going to stand out, she was going to stand out in her own way."

Davey nodded, again blankly.

"The point is…" Shane leaned in, not quite looking Davey in the eye. "When you stand out, you've got to own it. You've got to expect that butthead people are going to cluelessly rain on your parade."

"Shane," Ivy chastised from behind the counter.

"Let him run with it," Mitch said. Mitch was engaged to Laurel. He knew Shane wasn't feeding the kid a line.

"You've got to shrug those people off, because they don't matter in your life." *Voice of experience.* Shane rubbed his thumb over the scar on his chin. "You've got to remember every morning while you're brushing your teeth that if you step off the ranch, someone is going to notice you. And because you're one of a kind, they might not know the right way to talk to you."

The kid's frown deepened. At least it wasn't a scrunch.

"If you practice what to say in the bathroom mirror, next time you won't be caught off guard when someone comes up to you."

Davey turned sideways in the booth. He had his mother's eyes. "What should I have said?" The scrunch had returned.

Shane held up a hand. "What's past is past. That woman's not coming back. You're not getting a second shot at telling her to get her hands off you."

Davey drew a shuddering breath.

"Let's go over some things you can say in the future." Shane purposely laid his hand on the boy's shoulder. "Imagine. Here comes well-meaning, yet clueless person number one." He cleared his throat. "'Oh, look, Davey. You're missing a hand,'" Shane said in a high-pitched voice. "'Did you know you were missing a hand?'"

Behind them, the schoolkids giggled.

Davey started to smile.

Shane leaned in and whispered, "Go on. Give me a shove back."

"I'm not looking for a new hand." Davey took Shane's advice and built on it. He lifted Shane's hand off his shoulder. "But thanks for offering to loan me yours."

The boy had sass. Shane narrowed his eyes. "I'm thinking you watch a good bit of television."

Davey grinned.

The weight on Shane's chest eased. This kid was going to be all right. "Let's try another one. 'Hey, kid.'" Shane pitched his voice in the silly zone once more. "'What happened to your hand?'"

"The boogeyman ate it when I wasn't looking." Davey turned toward his classmates. "Watch out! There he is!"

Shane laughed. Their audience whooped and applauded in appreciation.

"You're good at this," Shane said in a low voice. The kid was a lot better at deflecting bullies than Shane had been at his age.

"I went to a camp for kids like me where we learned stuff. And…" Davey's eyes watered and his voice lost its confident tone. "And my dad used to practice with me. He gave me the boogeyman line."

Not only did the kid not have a hand, but he also didn't have a dad anymore.

Shane's throat threatened to close. "The boogeyman is a truly excellent response. Your dad would be proud of you." His mom, too.

"Thanks." Davey leaned in. "I should get back to my math test or the kids are gonna think this is weird."

"Right." Shane backed out of the booth, feeling drained, as well as oddly nostalgic for his grandfather, who'd excelled at talking to Shane, his siblings and cousins. Hard talks and pep talks had been his grandfather's specialties.

After Davey returned to his classmates, Mitch came to stand beside Shane. "You just keep on surprising me."

"I'll take that as a compliment." And yet, Shane was no closer to helping the town find its way to prosperity or safeguarding his grandfather's reputation.

CHAPTER FIVE

"Do you know how to saddle a horse, Uncle
Shane?" Alex gave Shane the kind of assessment only an almost five-year-old could.
He scratched the cowlick at his crown and
squinted at him. "You don't look like you do."

A day after coming to Davey Clark's rescue, Shane stood in the breezeway of the barn
at the Bucking Bull Ranch, flanked by his
twin nephews. The Clark boys were behind
him, clustered around their great-grandmother
Gertie, who sat on her walker. He'd led one
of his nephews' ponies out of her stall and
had tied her lead rope to a ring on the wall.
And now everyone was waiting for him to
do something else in the barn, the same way
his Monroe siblings and cousins were waiting for him to do something else with Second Chance.

In the barn, it was a question of how. How
did he saddle a horse? In Second Chance, it
was a question of what. What could he do to

lift the town's economic status without changing the tenor of the place?

"Uncle Shane?" Alex prompted.

"I've saddled horses," Shane answered. Maybe five times, but that had been fifteen to twenty years ago, when he'd tried out for his high-school polo team on a bet. A bet he'd lost, by the way. "It was just so long ago."

The Clark boys laughed like Shane was putting on the greatest show they'd ever seen.

"Hurry up and remember, Uncle Shane." Andy pressed his cheek against his pony's neck. "I want to ride Stormy."

"Mom says you have to be able to saddle your own horse if you want to ride." That was Davey, not giving Shane any leeway for the save yesterday in the Bent Nickel.

"That's a Clark rule," Gertie Clark called out in a half-scolding voice. "For Clarks only. Do you need help, Shane?"

"No—no. We've got it." Shane took out his cell phone and searched for a how-to video. How hard could saddling a pony be? "Here you go." He started the video on silent mode. "Step one is to brush down your mount."

Alex's eyes lit up. "I know where the brushes are." He ran to a room at the end of the row of stalls and disappeared inside.

"And I know where her blanket and saddle are." Andy scampered after his twin.

"Do you need help carrying anything?" Shane called after him.

"No." Andy banged into the tack-room doorway. "Ow." He disappeared inside.

Ten minutes later and Stormy had a saddle on her back, but based on the laughter meter from the Clarks, Shane had done something wrong. He rested his hands on the saddle and ran through the video again.

The sound of pounding hooves diverted attention from Shane.

"It's Mom." Little Adam Clark wasn't much older than Shane's nephews. "And Aunty Em!"

"The boys aren't supposed to be in the barn unsupervised." Franny brought her horse to a halt just outside the barn door and flung herself to the ground with the grace of a born horsewoman. She wore faded blue jeans, scuffed cowboy boots and a blue hoodie emblazoned with the word *Mom*, with a bright red heart where the *o* should be. Her cowboy hat was a richer brown than her hair, pulled low over gray eyes that flashed with annoyance.

"They're not unsupervised." Old Gertie had her back up. "I'm here." Sitting in her walker.

She turned to Shane. "You've got to pull that girth strap tighter, Shane."

Advice? He'd take it.

"Here?" Shane fumbled underneath the stirrup with one hand.

"No" came a chorus from Clarks of all ages and sizes.

Grinning, Emily stayed on her horse, looking content to avoid what was about to come.

"What's going on here?" Franny stomped toward her trio of laughing boys, bringing quiet with each booted step. Her big black horse followed her like a loyal dog. "We have rules on the ranch. The boys can't be outside unsupervised." Dark looks all around. "And Shane isn't qualified to handle stock."

Shane wasn't going to argue.

Gertie was. "*I'm* in charge." She tapped her chest, raising her thin voice. She wore boots, blue jeans, a blouse and a lightweight jacket that probably did nothing to keep her warm in the cool spring breeze. "It's okay."

Thunder rumbled on the slopes above them. The sky was growing dark.

It wasn't exactly blue skies in the barn, either.

"It's okay," Gertie said again.

"It's not okay," Franny snapped, stumbling

forward as her horse bumped her from behind in his haste to reach Gertie.

"There's my handsome boy." Gertie handed the black horse a carrot. She then raised her eyebrows at her granddaughter-in-law.

Scowling, Franny pulled the brim of her cowboy hat down low. "I swear, Danger likes you better than he likes me."

"You're Buttercup's favorite." The old woman gestured toward a stall decorated with plaques and trophies.

The tension in the air was thicker than the gathering humidity.

"I don't mind the extra supervision." Shane pulled a smile from his arsenal that he reserved for difficult high rollers. "In fact, I could use a little help here. I'm becoming the poster boy for saddling don'ts."

The Clark boys chortled some more, earning another stern stare from their mother. That same cold stare bounced off Emily, who'd perhaps foolishly decided it was safe to dismount and enter the barn. Finally, Franny swiveled her no-nonsense gaze at Shane.

This is a woman used to being in charge.

And yet, there was a note of resignation in her eyes, as if she knew no matter how fast she rode, she wouldn't win the race.

"I throw myself on the mercy of the Clarks."
Shane held out his hands. "I'm just a favorite
uncle who brought his nephews to visit their
ponies." It had seemed a good idea at the time.
He hadn't realized this wasn't a full-service
outing.

"Stormy bloats." Franny handed Davey her
reins and marched toward Shane.

"I was going to tell him that," Gertie groused.

Franny seemed weary as she explained.
"You need to give Stormy a nudge when you
cinch her up. Otherwise, when she stops holding her breath, that saddle and whoever's in it
will swing down to her belly." She came up
to Shane. Her frown was deeper than ever.

Shane didn't feel the impact of her frown,
though. His brain was short-circuiting. That
had only happened once before. Also on a
visit to the Bucking Bull. Also when Franny
had come near him. Her eyes... They were
a soft gray. The gray of baby rabbits, chubby
ponies and funeral melancholy.

That was what always drew him up short
when he looked into her eyes. Franny had
weathered life's disappointments and was still
standing, although not defiantly. No. She en-
dured. She was the kind of woman a powerful

man wanted at his side because she wouldn't break. And yet, those eyes…

She was breakable.

Deep down, where she didn't want anyone to see.

"What's this?" Franny pointed to the phone in Shane's hand, which was paused on that how-to-saddle video.

Davey couldn't resist. "He was teaching himself how to saddle a horse."

The Clark boys were beside themselves with laughter now.

Not immune to the ridiculousness of the situation, Shane's nephews, Gertie and Emily joined in the chuckle-fest.

Shane might have laughed, too, if not for the look of exasperation on Franny's face.

He didn't want her to be frustrated with him. He didn't want to be another encumbrance that a ranch owner with a large family had to deal with.

His mouth opened and a defense rattled out. "Gabby, back at the inn, always says you can learn how to do anything on the internet." Great. Now he was quoting a twelve-year-old. He had to get back to Vegas.

"Videos," Franny mumbled, the word punctuated with a weary sigh. She confiscated

Shane's phone and handed it to one of his nephews. "There'll be no more of that. Now, look. You've threaded the strap right. You just need to give her a nudge…" She kneed Stormy in the flank.

The gray pony exhaled, long and slow.

"And then you tug." She yanked the end of the girth strap firmly. "Now she's ready to ride. In the arena. Not the pasture." Her gaze drifted toward the door and the trees beyond the ranch house. "*Never* the pasture."

"Thank you." Andy hugged his pony, extending his small arms as far around his pony's neck as they'd go.

"What about me?" Alex asked, a whimper building in his voice.

"We're doing your pony next," Shane promised, looking around for a stall containing another pony.

"As amusing as this has been—" Emily walked her horse into the barn "—I've got to get cleaned up for work in town. Davey, can you put my horse up?"

Davey nodded. He may have been lacking a hand, but he was more skilled than Shane, and probably many others, with horses. He tied up both horses before Emily left the barn.

"Davey." Franny gestured for her oldest to

come closer. She leaned down and said in a low voice, "What's the first rule of ranching?"

Davey's smile fell quicker than a poorly thrown rock in a tranquil pond. "Safety."

"Should you be letting Shane saddle ponies for kids to ride when it's clear he doesn't know what he's doing?"

Davey scuffed his boots in the dirt. "No."

"Is it safe for a pony to have a saddle put on wrong? Couldn't she get hurt?"

"Ah, Mom." Davey didn't like to be schooled on responsibility, especially when his two younger brothers could hear.

Franny straightened, one hand around her son's solid shoulder.

Shane was touched. The scene reminded him of himself and his grandfather standing similarly on a trip to the Monroe Yacht Works.

"Whatever you make in life, do it with honor and pride," Grandpa Harlan had said.

The Clarks subscribed to the same principle.

The business-like facade fell away from Franny's gaze, letting the vulnerability shine through. "Thanks for standing up for Davey yesterday."

"You know—" Shane captured Davey's eye

"—I think he would have done all right without me."

Davey's chest swelled with pride. "I'll help you saddle Brownie, sir." But he paused to scowl at his younger brothers, who were giggling.

"I appreciate it, Davey. And you can call me Shane." He waved at his nephews, indicating they should come closer. "Come over here and watch. Maybe by the time Zeke gets home we can show him what we've learned about caring for your ponies." Too late, he realized. Good ol' Uncle Shane had essentially promised he'd bring his nephews back to the ranch more than once in the next two weeks.

Davey demonstrated how to put a bridle on Stormy—bit first, then hook the headstall over her ears. "Didn't you learn this in school when you were on the polo team?"

"It's coming back to me," Shane admitted. "Slowly, because I'm old." Slowly, because he'd had no true interest in becoming a polo player back then. "I didn't actually make the team. I fell off my horse too much when I swung the mallet at the ball."

Laughter filled the barn once more.

"I've fallen off a horse," Andy revealed in Shane's defense. "I landed in manure."

"Me, too," Alex said solemnly. "Zeke says if you're a true cowboy, when you fall off, you get back on."

Shane's brother-in-law would say that. He was a true cowboy.

Shane bent his knees until he was face-to-face with his nephews. "I fell off so many times I decided I wasn't going to be a cowboy or a polo player. But... No matter what you decide to be when you grow up, I'll always be there to support you." That felt like a sentiment Grandpa Harlan would approve of.

No one was laughing now.

Shane rose, feeling more than a little self-conscious. What was coming over him? His father would scoff if he heard that sentimental mush.

"Do you know what people always forget to do?" Grandpa Harlan had told Shane the day he'd graduated from that fancy prep school in Philadelphia. "They forget to say they care. Or they're proud. Or that they'll always be there if you stumble when reaching for those stars high up in the sky." And then, he'd hugged Shane. "Don't you forget."

Shane was trying hard not to.

"Some folk aren't born to ride," Gertie said sagely.

"That'd be me." Shane raised a hand as if taking an oath on the witness stand. "No regrets, though. Who knows? Maybe when I'm helping out here the next few weeks, I'll learn something about horses."

"You don't have to help out here," Franny said, starch plain in her words. "We'll call if we need you." Which sounded a lot like never.

"But I want to ride every day." Alex thrust out his chin.

"Me, too." Andy looked worried, as if he might cry if told he couldn't ride his pony every day.

Every day.

Shane looked at Franny. She returned that look with a breath-stealing stare. Not on purpose, Shane was sure. Nevertheless, Shane felt it all the way down to his toes.

Attraction. Mutual attraction.

It made the idea of "look but don't touch" seem like a test of wills.

His.

Franny was beautiful, with no makeup and a hoodie with a heart that was cracked down the middle. She was fragile, despite her backbone and business-like manner. She checked boxes Shane hadn't realized he had on a list of what would account for an engaging woman, despite the fact that he and Franny came from two different worlds. Strong, capable, independent.

Their attraction had no future. In that electrifying moment, it didn't matter.

And the scary, dizzying fact was that Franny didn't seem to care, either. Because she didn't look away.

"I knew it," Gertie mumbled, a smile in her voice.

Thunder rolled closer, breaking the moment. Its sound almost putting a physical distance between them.

"Oh." Gertie shivered as a chill breeze pushed through the barn.

Shane removed his jacket and wrapped it around the old woman.

"Charlie. Adam." Franny had returned to ranch-owner mode. "Please help Granny Gertie back to the house."

"Ah, Mom." Charlie edged farther away from Franny, his brown hair ruffling in the rising wind. "I want to see the boys ride."

"Can we ride, too?" Adam asked, trying to look angelic, which wasn't all that hard for her youngest. He had her soft gray eyes and a pair of dimples.

"Please," said a masculine-sounding cho-

rus. Everyone had chimed in, from Shane and his nephews to her own sons.

He could tell that Franny wanted to refuse. It was there in her expressive eyes. "All right. All the boys can ride."

Whooping, her boys scampered about, collecting tack and tossing good-natured taunts at each other.

"Shoot. No ride for this old bird." Gertie wrapped herself tighter in her layers. "I never have any fun."

"You're cold," Shane said. "I'll take you back to the house. That is, if that's all right with Francis." Shane used the formal version of her name on purpose, intent on inserting a layer of protocol between them.

While Gertie protested being put up like a spent horse, Davey said, *"Francis?"* He balanced a saddle and blanket in his arms, grinning. "Nobody calls Mom *Francis.*"

"No one but my dad and the loan officer at the bank," Francis murmured, meeting Shane's gaze once more.

"I'm not here to make you a loan," Shane murmured back with a reluctant smile. His plan to put space between them was officially over.

"Permission granted," Gertie said with a knowing smile. "To call her."

"I'll watch the young riders, Shane." Franny turned away from him. "If you watch the old meddler."

"Meddler? Me?" Gertie harrumphed. "You two need meddling."

Shane and Franny were quick to reassure her they did not.

CHAPTER SIX

PONIES AND PINT-SIZE horses plodded around the arena with no destination in mind.

Like my life.

Shane used to have a plan, one that involved world domination through his eventual control of the Monroe Holding Corporation.

Gertie bumped him with her elbow. "You think too much."

"You can never think too much." There were worst-case scenarios and permutations of possibilities to make contingency plans for. With the town. With the dissenting eight. With his father's hinted offer. With his hunch regarding the terms of Grandpa Harlan's will ending a year after his death.

"It's dangerous to second-guess in here." Gertie tapped her temple. "As dangerous as second-guessing yourself in here." She tapped a spot over her heart. "You miss out on life." She nodded toward the arena. "Take my Franny."

Now there was a comedic opening.

Shane smiled, refusing to accept the bait.

"She's been hiding out here on the ranch ever since Kyle died..." Grief seemed to steal Gertie's smile. "Blaming herself. Second-guessing her management of the ranch. It's all my fault."

"I'm sure that's not true." Shane glanced up at the scene before him and immediately felt as if his professionalism and detachment had been stolen from him when he hadn't been looking.

One look at Franny riding that big black horse earlier and he'd forgotten cowgirls weren't his type. And now...

Franny stood in the middle of the arena directing traffic—congestion caused by her boys and their horses. She also corrected riding technique—sadly lacking in Shane's nephews. Wisps of brown hair escaped her ponytail and cowboy hat and were flung about by the ever-increasing wind.

"Why don't ponies have steering wheels?" Alex's question elicited hoots and chuckles from the Clark boys. Alex had an insatiable curiosity, which would either lead him to become a top scientist for NASA or a cracker-jack private investigator.

"Heels down, Alex," Franny instructed. "That's it. Good."

"Look, no hands." Andy dropped his reins and extended his arms to the corrugated tin roof.

Shane was certain Andy was going to do something that involved speed and adventure—fighter pilot, downhill ski racer, human cannonball at the circus.

"Pick up those reins, Andy, or you'll have to get off." Franny had a way of delivering commands without sting.

Shane knew Franny's father couldn't do that.

Andy did as asked, looking only slightly abashed. He kicked his pony in an effort to get her to move faster. The pony ignored him.

Shane chuckled.

"Better," Gertie said. Despite her praise, she nudged Shane with her elbow. "Hear that?"

He cocked his head. Hooves plodded on dirt. Birds sang in the rustling trees. Cattle, mothers and their calves, called to each other in the pasture beyond the arena. Thunder rumbled again and was closer than before. "Hear what, exactly?" he asked. There were too many options to choose from.

"Emily's leaving. For work."

The rumble of a truck engine on the other side of the barn heralded as much. Emily was going into town to open Sophie's shop. Shane's twin had given him a choice—run her store while she was honeymooning or watch her twin boys. He'd chosen babysitting his nephews. Just his luck that his choice put him in proximity with a beautiful woman who wasn't in his long-term plans.

"Do you hear that?" Gertie interrupted his thoughts with the same question.

Shane dutifully listened once more and shook his head.

"Out here, you listen." Gertie gestured toward the other side of the covered arena. "Rushing water."

Shane heard it now—the gurgle of fast-running water in a stream or culvert.

"It's raining in the mountains. Soon—" Gertie gave him a smile made lopsided from the half of her face that had yet to recover from her stroke "—it'll rain here."

"We'll be okay, right? The arena has a roof." At her soft laughter, he added, "Will the ponies get spooked?"

She laughed some more, shaking her head as if enjoying a private joke.

"Granny, you should go back to the house

before the rain hits." Franny spared an instruction for her grandmother. "We'll ride a little longer and then put the stock away so the Monroes can get back to town safely." Her gaze flicked over Shane dismissively.

He didn't feel dismissed. He felt aware. Of her. And curious. About how she'd feel in his arms.

Franny Clark was a handful. And she had her hands full, what with raising three boys, running a ranch and caring for Gertie. Shane had his hands full, too, what with watching his nephews, worrying about his grandfather's legacy and formulating a plan to become the leader of his generation of Monroes.

He tucked away awareness and curiosity as he stood and drew a grumbling Gertie to her feet. He helped her to her walker. She set a slow pace to the ranch house.

"What a gentleman," Gertie said. "Harlan would be proud."

"You three—Shane, Bo and Holden—get ice cream last," Grandpa Harlan had said on one of his beloved road trips. "A gentleman waits until everyone he cares about has what they need before he sits down to eat."

Cousin Holden, then seventeen, had shoved his way between twelve-year-old Shane and their grandfather. Holden was the first Monroe grandchild and thought he was Heaven's gift to the family and the world. Cousin Bo, fourteen, had shoved his way between Holden and Shane, driving an elbow into Shane's gut for good measure. As the second Monroe grandchild, and having hit puberty early— *he'd begun shaving at eleven!*—Bo didn't let any of the remaining grandchildren forget he was the biggest.

Standing at the end of the line, Shane had been beside himself. *A gentleman?* Shane was just a kid. Besides, they were a party of thirteen. What if the parlor ran out of ice cream before Shane's turn? Or cones? Shane had a sweet tooth and a bottomless pit where his stomach was supposed to be.

But year after year, trip after trip, the message had sunk in. Family first. Always before his own needs. And strangers. Strangers came first, too. On Grandpa Harlan's road trips, they'd stopped to help more strangers than Shane could count. Flat tires. Engine trouble. People caught short, asking for gas money to get to the next town. Grandpa Harlan didn't discriminate or judge. He treated everyone as if they were trusted equals.

"Keep up." Gertie's words brought Shane

back to the present. She returned his jacket to him and pointed at a nearby tree. "Here."

"Am I supposed to listen to the tree?" Shane gave it a cursory glance.

"Pfft." Abruptly, Gertie sat on the part of her walker that acted as a seat, fingering something inside the pocket of her thin jacket. "Look up."

He did, sliding his arms into his jacket as the first raindrops began to fall. He nodded and then spotted what she was actually referring to.

An old photograph in protective plastic had been placed in the trunk of the tree, and the tree had grown around it until only a few inches of the couple in the picture was showing.

He moved closer and ran a hand over the bark, which acted as a sort of frame for the picture. "Is that a photograph of you?"

She smiled. "That's my husband, Percy, and me. In our prime." She blew out a breath, clearly challenged by the amount of words she wanted to say. "This darn cold wind... steals my breath. We were going to a dance. In Ketchum."

He should get her inside, but there was something unusual about a photograph in a tree. "Why did you put your picture in the bark?" She didn't do that with all photographs. He'd been inside the ranch house once before and had seen her wedding photo on display.

"We all did it. Young couples. Family. Friends. We put them near our homes and other important places." She frowned slightly, fingering whatever it was in her pocket.

Above them, a bird sang at the top of his voice as if doing so would keep the dark clouds away.

"If you all did it…" Shane tried to process her point. "Does that mean my grandfather has a picture in a tree somewhere, too?"

"Yes." She pushed herself to her feet impatiently, as if she'd been waiting for him to put two and two together the whole time. She headed toward the ranch house. "Harlan had many."

Shane snapped a picture of the photograph with his phone, planning to show it to Cousin Laurel when he returned to the inn. "Was that because he was a ladies' man?" Many female residents of the town, who'd known him, had told Shane as much.

"No. His pictures lead to Merciless Mike Moody." Gertie paused and peered at Shane as he caught up to her. "Do you believe me?"

"You're talking about Merciless Mike—the stagecoach robber?" Shane didn't so much as crack a smile. If the desperado had existed and she knew more about him, he could use that to protect and preserve the town. "Do you have any proof?"

Before she could answer, thunder boomed, rolling across the valley.

Gertie cocked her head. "Hear that?" she asked when the sky quieted.

Shane listened. "No. Everything is quiet."

"Exactly. No birds." She stood and aimed for the house. "Best get inside."

Once Gertie was seated in a living room chair with a cup of tea and Shane had a cup of coffee, she twisted her face into a frown. "Promise me that you'll help Franny."

"Of course." Not that he thought he'd be called upon for more than bringing them groceries or unstopping a clogged toilet. Even those things he imagined Franny could do just fine on her own.

"She's in over her head."

Shane found that hard to believe. "I'll help any way that I can."

Gertie studied him before nodding, satisfied.

Boisterous voices mingled with laughter

and the heavy raindrops falling outside. Feet pounded up the porch. Franny and the boys were back.

"I'd like to talk to you more about my family's history." Who knew what else he could learn from Gertie besides how sentimental photographs were left in trees?

"When you've seen more of the pictures, you can ask me." An odd stipulation.

The door banged open and five wet boys tumbled in. They talked and laughed over one another as they shed wet boots, jackets and hats. Franny brought up the rear, hanging her hat on a hook near the door before organizing the discarded outerwear.

Davey ran over to Gertie. "Mom taught us how to ride in a horse parade. Five across. I had to rein in Yoda." He leaned forward and whispered, "He doesn't like to parade with ponies."

"Me, neither." Gertie glowed at her great-grandson. "You rock, kiddo. Fireworks?"

"Fireworks." Davey thrust out his right hand.

The two fist-bumped and did a backhanded handshake, then performed a one-handed jazz-hand explosion, complete with the sound of firework bursts.

"Uncle Shane!" his four-year-old nephews said in unison as they scrambled onto his lap.

"We're cowboys," Andy announced, digging his toes into Shane's thigh.

"Franny said so," Alex echoed solemnly.

Shane made all the appropriate noises and shifted Andy's feet.

His gaze collided with Franny's in the hope he'd have gotten over his infatuation.

Nope, still attracted.

He glanced at Gertie, who was grinning. "Don't get any ideas."

"Too late." She chuckled.

Shane set his nephews to the floor. "We'd best be going before we wear out our welcome." He stood, pausing to kiss Gertie's soft cheek, ignoring Alex and Andy's protests about video games and feeding their ponies dinner. "Thanks for the cowboy lessons. We'll come back for another pony ride in a day or so."

Gertie grabbed his hand. "Look for more bread crumbs to Merciless Mike." Her voice was a whisper.

"Bread crumbs? You mean, the pictures in the trees." Shane glanced out the window, but the pouring rain obscured everything. "Here?"

"Everywhere," the elderly woman replied. "Follow them to find what you're looking for."

"Okay." The jaded side of Shane, the one that comped high rollers and planned corporate takeovers, wondered at the purpose of such a hunt. The gentler side of Shane, the one that was a good uncle and loved his grandfather, wondered what clue Gertie was giving him. Would he find Mike Moody's gold? Or something important about Grandpa Harlan? Both seemed a cold roll of the dice.

"I'll walk you out." Franny cut short any opportunity for more questions. She didn't waste time outside, either, helping Alex into Shane's tall SUV and buckling him into his car seat, while Shane did the same for Andy on the other side of the vehicle. "Can we talk before you go?" She gestured for him to follow her to a corner of the covered porch, away from the front door.

"My grandmother likes to spin stories about the past."

"You mean Merciless Mike?"

Franny nodded, looking grim. "Merciless Mike Moody. Buried loot. Riches like you've never seen."

"I've heard the tale before." From Egbert, the town historian, who'd helped fill in gaps about the historical significance of buildings in Second Chance.

"The gold is a myth," Franny said firmly. "Every kid for the past five or six generations has tried to find Merciless Mike's ill-gotten gains, including Gertie's husband and your grandfather. While it's amusing to most people in town, it's real to Gertie." Franny winced. "More so, ever since her stroke. I'm afraid my kids are going to take her seriously one day and go off into the woods and start searching. And be deeply disappointed." She punched her hands into her jacket pockets. "Please, don't tell anyone she brought up that old tale. It just keeps a silly myth alive."

"My lips are sealed."

"Gertie's lips should've been sealed," she muttered.

All this talk of lips…

Shane was struck with the need to stare at hers. No lipstick. No work done to plump them. They were just your average, run-of-the-mill lips.

And still, he stared.

"I…" Franny paused and for the first time seemed uncomfortable with him. "You don't need to come around anymore. I know you promised Zeke you'd watch out for me—*for us*—but that won't be necessary." There was a worried slant to her eyes, as if he'd discovered more than Monroe secrets during his time on the ranch today. As if he'd discovered *her* secrets.

Help her. Gertie's words came back to him. Maybe she did need help. In his experience, the people who vehemently turned down assistance were often the ones who needed it most.

The jaded side of Shane was convinced Franny wasn't his problem.

The sentimental side of him was convinced it would be an honor if she was.

He stared at his Hummer through the pouring rain. Water raced past his tires, easily two inches deep now. The ranch's dirt-and-gravel driveway was long, with switchbacks, potholes and deep ditches.

"You can see we're doing fine here," Franny said with just a hint of desperation in her tone. "We moved some of our prime stock down to the spring pasture this morning."

Some.

And her father had refused to help her.

"And how much more stock needs to be moved?" Shane zipped up his jacket.

Her eyes widened. "How did you...?"

"A lot, I'd imagine." Shane shrugged off her surprise at his assessment. "I'm a manager. I put information together and manage things." Like family trips to Second Chance and a one-thousand-room luxury hotel on the Vegas strip. He'd gladly push forward change in Second Chance if given the opportunity. "What are you worried about?" It couldn't just be him learning about a local legend from her grandmother or mentioning the fable to folks in town.

Franny put her hands on her hips and tried to look as if she was a successful, independent businesswoman who had everything under control. She couldn't pull it off. Her gaze wavered.

Shane jumped in, feet first. "You're behind in inventory management because Zeke broke his leg last January, aren't you? And now he's off honeymooning and you didn't have the heart to tell him you couldn't spare him. So, seriously, how can I help?"

"You can't." She frowned, clearly disliking his perceptiveness and his questions. "Ranching is dangerous work. We'll get by on our own."

Shane shook his head. "I can ride, a little." Western saddles had horns, didn't they?

It was a lot harder to fall off than from an English saddle while wielding a polo mallet. "I'll come back tomorrow and give you a hand."

"So, you're a corporate manager *and* a cowboy now?" Franny was trying to undermine his goodwill. But her gaze couldn't hold his, a sure sign there was more here than met the eye.

More than her pride?

He didn't know her well enough to decide. "I'm sure you have horses that know what to do around cattle. You just need someone to sit at the controls in case anything goes wrong."

The rain increased, coming down so fast that the sound nearly drowned out his words.

"You've just succeeded in boiling down the effectiveness of a cowboy into a simple drone." Oh, she was mad. Her hands were moving. And her eyes... They were moving, too. Giving him a once-over. A twice-over. Landing on his mouth.

Shane might have smiled if her gaze hadn't deepened into a glare at the first twitch of the impulse.

"I gave my word that I'd help," he said. "And help I will." He moved toward the steps to leave, but hesitated, noting the increasing depth of water around his tires, while struck with worry about his nephews and the drive to town.

"I suppose you always honor a deal." Franny came to stand next to him, hugging herself.

"Yes. And I suppose you don't accept help."

"I would from my ranching neighbors."

"You'd ask for a cowboy's help but at great cost to your pride," he said, thinking of her father. "I don't understand why my suggestions are so unpopular in this town. I always offer good advice."

"We're afraid whatever you suggest will raise taxes to pay for services more common to a city, like buses to ferry tourists from one end of Second Chance to the other. Up here, if you want to go somewhere, you find your own transportation."

"Ah." That might explain why his suggestions about tourism and festivals met with resistance from the town council. But he had bigger issues at hand. He pointed to the deepening water rushing across the gravel driveway. "Is this house in a flood plain?"

Franny scanned the yard, and then the dark sky above them. "You need to come back inside." She hurried down the porch steps and shouted over the downpour, "The road back won't be safe."

He ran after her through water that reached his ankles. "Are you sure inside is the best alternative?" It seemed like the flood was coming and they'd need an ark.

"The house is raised. We'll be fine. The highway has a history of washing out in springtime, rolling whatever is on it down the hill." She yanked the SUV door open and reached for Alex. "The safest place on the Bucking Bull is this house."

With her.

CHAPTER SEVEN

"THERE'S MY NEW partner in crime." Laurel Monroe, Shane's cousin, waved at Emily from the porch of the brick mercantile.

Tongue-tied, Emily ran through a litany of witty replies, like "hey" and "afternoon." None of which struck the sophisticated note Emily was looking for. Because she was used to talking to horses and cattle, not twin sisters of famous actresses. Silently, she climbed the stairs from the highway to the trading post, where she'd be working at least temporarily, settling for a wave as a reply.

"Let me know if you need anything." Laurel disappeared into the mercantile.

"Like my voice?" Emily's foggy brain didn't bode well for the next two weeks.

In a sea of log cabins that made up the heart of Second Chance, the brick mercantile stood out. One hundred years ago, women had bought calico and lace there. Today, Laurel's shop sold work by local artisans—quilts, hand-knit sweaters, blown glass, paintings and photographs of the Colter Valley. Laurel was a vibrant redhead who was pregnant and engaged. Needless to say, Emily was envious. Laurel had come to Second Chance and fallen in love with the local innkeeper and his daughter.

In a few short weeks, Emily would be thirty. She could practically feel the seconds ticking by on her biological clock. The girl who once only wanted to work on a ranch, now only wanted to be a mom. And the way Emily saw it, she had two choices: move to Alaska, where the male-female ratio favored single women, or find a job in Second Chance. So, she set aside her guilt over leaving Franny in a jam on the ranch and opted for town to reach for the brass ring. Or a diamond ring, as it were.

Emily turned toward the trading post.

Whereas Laurel ran a homey boutique, her cousin Sophie ran a secondhand store. What she sold wasn't exactly antique, but it wasn't exactly junk, either. And she knew how to let people know it was a store filled with unusual finds. The front end of a Ford Edsel was attached to the log facade and the porch railings were antique bicycles. Sophie also had an online store advertising what seemed like an endless stream of merchandise.

Emily unlocked the door and turned on the lights. It was like stepping back in time. A small horse from a carousel. A collection of oil lanterns and old oilcans. Delicate wooden chairs. A small potbellied stove. She peered into a glass case and wondered what Sophie had put inside this week. There'd been a display of silver sheriff's badges and cast-iron toy fire trucks last week. Pairs of ceramic salt-and-pepper shakers filled it now—brightly colored Chihuahuas, mallards, hula dancers, dancing bulls and more. Each priced around twenty dollars. They were cute, and she bet she'd sell some before Sophie returned home from her honeymoon.

Emily was always amazed at the items Sophie had on sale. Several pairs of used cowboy boots were clustered in the corner near some old ceramic gas-station signs that leaned against the wall. An ancient typewriter sat on the shelf, missing the *H* key. A display of tall, slender trophies lined a shelf beneath a high, narrow window.

There were lots of outbuildings at the Bucking Bull with similar collections of what Emily considered useless stuff. But, hey, people actually bought things here, and because they did, Emily had a chance to meet men.

Possibly eligible men interested in used cowboy boots, old oilcans and gas-station signs.

Slim pickings, but still.

Why was Granny Gertie so annoyed with her working in town?

Would you leave if you married a Monroe?

Leave her home for the chance at love and family?

Can I take my horse?

Emily sighed. She didn't want to leave the ranch, but drastic times called for drastic measures.

A truck parked in front of the Lodgepole Inn across the street. Two men got out and looked around.

Two men.

A shudder of excitement made Emily's heart soar.

I knew working in town would pay off.

Her brain matched faces to names. *Monroes!* And one of them was Bo!

She'd chatted with him at the wedding reception. He'd said he was leaving town, but here he was. Back again.

For me?

Thunder rumbled in the distance. Emily refused to take it as a bad omen.

"Jonah! Bo!" Laurel had stepped out on

the mercantile's porch. "What are you doing here?"

Perhaps not having heard, Bo trotted up the steps to join Laurel. Jonah, a skinny redhead with a messy goatee, turned and acknowledged Laurel with a nod.

Before the wedding, Emily had studied the Monroe family tree as if preparing for a midterm exam. Jonah was Laurel's brother. He was a scriptwriter with credits that included such classics as *The Good Witches of Sixth Grade* and *Christmas on Cleveland Mountain*. Kid fare. That didn't disqualify him. No. It was his lean frame. Clearly, he didn't eat beef or biscuits. And Emily had never been skinny in her life. That disqualified him.

It was Bo whom Emily had her sights on. He had muscles that went on for days, putting some of the rodeo cowboys she'd met to shame. Next to him, she felt petite. He had gorgeous thick brown hair and gray eyes, not to mention he'd been raised in Texas and wore authentic cowboy boots. He'd make beautiful babies. Burly cowboys and sturdy cowgirls.

"Did you forget something?" Laurel asked Jonah, as he made it to the porch to join her.

"I forgot not to listen to Shane." Jonah had a distant air about him, as if he was living too much in his own head. "I'm here to *contribute* and then I'm going to leave."

A car pulled into the lot in front of the general store, which was situated next to the inn. Four young women got out of the car, talking and laughing. They had on city-girl clothes—short shorts and cute blouses.

"Wow." Jonah had turned toward the newcomers entering the store and Emily's opinion of the scriptwriting Monroe went right along with them. "I'd forgotten what a great view the town has."

"I know you aren't enjoying a view of the Sawtooth Mountains or the wildflowers." Laurel didn't let her brother get away with anything. "Don't even try to pretend you aren't watching four sets of trouble."

Jonah grinned. "Okay. Not pretending."

Emily grinned. Back when Kyle was alive, she'd teased her brother mercilessly, too.

Tears gathered, and Emily retreated to the sales counter. Kyle's death had blindsided her. And now, the ranch seemed to be missing something.

What would Kyle think about her wanting to leave the ranch for love? She hoped he'd have said something like "We'll get by without you, squirt," and not "You're a quitter, squirt."

Granny Gertie was fond of saying "Clarks don't quit." But that hadn't applied to Emily's parents. A decade ago, they'd accepted a buyout offer from Kyle and Franny, and then retired to Padre Island in Texas. Nowadays, the only thing they rode was a motorboat. They were happy, proving Clarks could live off the ranch and still feel a sense of satisfaction.

As long as I can take my horse.

A figure appeared in the open doorway, startling her.

"You don't wanna be jumping like that when the paying customers show up." An elderly woman entered the trading post. She wore a burgundy corduroy skirt and a thick beige fisherman's sweater. Her short gray hair stuck out at all angles and her attitude stuck out, too.

"Odette." Emily tried to keep the surprise out of her voice, but she blurted, "What are you doing here?" Odette wasn't a people person. Instead, she hunkered down in her cabin with her sewing machine and knitting needles.

Odette didn't seem to take offense to Emily's surprise, or at least the older woman's prickly tone didn't get pricklier. "I delivered a baby quilt to Laurel. I'm one of her top sellers." There was pride in her voice as she turned to look out the door. "That Monroe improves the town scenery. I bet Laurel would get more people to stop if he stood in front of the mercantile."

"You mean Jonah?" Emily welcomed the excuse to join Odette and take in the view.

"No." Odette pointed a slim finger across the way. "Mr. Bo-dacious."

Although he was too far away to hear Odette, Bo tilted back his head and let out an all-encompassing laugh as if he was used to being the life of the party. He wore blue jeans, and filled out a red T-shirt that proved he didn't sit in an office all day writing scripts for teenage girls like his cousin Jonah. Emily wanted Bo to laugh with her like that.

I should have worn my black blouse.

The one she put on when she ventured down to Challis for line dancing in summer. It accented her curves and made her feel feminine.

The Monroes disappeared into the mercantile.

"Those Monroes make me feel lonely." Odette shook her head.

"I know what you mean," Emily murmured.

"Because Monroes like that won't stay here." Odette prodded Emily's shoulder with one finger as if needing to emphasize her point, which seemed to veer from the point Emily had thought she was making. "Those big-city fellas are fragile, just like birds who can't last the winter."

There was nothing fragile about Bo. Now Jonah… He was another story.

"Well, I'm off." Odette headed for the path in the trees that led to her cabin. "Did you know we still don't have a replacement for Doc? It's shameful, I tell you," she called out, and kept talking long after Emily could no longer make out her words.

"Okay then." There was work to be done. Emily logged into the computer and checked the online version of the store. Someone in Boise had purchased an old steamer trunk and left a question in the comments regarding pickup. Emily emailed the customer back, confirming store hours.

And then the air was filled with feminine laughter. The young women had left the general store and were climbing the steps to the mercantile and trading post. They wore flip-flops and the boisterous smiles of women who knew they were pretty, who knew how to wear makeup and who knew how to flirt with men without looking like they were calculating his years of fertility.

Emily fidgeted behind the counter and startled when she heard footsteps on the trading-post porch. A man appeared in the doorway.

Jonah, not Bo.

Their eyes met. His were a crystal-clear blue. She sucked in an unexpected breath.

Who knew a stick figure like Jonah could pack a punch of sexual attraction?

Emily wondered if every Monroe had a superpower. Bo had those muscles. Jonah had those eyes.

Jonah's gaze drifted to more interesting things. "So, this is what Sophie gave up being an art curator to do." He meandered through the trading post.

More footsteps.

Emily's body sent out a red alert—*be on the lookout for Bo-dacious hunks.*

Bo appeared in the doorway, filling it with his broad shoulders. "Holy secondhand store." He chuckled. "I'm sorry Sophie isn't here for me to tease her about this." He entered the trading post, making the room feel smaller. "Where are the ancient paintings and marble statues?"

"Cut her some slack." Jonah stared above the fireplace at a bear trap. It was one of several Sophie had on sale. "The things here seem to have a certain Sophie-like charm. Old stuff with a story behind it."

Both men spared Emily a glance, as if waiting for her to join their conversation. Her mouth was too dry to speak.

"Are you thinking of writing a story about cowboys, snow and bears?" There was a humor in Bo's voice and a twinkle in his eyes. "Hasn't that all been done before?"

"Everything hinges on a fresh twist." Jonah didn't rise to the bait, answering as if they were having a civil conversation. "There's a new breed of horror film. Everyone's clamoring for smart scripts."

"Horror would be a new genre for you." Bo winked at Emily. "That is, if you don't count all those smarmy teenage television shows and movies you wrote. Those horrified me."

Emily couldn't believe she'd been included in the conversation—with a wink, no less.

Jonah considered his cousin the way a cowboy considered a powder-blue tuxedo. "They may not have garnered me any awards, but it was all lucrative work."

"Sellout." Bo tried to disguise his dig as a cough.

"Muscle-head." Jonah copied his cousin's coughing jab.

The college girls flip-flopped into the trading post. Not a one looked at the merchandise.

Unless you counted Bo.

They completely ignored Jonah, who leaned on the counter near Emily and sighed, as if being ignored was a common occurrence for him. Considering he could double as a scarecrow, it probably was.

"Are you from around here?" a blonde asked Bo.

"Nope. Texas." Bo held up a silver baby cup. "Who would buy someone else's baby cup?"

Giggling, the women surrounded him, offering answers and vying for his attention.

"You should jump in there," Emily advised Jonah, feeling sorry for him. He may not have the brawn of his cousin, but he did have those amazing blue eyes.

"Why?" Jonah yawned, never taking his eyes off the preening spectacle in front of him. "They're not staying. And besides, those are just the kind of characters to put into a screenplay with a rusty old bear trap and a small town with dark, spooky cabins and a snowstorm."

"Hey." Emily took offense. "Don't be ragging on my hometown."

"Do you live in a dark, spooky cabin?" Jonah's gaze swung around to her.

So blue.

It took Emily a moment to remember he'd asked a question. "No. I live in a hundred-year-old farmhouse."

"Also creepy," Jonah murmured, which still annoyed Emily, despite his pretty eyes.

"You and I have a different definition of *creepy.*" Emily managed to smirk. "What's this I hear about your charity work in town?"

Jonah gave Emily a stare that tried to pass for blank, but there was too much intelligence behind all that blue to fool anyone.

Except maybe college blondes in short shorts. They, apparently, didn't know what they were missing.

Emily was out of practice talking to men. She had to search her brain for the thread of their conversation. Ah, yes. "Charity work. You know, you told Laurel you came back to town because you have to contribute something."

"Oh, that." Jonah shrugged again, his gaze

drifting to his cousin, allowing Em to breathe again. "I'm a writer. I have nothing to contribute. I just can't get Shane to realize that."

Kind of like her at the ranch. Any cowboy could fill her boots. "Kind of defeats the purpose of your return then."

"Can't prove I didn't try if I don't try," Jonah said cryptically as he quit leaning on the sales counter. "Bo, I'm going to find the nearest bar."

"There is no nearest bar," Emily blurted.

Jonah sighed, not looking at Emily. "Bo, I'm going to find the nearest coffee place."

"There's only the diner." Inwardly, Emily cringed. She sounded like Davey, leaping into conversations at the first opportunity.

"Bo, I'm going to the *diner* for a cup of coffee."

Emily pressed her lips closed, watching Jonah leave.

"Sounds good." Bo disengaged himself from the blonde's clutches and followed Jonah out the door, trailed by his entourage.

Emily watched them go, wishing she was blond or had gone to college, or wasn't the kind of girl who was invisible to Bo-dacious hunks.

Laurel appeared in the doorway after they

left. "Mitch wanted me to tell you it's raining cats and dogs in the high country." Mitch being Laurel's fiancé, the manager of the Lodgepole Inn across the street and the mayor of Second Chance.

"Oh." Emily broke free of her Bo-inspired stupor. "Oh, no."

Her cell phone rang as the raindrops began to fall outside the trading post.

She didn't have to hear what Franny had to say to know she wasn't getting back to the ranch tonight.

"Oh," Emily said, less demoralized this time.

She was stuck in town and Bo was back.

Her odds of finding a man were improving.

CHAPTER EIGHT

"Thanks anyway, Jason." Franny ended the call on her cell phone and dropped the device on top of the dryer. "Blast." That was her last contact from her list of cowboys.

No one was available to work during the next two weeks. No one.

Her stomach was tied in knots and the weight of the Clark dynasty pressed on her shoulders heavier than ever.

The rain had been coming down for hours, thick and depressing, like her mood. The property was flooded with several inches of water. There was no way Emily was getting safely home tonight. And Shane wasn't leaving, either.

"Hey, Franny. Did you get anything to eat?" Shane came to stand in the mudroom doorway, as if drawn by her thoughts. "Anything I can help you with?"

"Help me?" Franny eyed the other door that

led outside. Escape wasn't an option. She blew out a breath. "No."

Not unless you can rope a bull from horseback. Not unless you can give a few young bulls a go at an eight-second ride. Not unless you can leave the ranch and let me return to not remembering what it felt like to stand in the circle of someone's arms.

"Help me?" she repeated. "Not unless you can wave a magic wand and—" Holding on to the dryer, Franny closed her eyes and attempted to focus on good things.

"It sucks going through a rough patch, doesn't it?" Shane interrupted her before she could make a mental list of goodness.

"Rough patch?" Franny opened her eyes, anger elbowing back despair as she turned to face him. "That's it? That's all you've got?" This was so much more than a rough patch. She gripped the collar of her T-shirt.

"Well, to be fair, I didn't have much to go on." He sighed as wearily as if he was the one carrying her burdens. "Listen, you and I both know magic wands don't exist. And pretending's for the weak. You have to be honest with yourself. Lay it all out there with your team." He paused, his soft gaze lingering on her.

Franny looked down. She was clutching

the collar of her T-shirt, stretching it out and down and...

Oh.

She tugged her T-shirt upward.

"I can't talk when you..." Shane made a strangled noise. "You should sit." With a deliberate, smooth motion, Shane freed Franny's hand from the purple cotton and led her to the bench where the boys were supposed to sit and take off their boots when they came in.

But boys being boys, they left their boots everywhere except the mudroom.

In the living room, Gertie asked Shane's nephews if they'd ever heard of Merciless Mike, the famed stagecoach robber. Davey and the boys began talking over each other about gold-filled cash boxes just waiting to be found on the mountain. Shane's nephews were insisting they'd heard the story before, but none of the Clarks listened.

"Logistics are my forte," Shane said in that take-charge tone of his that people in town took offense to. "Tell me what's going on. Lay it all out there and—"

"Logistics won't help me." She'd called everyone, hadn't she? "I need man power of the real cowboy variety." Franny blew out a breath and stared at her stocking feet. There was a hole working its way to life at her big right toe, the stitching unraveling the same way her life was. "I need a way to keep the ship afloat without letting my family down."

"I can relate." Shane took her chin in his hand and turned her face toward his. "Start at the beginning. Tell me everything so I know what to do."

His touch startled her, thrilled her, threw her into more of a panic than she'd been earlier. "Why? Why help me?" Why would a man like Shane, who—if town scuttlebutt was accurate—didn't own a pair of blue jeans. Why would Shane want to help someone like her, who only had two dresses in her closet— one for weddings, one for funerals. "And don't tell me you gave your word to Zeke."

"Okay." Shane shrugged those sturdy shoulders. "I want to help you because I see something of myself in you. The need to helm an old ship. The need to protect those who don't see beyond today's horizon."

The wind rattled the windowpanes. His gaze rattled her.

Kyle had never rattled her. Their romance had been comfortable. Inevitable. Predictable.

Franny didn't want to feel attraction that unsettled her. She didn't want her problems to be drawn out and exposed. It was easier to go it alone and keep all her fears and insecurities inside, hidden behind the mask of bravery that may not be fooling anyone.

"My grandfather used to say the only successful businesses he owned were the ones that scared the living daylights out of him." Shane rubbed a hand over his chin, over a small scar she hadn't noticed before that was barely visible beneath his dark stubble. "He once told me he'd never taken on a business where he hadn't stayed awake at night wondering what he'd gotten himself into and how many different ways he might fail."

"That can't be true." A knot in her stomach untensed, anyway. "Your grandfather was a millionaire. Many times over."

"My grandfather was just a man. He had fears when it came to business just like you and me. And he made mistakes."

Franny took in Shane's business khakis and polo shirt. "You don't look like you've ever misstepped, either."

Granny Gertie had come to the sad part of the Merciless Mike saga, where there was an earthquake on the mountain and the bandit was crushed by a boulder. He probably hadn't known what hit him.

It was almost better to never see it coming.

"You think I'm perfect? Flattering, but no." Shane rested his elbows on his knees and stared at his hands. "When I was in high school, I developed a problem with authority. As you can imagine, in a family of Monroes *that* didn't go over well, especially with my father. I was a Monroe. And with that came high expectations for me. Nobody wanted a troublemaker. I was sent to live with my grandfather in Philadelphia. I thought... I thought it was the worst thing to ever happen to me." He laced his fingers together and flexed them tight. "Grandpa Harlan enrolled me in this fancy prep school. I had to wear a uniform every day. And when I'd fallen off a polo pony enough times to knock some sense into me, I was ready to go home to Vegas, but..." His entire body stilled. "My dad said I couldn't come home."

Franny forgot to breathe for a moment. And after she did draw in air, she admitted, "My dad had high expectations for me, too."

"Sucks, doesn't it?" Shane eased open his hands and stared at them.

There was no more rattling. No more disbelief. There was just a patch of shared turf in the midst of life's storms.

"I've been trying to make up ground ever since," he admitted.

For her, with her father, that wasn't possible.

"I…" Franny didn't talk about the past. But, she realized, in the big scheme of things, she didn't talk about the future, either. She just kept putting one foot in front of the other. "My father was a very successful cattle rancher north of here. He wanted me to follow in his footsteps. To expand the ranch." She drew a deep breath. "When I became a Clark, when Kyle and I decided to buy this place and leave the Silver Spur to Dad, he was disappointed. But then we started a breeding program. Dad's a proponent of purebred lines in cattle. What we do out here… We don't follow breeding lines or pedigree. We let nature take its course."

Shane still wasn't looking at her. He stared at the washer across from him instead. "We're alike, you and I, not because of a shared past, but because we've both been raised to be competent at what we do. That doesn't mean things don't sometimes get intense or that we don't find ourselves facing a dead end." His gaze found hers. His lips moved upward in a smile reminiscent of Gertie's, lopsided yet genuine. "By the way, I've been told recently—*repeatedly*—that asking for assistance is better than pushing an agenda alone. The whole team-work-makes-the-dream-work cliché." He scoffed. "You and I both know what makes dreams happen. Hard work. Tough sacrifices by a fearless leader. And luck."

His words resonated. All except the fearless part.

Franny let silence fall between them. Listened to her boys talk about what they'd do with Merciless Mike's gold. Davey mentioned purchasing his expensive summer camp so anyone could go. "Telling you my predicament isn't going to help," she told Shane. Franny wanted to look away from those steady brown eyes, but she couldn't.

"You won't know until you try, will you?"

She shouldn't. Clarks kept their problems to themselves. Or, Kyle and his family had. But Franny was only a Clark by marriage. And Shane was so certain he could do something to help. The truth was, she needed a miracle or, at the very least, a giant dose of good luck and a posse of cowhands like the ones who'd gone after Merciless Mike.

"Come on," Shane said softly. "Give me

one fact about your situation. It'll make you feel better. You'll see."

He was offering her hope, something she hadn't felt in a long time on this treadmill of hers.

Hope filled her chest the way focusing on good things was supposed to. Hope made her think anything was possible. "All right. Fact—there's a man coming in less than two weeks expecting to see ten to twenty young bulls ready for the rodeo circuit. We need the money from the sale of those bulls to stay afloat." To keep food on the table and the lights on, not to mention regular payments flowing to her in-laws in Texas and to pay for Davey's camp this summer.

Shane didn't throw her a pity party. He simply nodded. "And your immediate task to make this happen is…?"

"Capturing the bulls." She struggled to keep her voice even. "Some of our branded stock is missing. Meanwhile, the two- and three-year-olds we have need to be trained to provide an exciting bull ride." At the crease in his brow, she added, "It's a dichotomy. The bulls have to be workable—herdable into stock trailers and chutes, willing to stand relatively still while the straps are put on and—"

"Docile, but mean-spirited when a cowboy gets on their back."

"Exactly." She squirmed, trying to hold back more truths, but not succeeding. "Fact—my husband died two years ago—" she carefully avoided the details surrounding his death "—and I haven't trained a bull since." She'd left that to Emily and Zeke, neither of whom had the ability to see the devil in a bull's eyes and tease it out. Not the way Kyle or his father had been able to do. And maybe not the way Franny had been able to, either.

"You used to train bulls?" Shane asked, leaning back and looking at her in awe.

"Don't be sexist," she snapped, pushing him farther away because his admiration might be her undoing.

"Gentlemen are rarely sexist. And you definitely deserve props for that." He held up his hand for a high five. "Bull trainers deserve respect, male or female."

Mollified, Franny touched her palm briefly to his, then admitted, "I can train, but I don't ride. I have an aversion to being trampled or gored." Although rodeo bulls were all dehorned. She held up her phone. "No one who can ride is available."

"Let's recap the steps. First you catch them

all." Shane smiled that nonthreatening smile of his, the one he'd used when he'd admitted he had no skill prepping horses to ride. "I'm sure word will get out that you're looking for bull riders. Maybe you should advertise that you'll train young cowboys how to ride, or let them practice bull riding for free. Like an internship. Or, maybe you should open up your call list to women."

"No." She scowled. "And no."

He gave her a funny look.

"No," she said again, this time louder. "It's not a summer trail ride on some dude ranch. These are large animals with small amounts of patience. And those are the domesticated ones. These aren't starter bulls with training wheels."

He frowned. "Life isn't safe. Accidents happen. Things go south. I get it now. You need bodies, preferably qualified bodies to—"

"Would you stop using the word *bodies*." Franny's stomach had plummeted back into knots, and she rubbed her hands over her face. "That's exactly what I'll get if I follow your suggestions." All it would take was another injury or—heaven forbid—death for her insurance to skyrocket and her resolve to keep things going to crumble.

Shane stopped talking. He stopped being the attractive man sitting next to her on a wooden bench that needed a coat of paint. There was a quietness to him that spoke of empathy, not teasing attraction. "There's something you aren't telling me."

There was. "My husband... Kyle was..." Franny swallowed thickly. "Kyle was killed by a bull while trying to bring in our strays alone." Although she sometimes suspected he'd gone out to capture a feral. "He was killed by a wild bull on the ridge above our property." Gored. Organs punctured. Limbs trampled. His face. His sweet, handsome face...

Franny held her breath, held in the grief and the hurt as it welled behind her eyes.

In the living room, the boys cheered over the performance of someone playing a video game.

In the mudroom, Shane took her hand. His face was a different kind of handsome than Kyle's had been, more refined and in some ways harder. He brushed a lock of her hair into place. "You aren't planning on training those bulls alone, are you?"

"No." She shook her head. "I need another type of bull."

"I don't understand."

Franny sighed. "Fact—this ranch used to make a fortune at selling killer bulls to the rodeo circuit."

Shane didn't say anything for a beat too long. "How long ago?"

His question confused her. "How long since Kyle died?"

"No. You said this place *used to make a fortune*. How long has it been since the Bucking Bull earned a generous profit?"

Franny pressed her eyes closed. She'd married Kyle ten years ago. They'd never made a fortune since she'd lived on the ranch. "Maybe six years ago, when Gertie's husband, Percy, died." She opened her eyes. And wasn't that a revelation. She let out a half-hysterical laugh. "I'd been thinking it was all my fault. That our financial woes were recent." When in fact they'd been there all along. Franny blew out a breath. There was still fear riding in her chest, but there was an ease to her shoulders that hadn't been there before.

"My offer still stands," Shane said. "I can ride a horse and say get along little doggies."

Franny leaned back to take him in—from his disheveled black polo to his wrinkled khakis. "Tell me the truth. You're not really a

Monroe, are you?" He couldn't be if he was offering to help a struggling rancher.

He chuckled, spreading his arms. "Don't believe what you read in the press." Instead of returning his hands to his lap, he captured one of hers and gave it a gentle squeeze. "In business, you have to decide if the fight to stay in business is worth the effort. Or the risk. And it sounds like, in your business, the physical risk is great."

The image of shadowy eyes in the trees pressed on Franny's chest. She explained about the feral bulls. She told him about the cunning one that had hit the post rail defending his herd.

"How many wild bulls do you need to satisfy the stockman?"

Franny's mouth fell open. "How many?" It was overwhelming to think beyond one.

"Remember?" His hand was warm on hers. His gaze steady as a rock. "Stick to the facts. Let's say you train a few of your own stock to round out the package and make the whole thing look attractive for sale—how many feral bulls would you need?"

"Two or three if he's looking for ten. Five if he's on the market for twenty." She pulled her hand free. "But don't. Don't try and plant hope in my heart. I can't find cowboys to even train our stock, much less catch ferals."

Shane tapped his forehead. "Logistics, remember. Two of my cousins came back to town today, one of which is my cousin Bo, who was raised on a ranch in Texas. That's enough bodies to round up the rest of your herd. And if need be, I can cover for Emily at Sophie's shop. *Retail* should have been my middle name."

More weight was lifted from her shoulders, just enough to keep hope alive. "And the bull riders?"

"This country is full of cowboys. Make some more calls. You'll find someone. Keep your spirits up."

And pray, she added.

Because someone was bound to get hurt.

And she wished with all her might it wasn't Shane.

Andy snored.

He was lying across the top of the sofa in the Clarks' living room, arms hanging down on either side of the couch where Shane was trying to sleep.

On the opposite end of the couch, Alex was lying across his legs and snoring, too.

The rain had moved on. But everything dripped outside. *Drip, drip, drip.* The moon moved in and out of the clouds. And there was the snoring.

"Listen," he muttered, thinking of his conversation with Gertie. Oh, he was listening, all right.

On the floor near Shane's shoulders, Bolt, the Clark's Labrador, was lying on his back, feet in the air, also snoring.

Shane wondered if he snored. He wondered if establishing the historical significance of Second Chance would be enough to spark tourism and protect the town from vultures like his father. He needed things to prosper in town if he was going to head all the family's businesses one day. He wondered why he'd told Franny about his past. He wondered if it was wise to help Franny when, increasingly, he wanted to kiss her.

It wasn't in his nature to renege on a deal, although she had the most kissable lips and he wasn't going to stick around town forever. He wasn't setting down roots here. He wasn't a cowboy looking for a ranch to work on. He wasn't looking to be a father to three rambunctious boys. Franny needed all that from a man and more. And yet...

I promised.

Not just Franny, but Zeke and Gertie.

Bolt pawed the couch cushion near Shane's head.

Shane inched closer to the back of the couch and bumped Andy's hand with his head. His nephew startled and clutched Shane's short hair, trying to find balance. Shane stifled a cry and steadied his nephew's arm. Alex sat up, as if sensing his brother's distress, and then flopped forward and drove his elbows into Shane's legs. Bolt sat up, surveyed the situation and put his two front paws on the cushion beneath Shane's shoulder.

"No," Shane whispered, shooing the dog aside.

With one hand on Andy to keep his nephew from falling off the couch, Shane sat up. He scooped the boy into his arms and walked down the hall to Emily's room, then tucked him into bed because that's where the twins had started the evening. Shane returned for Alex and slid him beneath the quilts next to his brother.

With a running start, Bolt managed to leap on the foot of the bed. He circled, pawed the quilt to his liking and then settled down with a sigh.

"Stay," Shane whispered, backing out of the room. The couch would be ten times more comfortable without this trio, lumps and all.

He padded to the living room, pausing to put another couple of logs on the fire.

Movement outside the window caught his eye—a large, four-legged body moved in and out of the trees on the other side of the barn. Except the longer he stared in its direction, the less it seemed to be anything other than a shadow from a cloud drifting overhead.

Shane settled on the couch, wondering…

If that had been one of Franny's feral bulls, it had been big.

But it couldn't have been a wild bull this close to the house…

Could it?

CHAPTER NINE

FRANNY CAME DOWN the stairs early the next morning with her mind made up.

First order of business? Put distance between herself and Shane. She'd kept herself awake last night marveling at his no-nonsense approach to her problems.

And the warmth in his brown eyes.

She pulled herself up short at the thought.

There will be no appreciation of the warmth in his eyes.

She continued down the stairs.

Second order of business? Ride Danger to check to see if the road was passable for Shane in his SUV. The rain had finished moving through the valley sometime after midnight.

It'd be so much easier to ignore how the warmth in Shane's eyes sparks an answering warmth in my chest if he was gone.

She stopped on the landing, staring out the front window to confirm the water wasn't rushing through the yard the way it had been yesterday.

It wasn't.

She stared at it a while longer because she knew what she'd see when she walked through the living room to the kitchen—Shane sleeping on the couch.

Third order of business? Ride the fence line in the ATV looking for breaks. *Note to self: bring supplies to make repairs. And Kyle's gun.*

That struck a little fear in her heart, enough to bolster her courage to face the handsome man sleeping on her couch.

She turned.

Shane was lying facedown on the sofa in front of the dying fire. Alex was sprawled on top of him. Andy was draped across the couch back, arms and legs dangling on either side. And Bolt was curled between Shane's legs.

This is worse than gazing into his eyes.

Franny swallowed.

He's adorable.

Not that it mattered. He was like a lost show pony. Eventually, he'd find his way back to the bright lights.

Franny walked on near silent feet to the kitchen because no day truly started without at least a little caffeine. She knew the coffeemaker was set to finish brewing a pot right about now.

Shane extricated himself from his human and doggy blankets as she passed, easing Andy from the couch back onto the cushions without waking him.

His nephews and Bolt slept on.

"Need any help?" he asked as he followed Franny into the kitchen. He contorted himself as if he needed to work the kinks out of his body.

With effort, she kept from staring. "I'd ask you how you slept, but I think that's obvious." The coffeemaker was in the final spitting stages of finishing the brew. Franny took two mugs from the cupboard. "You look like the sandman left sand in your eyes."

"My nephews don't know the meaning of the words *personal space*." And yet, he'd sacrificed his personal space for their comfort. The tenderness in his voice was likely to have spilled into his eyes, so she didn't look. "I carried them back to bed twice during the night."

Bolt joined them in the kitchen and sat on top of Shane's bare foot. Traitor. He rarely got up in the morning until Adam did.

"Stay here while I get the barn chores

done." Franny poured a cup of coffee and handed it to him. "Enjoy the peace and quiet."

Staring at the gray-muzzled dog, Shane shook his head. "You can show me how to help in the barn. Even if it's only picking up eggs."

"You should dress like a local if you're going to pitch in like a local." Franny froze in midpour.

"Visitors can pitch in." His voice was low and intimate. "No matter how they dress."

"Regardless…" Was that her voice? It was equally low, equally husky. Her cheeks heated. "If you want to help out on the ranch, you'll need a pair of cowboy boots. Blue jeans are recommended, but optional."

"I know where to find boots in town. And contrary to popular local belief, I do own blue jeans."

She wanted to lift her gaze and see his face. She kept staring into her coffee mug. "Yes, but did you bring the jeans you own with you?" Because no one in town remembered seeing him wear them.

"If you're willing to let me help with those bulls, you'll find out, won't you?" The warmth. The tease. The magnetism.

Franny closed her eyes. "You make me

afraid." Afraid she'd find out too many other things about Shane Monroe, appealing things, and fall for him.

"I scare you?"

"Yes." She opened her eyes and met his gaze, firmly, the way a woman with responsibilities would. "Because you aren't a cowboy. Because you don't aspire to the ranch life. And because you aren't going to stay in Second Chance."

"Meaning these long glances we exchange aren't predictive of a future together."

"Yes." Her pulse raced. She couldn't believe she'd told him that nothing was going to happen between them. That nothing *could* happen between them.

Shane cleared his throat and gestured toward her with his mug. "I appreciate your candor."

"I appreciate you not arguing my points." She slurped down her hot coffee, suddenly aware that Gertie's bedroom was just off the kitchen.

"You're the boss." Shane drank his coffee without a sound. His gaze on hers was as soft as a caress. "What else is there to do besides collect eggs this morning, boss?"

"Mucking out stalls."

Humor lit his dark eyes. "My cousins would say I'm good at shoveling—"

"Shhh." She clapped a hand over his mouth, removing it almost immediately. But not before she felt his warm breath on her palm. Her heart was off to the races again. "We don't use that word."

Shane grinned. "I was going to say shoveling fertilizer."

"Sure you were."

There it was again. That warm-eyed smile that made her forget she'd been married and widowed.

"Finish your coffee," he said. "I need a minute to wash up."

Together, they made short work of the chores in the barn and chicken coop. Franny lingered at Buttercup's stall. The old bull ate slowly, as if he'd lost his appetite.

"You keep a bull in the barn?" Shane had returned from dumping manure in the compost pile and parked the wheelbarrow near the equipment room.

"Buttercup is special." Franny explained about his storied past. "He's actually Buttercup number four. When the Clarks find a feral bull that's successful on the rodeo circuit, he retires with the name Buttercup."

"He's tame then?"

The old bull raised his head and stared at Shane, as if offended by his remark.

"No. He's far from tame." She made sure his stall latch was secure. "That's why I open the door to let him out in the paddock before I clean his stall."

An engine roared to life outside.

Shane frowned. "Does Gertie drive?"

"No. That's Davey. He probably noticed we're out of milk and decided we need to go to the store." Without realizing the road might still be flooded—or worse—washed out. Franny opened the barn door as Davey drove the truck toward her.

"Whoa." Shane came up behind her. "He's not just warming up the truck. He's driving." He elbowed Franny out of the way. "Can he reach the brake?"

"He's fine. We teach kids early how to operate machinery."

Davey stopped the truck safely and rolled down the window. "Mom, we need milk."

"I've got to check the road first."

"I'll do it." Davey shut off the truck and hopped out. He ran into the barn. "Yoda loves to ride in the morning."

"Okay. Breakfast in thirty minutes." Franny

picked up the bucket with eggs and headed for the house.

Shane dogged her steps. "You're going to let a kid ride down the mountain alone? What about—" he lowered his voice "—the feral bull?"

"There are too many fences between the pasture where I saw the bull and the road." Franny was already shifting gears, thinking about how to round out a meal of eggs for a crowd.

"Are you sure?" Shane glanced back toward the barn, frowning.

"History has proven me correct." She reached the porch steps and hurried up them. It was only when she got to the front door that she realized Shane wasn't with her.

He stood at the corner of the barn, looking at something a few feet away on the ground.

"Are you coming?" she called out to him.

Shane shook his head. "I'm going to ride the road with Davey."

"THANKS FOR SADDLING Zeke's horse for me." Shane rode the sleek brown horse along the gravel road next to Davey. He searched the ground for hoofprints and the trees for large, oblong bodies.

"Pandora likes to be ridden." Davey sat tall in the saddle and surveyed the land like a king enjoying the view. "Someday I'm going to have a horse like her. A true cattle horse trained by Grandpa Rich."

They rounded a corner made blind by overgrown brush. Water rushed in the stream to their right. And the stream had carried the dirt and gravel road away. There was a huge gulley where the road used to be, too steep of an incline to traverse in a vehicle without ending up balancing on its headlights.

Shane pulled at his horse's reins. "Well, this is unexpected." He was grateful Franny hadn't let him attempt driving away yesterday.

"We have to make sure this is the only bad part of the road." Davey sounded more like an adult than a nine- or ten-year-old. "Come on." He urged his small horse into the cut, through the stream and up the other side. Davey slowed his horse and waited for Shane to follow.

The good news was there were no humongous hoofprints.

The bad news was he couldn't let the kid go it alone. He stared down the steep slope.

So much for learning anything about riding on the polo field.

Oh, he'd learned something, all right. He'd vowed never to ride again.

He eased up on the reins and Pandora took off, eager to catch up to Davey and Yoda. Shane managed to stay on her, heeding some of the advice Franny had given his nephews yesterday—heels down, hands on the reins, sit back.

They followed the switchbacks down to the highway. Luckily, they were muddy from the deluge of water, but there was only the one section that had been washed out completely.

Davey stopped near the ranch gate and cattle guard. "See that?" He gestured with his wrist to a lake and a cluster of small cabins. "That used to be a kids' camp. I'm pretty sure it closed before I was born. Still, my dad used to take us down here in the summer to skip rocks."

There was a faded sign on the side of one cabin with what looked like an insignia of a tent among some trees and a river.

"That's a shame that you never got to camp here," he said.

"I go to a different camp." Davey straightened in the saddle, eager to talk. "I go with other missing kids."

Shane frowned, trying to process Davey's

words. Missing kids? Kids who'd been kid-napped? That didn't seem right. "I don't follow."

Davey held up his wrist. "Kids who are missing pieces, like me."

"Oh." Shane caught on. "The title threw me. I don't consider you missing anything."

Beaming, Davey sat taller in the saddle.

"You know…" Shane wracked his tired brain. "I think my family owns that camp."

"What are you gonna do with it?" Davey stared at Shane.

"I don't know." Shane leaned his forearm on the saddle horn the way he'd seen Emily do. "Maybe skip some rocks."

"I can teach you," Davey said solemnly.

A branch snapped in the brush behind them.

Shane swung around in his saddle but saw nothing. "We should get back. I need to ask your mother something."

"Like what?" Davey led the way.

"Like when she'll get the driveway fixed," Shane said, peering into the brush.

Or how sure she was that feral bulls couldn't reach the road.

EMILY HAD ALWAYS been envious of folks who lived in the heart of town.

They had the option of gathering for a cup of coffee in the Bent Nickel Diner, where they could hear the latest news or see their favorite people before work. Emily's visits to the diner were limited to specific opportunities created when she dropped off and picked up her nephews from their independent studies with Eli Garland, the education coordinator for their rural county. On those trips, she was usually in a hurry, fitting a visit to the grocery store into her time in town, rather than lingering over coffee or a meal.

Emily sat at the diner's counter, cradling a mug of coffee in her hands. She watched Bo in a booth near the front window. He put away a breakfast of steak and eggs as if he hadn't eaten in days.

"Don't make it so obvious." Jonah sat down next to her on a bar stool and ordered hot tea from Ivy, who ran the Bent Nickel.

"I beg your pardon?" Emily made a show of selecting a sugar packet and tapping it against her fingers to loosen its contents. Not that she put sugar in her coffee.

"Bo is like a tomcat." Jonah stroked his red goatee and gave Emily a sideways glance. "He only likes women who play hard to get. Don't chase after him."

Emily's spine stiffened. She returned the sugar packet to its small basket. "I'm not chasing after him."

"Chasing, mooning... Same thing." Jonah turned his stool so that he faced Emily. He seemed to be studying her. "I hear you were stranded in town because of the rain. But I didn't see you here for dinner last night."

"I ate at the inn." Laurel had invited her. "Not that it's any of your business." Not that she'd admit she'd been too nervous to hang out in the common room with the Monroes after being tongue-tied with Laurel. What if she couldn't think of anything to say to Bo?

"I'm a writer," Jonah said. "Everything is my business." He continued to stare at her with those brilliant blue eyes of his. "Why are you working in Sophie's store?"

"Seriously. It's none of your business," Emily snapped, unable to keep from sneaking a glance at Bo.

"Let me explain why I disagree." He leaned closer. "Shane wants Bo and me to contribute to town. You know, help out wherever we can. Be a good citizen and so forth. Sophie and Laurel have been doing it, too."

A strange feeling came over Emily. A strange cold feeling. It closed around her as if she was a goose caught napping in a rapidly freezing winter pond. "You think Sophie asked me to work in her store because I needed the job? Like I'm penniless? A charity case?"

There was too big a pause between her question and his answer.

"No," he said unconvincingly.

"My family—the Clarks—didn't sell to your grandfather." Emily tossed the words at him with as much venom as was possible, given she was whispering. "I'm not like *them*." She gestured to the residents who had sold.

"This is interesting." Jonah leaned closer. Those eyes. They were hypnotic, inviting her to spill her most intimate secrets. "Do you figure they sold their souls to the devil when they took my grandfather's money?"

"That would work for your horror-story script." She mentally shoved him back into his space. Physically, she didn't back down. "You read too much into things."

"It's my overactive imagination." He was unrepentant. "Are you sure there's no bad will in town? No…envy?"

"Shouldn't you be sitting with Bo?" He was so annoying.

"Nah. Anything he's got to say, I've heard before."

Ivy delivered Emily's breakfast—eggs, bacon, hash browns, pancakes, a slim orange garnish—and Jonah's tea, and then disappeared into the kitchen once more.

"Wow, that's quite a breakfast." Jonah stole the orange slice from Emily's plate. "Are you headed back to that ranch of yours to rope and ride before returning to open Sophie's shop?"

She was heading back for a clean change of clothes. "Breakfast is the most important meal of the day." Emily shifted her plate as far away from Jonah as she could without moving to another seat. "Are you counting your calories?" She nodded toward his tea.

Nothing like a man with no appetite to make a healthy gal feel cranky.

"And now I've hurt your feelings." Jonah grinned, an expression that highlighted his blue eyes. "I'll let you in on a secret. Writers—" he tapped his chest "—sit too much. We burn less fuel than cowgirls—" he tapped her shoulder, grinning broader when she shrugged away from him "—who are more than welcome to eat what they need to in order to do all the things cowgirls do. Writers—" he tapped his chest again "—are prone to writer's butt. Cowgirls are not."

Emily shoved a bite of eggs into her mouth to stop herself from gaping. She'd had some odd conversations with men over the years, everything from best practices for bull-semen collection to proper tack for headstrong horses—a product of her being just one of the guys—but this had to be the oddest. Where did the conversation go after a writer's butt?

Across the room, Bo got to his feet. He wore a blue checked shirt, blue jeans and cowboy boots. Jonah wore sneakers, white cigar jeans and a red T-shirt featuring an eighties rock band. Bo walked out the door with purpose. Jonah sat next to her for no reason.

Emily felt like she was on a blind date that was going poorly. She prayed for Franny to call her and let her know the road to the Bucking Bull hadn't been washed out.

"Did you hear the coyotes yipping last night?" Jonah didn't seem to notice or care that Emily was shoveling food into her mouth too quickly. "Scary, right?"

"Second Chance isn't frightening." Emily set down her fork and tried to set aside her annoyance with this man. "Don't tell me. Let me guess. The only creature you hear at night in Hollywood is the occasional stray alley cat."

"Hey, I've been camping." His eyes flashed with an emotion she couldn't immediately identify.

"In a motorhome, I bet."

"I've slept under the stars." The emotion revealed itself—amusement. His face blossomed into a grin.

I'm his entertainment.

Emily picked up her fork and stabbed a chunk of egg. "There's an abandoned camp by the entrance to the Bucking Bull. I bet you'd find plenty of inspiration by sleeping in one of the cabins." If he accepted her challenge, she'd sneak into the grove of trees bordering the camp during the night and make ghostly noises, rustle branches and toss pebbles onto the roof of his cabin.

His smile never wavered. "A research opportunity. I love it. You'll have to show me where it is."

She chewed her egg and nodded.

Oh, she'd show him, all right.

CHAPTER TEN

"YOU DIDN'T HAVE to c-ome with me," Franny shouted over the ATV's engine as she gunned it along the fence line.

"Oh, yes. I did." With his pulse pounding in his temples, Shane held on to Franny's hips from his spot behind her as he searched the wooded terrain ahead for large moving objects, like bulls who sneaked down to the barn in the middle of the night.

By the time he'd gotten back to the Bucking Bull, helped Davey put up the horses and found Franny, what he'd thought had been a bull's hoofprints by the barn had been obliterated by five young boys playing hide-and-seek.

"Here." Franny brought the ATV to a stop next to a set of fence poles that had been pushed over. "The ferals are coming in here." Pieces of short, dark fur clung to wire barbs like feathers tied to fly hooks. "At least the wire didn't snap this time."

There were rocks surrounding the base of each metal pole. They'd tumbled several feet downhill.

"I'm guessing from the rock piles that they've come in this way before?" Shane pointed at the potato-sized stones. It was the first he'd seen of their use.

"Yes." Franny unstrapped the cargo hold and removed a shovel. "There's a trail they take down the mountain." She pointed toward a wide, trampled track disappearing into the trees, and then she gestured down the hill. "You can see the pasture from here."

And no doubt smell the green grass.

"I don't see tracks." Shane gave the ground a quick perusal, hoping to see something dissimilar to what he'd seen around the barn this morning. He wanted to disprove the nagging suspicion that he'd seen a bull last night.

"They'd have been washed out by the rain."

Shane took the shovel from Franny. "Hold the post up while I fill in the dirt." So they could reposition the post vertically and shore it up with those rocks.

Franny righted the pole and cocked her head. "Do you hear any birds?"

"No." He planted his feet and began digging. His leather loafers sunk in the mud. His spade cut through soupy earth. "Should I?" He was reminded of Gertie telling him to listen. "Do you want me to whistle?"

"No on both counts." Franny stared toward the trail above them, and then over her shoulder, eyes darting nervously.

Shane spared the trees a glance. A pair of eyes stared back at him. He stopped shoveling. "Look."

"What? Where?" Franny let go of the post and rushed to the cargo hold, grabbing a shotgun.

"Stand down." Shane pointed. "That's one of those tree pictures your grandmother was talking about." He stepped carefully over the wire and climbed the ten feet or so over to the tree.

"What are you doing? Get back here." Franny's voice was filled with fear.

Curiosity and quiet overrode Shane's apprehension. "I want to see who's in this picture." The one framed in the tree trunk. Shane expected the photo to be of Percy and Gertie. He was surprised to recognize his grandfather's young face staring out at him. Harlan was flanked by Percy and a man who was the mirror image of Harlan. "What the...?"

His grandfather had no siblings.

"Shane, I think you should get back on my side of the fence."

"Agree, but…" He tugged his cell phone from his pocket and snapped a photo of the picture. "Do you know anything about my grandfather's family?"

"No, and I don't care. Shane, I don't hear any birds."

"That's probably because you scared them with the booming engine of that ATV." With his back to Franny, Shane stared at the yellowed photograph. The three men stood leaning on shovel handles. Had they been digging for Merciless Mike's gold or…? "Did my grandfather help Percy build this fence?"

"I don't know." Franny's voice was high-pitched, stressed-out. "Shane, the birds go silent when there are ferals nearby."

A twig snapped behind him.

Shane spun.

Franny had her gun raised.

A hulking bull stood twenty feet away on Franny's side of the fence. His long horns were caught in the branches of the trees he stood between. He moved his head slightly, cracking the thin branches. But his gaze never wavered from Franny.

"Don't move," Franny said just as Shane picked up his foot to rejoin her.

"Is he feral?" Shane asked as quietly as he could above the roaring in his ears. "Are you going to shoot him?" Were they going to have steak for dinner?

"It's no big deal," Franny said in a half whisper. "Just stay still."

Shane went cold. He had to get to Franny. To protect her. "Shoot him." There was no way he could reach Franny and get her to safety. Thanks in part to the slick slope. Not to mention the barbed wire. While the bull had a clear path to her.

"He's on the Bucking Bull side of the fence," she said, still in that hypnotic half whisper. "It's no big deal, fella. *I'm* no big deal."

Shane begged to differ. She was a big deal. To him. To those boys back at the ranch. To Gertie and Emily. He didn't know how that could be. He'd met her twice before yesterday, albeit it hadn't been a run-of-the-mill twenty-four hours. Now, death was staring them down.

And he was helpless.

He'd never shot a gun before and, standing there, he regretted it, more than he regretted not learning how to ride a horse properly. Why hadn't his past prepared him for this? He was going to fail Franny.

Shane lifted his foot again just as the bull huffed and turned away to amble down the hill, breaking branches as he went.

A flock of birds took to the air in his wake, silent in their escape.

"Get on the ATV, Franny." While the bull's back was to them. Shane picked his way carefully down the slope, over the wire, and made it to her side.

Franny hadn't moved.

The sound of cracking branches receded until, finally, there was silence.

"I need you to fix that fence." Franny rested the gun in the crook of her elbow and pushed up the fence post with a hand that trembled.

"You can't be serious. We need to leave." Race down to the ranch house and move everyone into town. Shane clenched his hands into fists, sucked in air, tried to tamp down the adrenaline. "That thing is in your pasture. He pushed over the fence posts like they were candy canes in the snow."

"That's not the biggest of the bulls, Shane. He's workable. I need him to stay in my pasture. You can go back to the house if you want, but I'm not leaving until this fence is fixed." There was no fear in her voice. She was sounding more like her competent, determined self. "He's worth more than Merciless Mike's gold to me."

"I'm lodging a formal protest." Because Shane couldn't leave her. He started to dig, listening for birdsong and formulating all kinds of contingency plans.

FRANNY COULDN'T STOP SHAKING.

Not even when she and Shane closed the pasture gate behind them.

Not when she parked the ATV in the shed.

Not when Shane got off the ATV and stood berating her while she put away fencing tools and the other supplies.

"I can't believe you made us go the entire circuit," Shane ranted. "All around the pasture."

"There was more fence down." Details. She had to focus on details, or the shaking might get worse. Might make her realize feral bulls were a big deal. A very big, dangerous deal.

"You knew there would be."

Franny shook her head.

"Everything we fixed had been fixed before, shored up with rocks." Wow, he sounded angry.

"I didn't know." Franny couldn't remember the last time she'd repaired the fence. She finished putting everything back where it belonged and faced Shane squarely. "But Shane... It's okay to be scared. A healthy dose of fear makes you careful." That was her father talking.

"What we did out there was anything but careful." Shane stood his ground, muddied, red-faced, upset. "That was too much of a gamble."

"Were you calculating the odds?" She attempted a smile, but her lips quivered just as unsteadily as her knees. "Haven't you ever just gone with your gut and taken a chance?" He was from Vegas, after all.

"I've played hunches." He stared across the ranch yard at his SUV. "That hasn't always ended well."

At the mention of bad endings, the shaking grew more severe.

Franny paced in a small circle and shoved her cowboy hat more firmly on her head. Began talking in the hope that words could help her return to a normal state so the boys wouldn't see her like this. "I grew up on the other side of the valley. Our ranch wasn't as large as the Bucking Bull or as high-profile," she told him. "We raised Black Angus. I know my dad wanted to have boys—lots of boys to ease the workload and eventually inherit the place." She shrugged. Still loaded with adrenaline, her shoulders practically bounced off her ears. "All they got was me. Mom was thrilled at having a girl. Dad made do. I was taught how to apply makeup with a steady hand." Life on the Bucking Bull had taken that skill away from her. "Noticing that steady hand, Dad taught me how to shoot, ride and rope. And here's the thing about roping..." She settled her hands on her hips, gripping the denim to hide the shaking. "It's all about instinct. Oh, there's rhythm. There's grip-and-release." There was the pressure of the knees and legs around your horse. "But it all comes down to gut feel. When you feel the bull will stay the course. When you feel you've got the arm strength to handle the distance of the throw." When you feel luck is on your side. When you're certain you won't miss because you'll disappoint your father if you do.

"Instinct?" Shane huffed harder than the bull had on the mountain. "You're calculating odds in your head the same way professionals count cards dealt and played."

"I'll go with instinct, thank you very much." Why wouldn't her hands be still?

"Instinct," Shane huffed again, staring at her. And then he closed the distance between them and wrapped his arms around her.

They were strong arms. She leaned into him and he was like a rock. Her arms slid around his waist as she drew a shuddering breath and admitted, "It was scary, but everything's going to be all right. All I need to do is prep them for the rodeo."

"Them?" Shane drew back and tilted up Franny's chin so he could see her face.

"You didn't see? There were two bulls with horns in the pasture." Bradley Holliday was going to be pleased with that. "I need to bring them to the arena, dehorn and deworm them, and get them used to captivity."

"A move that's simultaneously hazardous and brilliant. Franny..." There was wonder in his voice. And then he was kissing her as if they'd survived the sinking of the *Titanic* but might not make it out of the lifeboat.

He was right, of course.

But she rather liked the image of herself as the "Unsinkable Molly Brown."

And she rather liked the intensity of his kiss. It reminded her of who she used to be.

CHAPTER ELEVEN

"Did you guys have a good time?" Shane asked his nephews as he slowly navigated the Bucking Bull's repaired driveway.

Franny had contacted a neighbor with heavy equipment and arranged to have him repair the washed-out sections of the private road in exchange for beef or manual labor. Someone had called as they returned from mending fences to say her driveway was as good as new.

"I had the best time," Andy said from his car seat in the back.

"Being a cowboy is almost as much fun as being in school." Alex built on his twin's review.

"Better," Andy said. "Did you see any bulls, Uncle Shane?"

"Yes." Oh, Shane had seen a bull, all right. He'd had a front-row seat as Franny had faced down that monster, knowing she needed the bull for the stockman. Shane would've shot the darn thing. Instead, he'd kissed her.

That wasn't what Zeke had in mind when he asked me to help her.

Guilt had its hot hand pinching the base of his neck, right next to where regret was clasping him.

Not that the kiss had gone poorly. They had chemistry to spare.

But that hadn't been the right place or the right time. Possibly not even the right woman.

"I wish we lived on a ranch." Andy yawned his words. "I could ride Stormy whenever I wanted to."

"We'd wear cowboy boots all the time," Alex said through an equally deep yawn.

"There's no falling asleep in the car." Shane eased around a corner. If they fell asleep during the ride to town, it would throw off their bedtime tonight.

Speaking of sleeping, he'd been unable to ask Gertie about seeing double in Harlan's photograph because she'd been napping when he and Franny had returned from mending fences.

His nephews were eerily quiet.

Shane glanced back. They were both asleep. Snoring.

"Just my luck," he muttered as they reached the main highway.

A truck and trailer were parked alongside the road. And a man wearing a straw cowboy hat was securing a very muddy tractor with a scoop onto the bed of the trailer.

Shane got out of the SUV and approached him. "Hey, thanks for fixing the driveway for Franny. Can I give you gas money or something?"

The man spared him a glance, which turned into a curious stare. It was the older cowboy he'd seen in the diner. Rich, Franny's father. He stopped ratcheting the broad straps and looked Shane up and down with cold gray eyes. "Are you coming from the Bucking Bull?"

"Yes, we…" Shane reached for the smile he used with dissatisfied high rollers. "My sister married Zeke Roosevelt, who works at the Bucking Bull. I brought my nephews over yesterday to ride their ponies and we got trapped by the rain. I'm Shane." He held out his hand.

Rich chewed on his answer, likely searching for bones to pick. "Huh." He went back to tightening the straps without introducing himself or shaking Shane's hand.

"You know, Franny needs help with those bulls. She's got a stockman coming and—"

"*Francis* chooses to run this ranch on the backs of mongrels and strays." Rich moved to the next strap.

"My grandfather used to say there's a market for everything." Who cared if Franny made a living selling feral bulls? "If you think about it, she's running a bit of an animal rescue. Those bulls will get good medical care and guaranteed meals." A stretch, but hey. He had to say something in her defense.

Rich scoffed. "You're a Monroe."

"Yes, sir." Shane wasn't going to apologize for that.

"I have no gripe with Francis selling bulls to rodeo stockmen." Grunting, he struggled to lock the ratchet in place. "It's her breeding practices that dilute stock. Crossbred bulls don't produce stronger cattle."

"Aren't they breeding for rodeo purposes? To produce a meaner bull for the circuit?"

"No." Rich scowled, pulling off his work gloves and slapping them against his palm. "Don't get me wrong. You have to introduce crossbreeds into your lines every few generations to prevent inbreeding and defects.

But you do it through the crossbred cow, not the bull."

Shane didn't pretend to understand the man's diatribe. "If that's the case, why is that part of her business so lucrative?"

"Because *some* ranchers *assume* a bigger bull will produce bigger calves, meatier calves. They don't study ranching. They just plunk some cattle in a pasture and hang a shingle." Rich shook his head and pushed past Shane, opening the door to his truck. He tossed his gloves inside and turned around. "Ranching is about sustainability and responsibility, not just of one ranch, but of the industry."

"So you won't help Franny train the stock she needs? And all because you disagree with one aspect of the way she puts food on the table?" Didn't he care about his grandkids?

"Mr. Monroe…" Rich tipped back the brim of his hat and glared at Shane. "Everyone has to decide how they want to live and what they believe. They have to draw the line and decide how far is too far." He pointed his finger at Shane. "Your grandfather knew that. It was the one thing I respected about him." Rich climbed in his truck and drove away.

Leaving Shane to wonder what line Grandpa Harlan hadn't crossed.

"WHAT'S TROUBLING YOU?" Gertie came through her bedroom doorway into the kitchen and rested on her walker.

"Nothing." Skin chilled, Franny closed the freezer door and set the roast on the counter to defrost.

Gertie wasn't buying it. "You were staring into that freezer for a good minute or two before you noticed me."

"I was distracted." Huge understatement. "I need to bring the ferals in the pasture to the ranch proper." Brand, tag, inoculate, deworm, dehorn. "I need someone with better arm strength than Emily or I have to do it properly." The dehorning tool was like a heavy branch trimmer and required leverage.

"There are sturdy men in town." Gertie settled on the walker's seat. She wore a stretched and faded red sweater, loose pants and slippers. "Not to mention Shane."

"Please. Let's give the idea of Shane a rest." They'd kissed. And then things had gotten a little awkward between them. They'd returned to the ranch house walking at least six feet apart. And he'd shaken her hand when he left.

She hadn't even merited a hug or a kiss on the cheek. If that wasn't writing on the wall, she didn't know what was. "I'd rather not lean on a man who has no experience on a ranch."

And yet, Shane had promised to return tomorrow with his cousins.

"Pfft. No experience on a ranch? That sounds like your father talking." Gertie thrust her hands in the pockets of her sweater and worried whatever was inside.

"No. It's me who's talking." The woman who was so flustered she couldn't remember what seasonings went in pot roast. "It gets harder every year to run this place."

"You're only saying that because it's been a difficult two years. I felt the same way after Percy died. But I had you and Emily, and the boys here every day, giving me a reason to push on. And, of course, there's Merciless Mike Moody."

A shiver went down Franny's spine at the irrationality of Gertie's reference to the bandit. Why would he give Gertie the will to live? Franny refused to acknowledge her grandmother's mention of the myth, which meant she couldn't chastise her for telling Shane about those photographs in the trees. "Maybe we should sell. The Monroes might buy us out. And if we lived in a city, Davey would have a better support system."

"No!" Gertie looked horrified. "Davey has the best support system any kid could ask for. You're just restless." She tugged out whatever she'd been worrying in her pocket. It was something wrapped in a white embroidered handkerchief. She clutched it with both hands. "You need a man, if only for his biceps."

"Let's not start with Pauline Willette's nephew's grandson." The man Gertie tried to push on Emily all the time.

"That wasn't what I meant." Gertie's voice had turned gruff. "You need a little influx of money, is all. I told Kyle as much." She stared at her handkerchief.

Kyle. He wouldn't want Franny selling his heritage.

"Don't get me wrong," Gertie continued. "A little romance with a Monroe would do you no harm, but you need a temporary man to help you find Merciless Mike's gold."

Merciless Mike's gold?

Franny gripped the counter and hung her head, convinced that Gertie's stroke had short-circuited a part of her brain. The woman believed in Merciless Mike. Really believed. For her, it was no longer just a beloved story with a family connection.

"I…" Franny couldn't look at Gertie. "Excuse me. I need to check on the boys." She raced upstairs, sat on her bed and put her head in her hands.

Emily was going to leave the ranch. Gertie was becoming unstable.

The clock was ticking on the Bucking Bull's future.

Franny had one hope of continuing. Shane Monroe.

She only hoped her trust wasn't misplaced.

"WELL, WELL, WELL." Shane held his sleeping nephews in opposite arms and kicked the Lodgepole Inn's door closed with his foot. He couldn't as easily kick closed the memories of Franny's kiss or the danger of those large bulls on the slope. "Look what the cat dragged in."

Bo and Jonah lounged on the couch in the common room. They were staring at the latest sports update on the television mounted over the fireplace, and looked bored. He'd known they'd arrived. Laurel had called him last night. But he couldn't quite believe it until he saw it for himself.

"We could say the same for you." Bo grinned

broadly, taking in Shane's mud-stained attire. "You look like the cat dragged you through the nastiest mud puddle in history."

"You dared us to come." Jonah closed his laptop and considered Shane while he stroked his goatee. "At least give us some respect for showing up. Unlike you, we showered and everything."

"We gave Laurel moral support at her little shop across the street." Bo stood and stretched. His cowboy boots rang on the wood floor as he closed in on Shane. "But other than that, I don't see how we can do anything here that increases the town's value. It's not as if they have an oil rig that needs fixing."

He was right. The twins felt heavy in Shane's arms.

Bo needed something concrete, an achievable goal that he could see and measure. Shane wasn't sure he had that where the town was concerned. As for what Franny needed...

"This isn't as straightforward as picking up roadside trash or cleaning up an old lady's garden," Shane explained. Not the usual charitable contribution. Just like Franny wasn't an average woman. She'd kissed him as if he was her lifeline. She hadn't been put off by his need to hold her close and reassure himself she was safe. If anything—

"Your point?" Bo approached and took Andy from Shane's arms.

"I'm not sure he has one." Jonah drummed his fingers on his laptop case.

"Ice cream," Alex murmured, drooling on Shane's neck.

"Hold that thought, everybody." With Bo's help, Shane got the sleeping boys upstairs and settled on his bed. A quick shower. A set of clean clothes. A loose plan to pitch his cousins, with the hope that his proposal would go better than the one to the town council the other day, and he was back in the main room.

Shane sipped at a cup of coffee from the inn's kitchenette and picked up the contribution conversation where he'd left off. "I have a little project for you two."

Closing his laptop again, Jonah eyed him suspiciously. "Your little projects are never little. The last time you had a little project for me, you asked me to write a script for a Vegas cabaret."

"Which was a hit and bulked up your résumé." Shane sat on the hearth and got down to business. "I received a report from a consultant I hired with recommendations concerning improving the town's economy and long-term viability. The first option was long-term—develop this into a luxury destination."

"There's little about this place that seems luxurious." Smirking, Bo gestured toward the log walls of the inn.

"Not to mention, it would take more capital from the twelve of us and it would be a gamble." As a storyteller, Jonah knew how to play out the thread of possibility. "And the alternative?"

Shane liked how Jonah segued for him. "Earn the historical-significance label for most of the downtown area. Make it a walkable tourist stop. Charming shops. A range of dining experiences. All kinds of field trips that would involve highlighting local history and legends."

Jonah's eyes gleamed with interest. "Ah, you need another script."

"This town needs lots of elbow grease. The diner. The stores." Bo shook his head. "I can't help you with any of this." He headed toward the stairs. "Pack up, Jonah. We gave it our best shot."

"Wait." Shane's neck tweaked, just as much a product of his stress as his night spent on the couch. "There is something you can do."

Help Franny with the bulls. Keep her safe.

Shane knew he couldn't ask Bo outright. He'd need another goal, one that mattered to the Monroes.

"Keep looking for pictures," Gertie had said. "Everywhere."

Of course!

"What do you need us for, Shane?" Bo asked impatiently, arms crossed, a wall unto himself.

"There are loose ends." Shane told them the legend of Merciless Mike Moody, adding the part about the pictures in trees being bread crumbs. He didn't tell them his theory that Grandpa Harlan had found the gold because the existence of the pictures called his hypothesis into question. Who left bread crumbs leading to nothing?

"You want us to go on a scavenger hunt?" Jonah sat on the edge of his seat on the couch, looking suspicious. "Searching for markers in trees?"

Shane nodded.

"How big is this town again?" Bo came to stand behind the couch, then leaned on the back and faced Shane, studying him as if this was a high-stakes poker game and he was looking for tells. "The part we own?"

"Two thousand acres." Shane tried to act as if this wasn't a daunting task.

"Have you made a search grid?" Jonah asked. Apparently, writers were just as interested in logistics as hotel-chain managers.

"I haven't. But I have the perfect place to start." Shane kept his expression neutral. "The Bucking Bull Ranch."

Bo frowned. "Do we own that?"

"No." Avoiding a stare-down with his cousin, Shane set his mug on the coffee table and put a small log on the fire.

"Why would we start our search at this ranch?" Bo's scrutiny tried to poke holes in Shane's motives as much as his question did.

"A ranch we don't own, by the way," Jonah added. He may have been intrigued by the story of Merciless Mike, but he didn't seem to be eager to join in.

But they were interested. And they hadn't walked away.

So Shane kept at it. "I'm betting it's there because Grandpa Harlan didn't buy the ranch. It's the perfect place to put something you don't want found."

We ride around the property, look at some trees, round up some cattle.

Two birds, one stone.

Shane allowed himself a small smile.

"You should have gone into fiction writing, Shane." Stroking his red goatee, Jonah eased into the couch cushions. "That's a little too predictable."

"Yeah. What if there's nothing at the end of this trail?" Bo demanded. "Didn't you say residents have been looking for Merciless Mike's hidden gold for decades?"

Shane began to doubt he could convince them to help. Elation drained out of him. He felt the exhaustion of the day, of his extended stay in Second Chance, of the roadblocks he encountered at every turn.

Shane pulled up the picture of the Clarks on his phone and showed his cousins. "I found this picture on a trail leading up the mountain." He toggled to the photo of their grandfather, Gertie's husband and the mystery man.

"Am I seeing double?" Bo squinted. "Two Harlans?"

"Could be a cousin." Shane shrugged. "Or a brother."

"The plot thickens." Jonah couldn't hide the interest in his tone. He'd never been good at cards, either.

"I'm going to contact the county recorder's office." Shane planned to request all records of Monroe births. "We'll find out who's in that picture with Grandpa Harlan. But if we can find out where the trail leads, we can use that as a draw for tourists."

"Hike Merciless Mike's trail?" Bo's expression was dubious. "That sounds like an amusement-park attraction."

"People hike to waterfalls for a good view," Shane pointed out. "They walk the Oregon Trail to experience history. A legend like this adds to the mystique of Second Chance. More so if there is gold waiting there to be discovered."

"'Adds to the mystique'?" Bo grumbled. "It's the only mystery here."

"I don't care." Jonah was definitely in Shane's camp now. "I claim dibs."

"Dibs? On what?" Bo frowned at Jonah. "Pictures in trees?"

"No. Grandpa Harlan's twisted story. Forgotten relatives." Jonah picked up his laptop and began pounding on the keys. "And yes, I suppose photographs in trees. 'Gold in them thar hills.' All I need now is a villain."

"One who'd use that bear trap from Sophie's store?" Bo chuckled, but only briefly. "Hey, are the owners of the Bucking Bull going to be okay with us traipsing around their ranch?"

"It's kind of a quid-pro-quo situation." Shane delivered his proposition slowly. "They'll provide us with horses and lead us around the property if we agree to help herd any stray cattle back to home base." Should he tell them about the granddaddy of all bulls? He decided not to.

There was safety in numbers, right?

Bo crossed his arms. Again, Jonah closed his laptop. They both waited for Shane to say more.

"It was the only way I could get us access to the property." That wasn't the reason at all. Shane was glad Franny wasn't around to hear this.

But someone else was.

"Shane." Roy tottered out of the guest room located to the right of the fireplace. He hadn't combed his white hair or ironed his bright green bowling shirt. Since he'd suffered a heart attack a few weeks ago, he hadn't been comfortable enough to move back into his cabin alone. "You could ask me about the man in the picture." Roy sounded hurt. "Or the pictures in trees."

"If I asked, would you tell me?" Shane knew better than to get his hopes up.

"You know I'm not legally allowed." Roy sat down in a wing-back chair near Bo, having the good grace to look remorseful to have signed a confidentiality agreement. The town's handyman did enjoy being helpful. "Doesn't mean I don't want to be asked."

"And there you have it, gentleman." Shane pointed to Roy. "A nonanswer. Proof that there is something out there. Something Grandpa Harlan wanted us to find."

"Or it's a wonderfully plotted red herring." Jonah studied Roy, no doubt cataloguing him for characterization in his script. "I don't care. I'm in."

Relief relaxed the kink in Shane's neck.

"I suppose I could spare a few days," Bo said, relenting.

"Fantastic!" Shane couldn't believe things were finally going his way. "Plan on a horseback ride tomorrow."

"Can't we rent a quad or something?" Jonah had never enjoyed athletics.

"We don't have enough ATVs," Shane said. The Bucking Bull only had the one quad.

"Cattle can hear engines…" Roy trailed off,

rubbing his collarbone and grimacing like he was having another heart attack.

"Roy?" Shane hurried to the old man's side. "Are you okay?"

"If my heart's still beating in a minute, I'll let you know." The old man levered himself to his feet just as Laurel came out of Mitch's apartment behind the check-in desk.

"Hey, Dr. Carlisle. Thanks for taking my call. I'm sure it's nothing," Laurel said in to her phone as she massaged her lower back and told the former candidate for town doctor her symptoms. "I'm about twenty-two weeks along and…"

Behind her, Mitch filled the doorway, worry lining his strong features. Roy's glazed eyes didn't stray from Laurel.

"*Practice* contractions?" Laurel beamed at Mitch. "That's great to hear… Yes, Mitch made me call."

Roy's breath hitched, which had Shane lurching across the room and taking the phone from his cousin.

"Hey, Dr. Carlisle. It's Shane Monroe." He spit out words quickly before the doctor could protest or hang up. "I'm standing here looking at Roy. You remember Roy, right? Older gentleman who's skinny enough to play

C-3PO in *Star Wars*?" He paused to draw a breath and take hold of Roy's arm. "Anyway, he had a heart attack a few weeks ago and stents put in. And right now, he's rubbing his chest, looking pale and not at all annoyed that I just compared him to a robot."

Mitch took Roy's other arm and together they sat the old man in a chair. Laurel bent behind the check-in desk and then joined them, carrying a large first-aid kit.

"Dr. Carlisle?" Shane checked to make sure the call hadn't dropped. His palms were damp as he tried to recall his CPR training.

"Shouldn't we call 911?" Jonah hovered nearby.

"It'll take them thirty minutes to get here," Mitch explained calmly.

"Is he having chest pain or shortness of breath?" Dr. Carlisle sounded weary but had committed to stay on the line.

Shane relayed the question and got his answer. "No."

Laurel slipped a portable blood-pressure cuff on Roy's thin wrist.

"Tell her I felt a little ping in my heart." Roy cleared his throat. "Ever since it happened... It's probably nothing." But he still looked shaken.

Shane was shaken, too. "His heart pinged. Is that normal? Laurel's taking his blood pressure."

"He needs to be checked out in person by a medical professional. I've seen your equipment up there. You can't trust the readings." She sighed. "Ask Laurel if she can come down to Ketchum for an office visit and bring Roy to see his doctor as well. Today."

Shane relayed the message, setting the group in motion. "Thank you, Dr. Carlisle. I don't suppose you'd reconsider our job offer. You should see Second Chance in spring. The wildflowers are in bloom."

"Amazing." She didn't hang up on Shane. "Holden warned me you'd find a way to repeat your offer."

"Did he now?" Anger shuddered through Shane, questions and accusations pressed up the back of his throat.

His cousin and Dr. Carlisle had spent a long, romantic evening getting to know each other two months ago when the town was snowed in.

"Holden also suspected you might make me an offer to consult on updating your clinic."

"That was the furthest thing from my mind." But a wonderful idea. Shane wished he'd thought of it. Second Chance took time to grow on some people. It was the perfect way to win her over. "Do you still carry that black purse of yours?" The one she used in self-defense.

She chuckled. "Yes, I do."

"You don't use it on Holden, do you?" *Use*. Present tense.

"No." She chuckled again. A feminine chuckle. A self-conscious chuckle.

An I've-seen-your-cousin-recently-but-it's-our-little-secret chuckle.

Shane's fingers curled so hard his knuckles cracked. What was Holden up to? He lived in New York and was dating an Idaho doctor? Why? Shane took a deep, calming breath. "I hope Holden took you someplace nice in Ketchum for dinner last weekend." The weekend he'd returned for Sophie's wedding.

"It was a lovely dinner. I made sure I met him at the restaurant." Her tone gave away that she'd fallen for Holden's considerable charms. "The last time I got into a car with a Monroe I was in Ketchum, but ended up in Second Chance somehow."

"Yes, well. I apologized for that." Shane rolled his shoulder where she'd hit him with her suitcase-sized purse. "Since I can't get you to consult on updating the clinic, can you recommend someone?"

Mitch and Roy headed out the door. Laurel held out her hand for her phone. Someone on Dr. Carlisle's end called her name. Shane wanted to keep the doc on the line, but he couldn't decide which of his thousand questions to ask next.

"I have to go," Dr. Carlisle said. "I'll be in touch."

Shane relinquished the phone and waited for Laurel to leave, then asked Bo, "Did you know your brother was dating Laurel's doctor? Why would he do that?"

Bo shrugged. "Is she pretty?"

"Yes."

Bo yawned. "Is she smart?"

"Yes."

"Pretty, smart, a doctor." Bo ticked off her attributes. "Need I say more?"

Jonah opened his laptop. "He must have run out of smart, pretty doctors to date in New York City."

That was the simplest explanation. But this felt different to Shane.

He added Holden interfering with his doctor search to his list of things to worry about.

CHAPTER TWELVE

SHANE WASN'T NORMALLY a breakfast person.

He was particularly *not* fond of Ivy's breakfast at the Bent Nickel Diner. She wasn't the best of cooks.

But the coffee was good, the rain had moved on and Laurel and Roy had passed their health checks yesterday, so things in town were quiet. And Shane needed to eat since he'd promised Franny he'd return to the ranch today to help bring in strays.

The Clark boys scurried in with their backpacks, dropped off by Franny, who drove off in a hurry. Charlie and Adam headed for the back, where Alex and Andy were serving time in pre-K. The twins would be finished after an hour or so and Laurel had agreed to watch them while Shane returned to the Bucking Bull. He didn't want to take them to the ranch until he was sure it was safe.

Davey paused at Shane's table. "Are these your brothers?" He shouldered his backpack, holding the arm with his missing hand to his chest, where everyone could see. Owning it.

"Cousins," Shane clarified. His brother was too busy being a chef in Vegas to stay in Second Chance. He introduced Jonah and Bo. "This is Davey, one of the cowboys from the Bucking Bull."

Davey's chest swelled with pride at his title. "Mom says if I grow, by next year I can help her with strays the way you guys are today. Well…if I grow and get good grades. I better go." He leaned down and whispered, "I didn't finish my vocabulary."

The Monroes wished him luck as he scurried to join his brothers. Conversation rolled around the back tables as children greeted Davey.

"Look at all those kids." Shane gestured with his coffee cup. "There must be at least fifteen. If it was me leading them, it'd be chaos."

Jonah craned his neck to see behind him. "That teacher has the Pied-Piper look about him, like Grandpa Harlan used to have."

"The old man always did seem happy to see us," Bo allowed, scratching the dark stubble on his chin. "He'd cram us in that old motorhome and drag us off for an adventure."

"I don't think he always knew where we

were going." Shane smiled as nostalgia took hold. "Remember how he'd spread his highway map out, hem and haw, and then announce where we were going."

Jonah turned back around. "Yeah, it was like he was thankful to us for an excuse to get away. Anywhere."

"Our fathers didn't make it easy on him." Bo returned his attention to his plate and a steak drenched in white gravy. "Questioned his every move. At least, until they took over."

"It's hard not being in command." Shane tamped down the rising frustration as he thought of the town council ignoring his suggestions for a fair or festival.

"Grandpa Harlan would say it builds character." Bo mopped up gravy with a biscuit.

"I miss him," Shane admitted. "Seeing his picture at the Bucking Bull... I miss him." He cleared his throat. "But I have to wonder why he never brought us here."

His cousins shrugged.

Suddenly, Jonah laughed. "This conversation with you is surreal, Shane. Tell us the truth. There's an evil force in town. A presence who devoured my cousin Shane and lives in the shell of his body."

"Very funny." Shane buttered his toast, even the burned crust.

"Is this what happens when you move to Second Chance?" Bo stopped eating. "You lose your edge?"

Shane set down his knife. "If that loss makes you more like Grandpa Harlan, then yes."

NOT ONLY DID Shane show up the day after he'd left the Bucking Bull, but, as promised, he also brought two of his cousins.

Franny very nearly threw herself in his arms again. An unwise impulse she fought hard to control.

My luck is changing.

"What are *they* doing here?" Emily joined Franny on the front porch. She scowled, but her downtrodden expression was reserved for the redheaded Monroe with the goatee.

"They're going to help me bring in the strays." And maybe Mr. Muscles could be prevailed upon to dehorn the ferals.

"Bringing in strays is my job. And Zeke's." Emily hadn't taken her eyes off that one Monroe, which was surprising considering it was Mr. Muscles she'd had her heart set on at the wedding last week.

"I can't wait for you or Zeke." Franny tilted her head toward the house. "Our stockman is coming. Go on. Get ready for work in town."

Emily took her sour expression into the house, slamming the screen door behind her.

Shane ascended the porch steps. He wore jeans, a gray polo and cowboy boots that looked broken in. "Problem?"

"Always," Franny answered, resisting the urge to greet him with anything other than a contained smile. *Where had he gotten those old boots?*

"I told you." Gertie took Emily's place on the porch, leaning on her walker. Her hair was flat on one side and curled up like a rising white wave on the other. She wore baggy burgundy sweats, a cozy purple sweater and her signature slippers. Not the best of impressions for meeting out of towners. But her smile was wide and nearly normal. "I told you the Monroes will help."

Shane introduced his cousins to Franny and Gertie.

"I like your boots," Franny teased Shane, unable to resist any longer.

"My sister Sophie found a roomful of used boots stored in the old schoolhouse last month. Jonah and I bought them from Emily at the trading post yesterday afternoon." Shane looked at his toes and then at Franny, a sly grin on his face as if he was thinking about kisses rather than boots. "I thought Emily might have told you." His grin expanded as the temperature in her cheeks rose.

Emily slammed out of the house.

"I'm still part of this family, you know." Emily marched down the stairs and to her truck. "Don't exclude me just because I'm working in town," she called over her shoulder.

Jonah made a derisive noise that elicited a growl from Emily.

"I didn't mean to go behind your back, Em." Franny rushed to soothe her sister-in-law's ruffled feathers. "I just wasn't sure they'd show up this morning."

"Monroes are dependable." This from Gertie. Her gaze was more settled than her coif.

Unable to stand it any longer, Franny finger-combed Gertie's hair while Emily backed up, truck tires spitting gravel.

Jonah leaped out of Emily's path before she ran over his toes. "I don't know about Monroes, but Shane is dependable."

"Grandpa Harlan always thought so." Bo

frowned at Jonah. "Did Emily just try to run you over? Is there something you're not telling us?"

"She thinks that I think…" Jonah shook his head. "Never mind."

Wasn't that interesting?

Gertie chuckled. *"Monroes."*

Only when the dust from Emily's truck dissipated did Franny realize there was no one around to stay with Gertie. She faced her grandmother-in-law and her walker.

"I'll be fine," Gertie reassured her, reading Franny's mind. "We need riders. Don't argue."

Franny couldn't. She was backed into a corner, and Gertie knew it. "You'll keep the cordless phone with you?"

"Cross my heart." Gertie nodded. "I'll be fine."

Franny hoped so. "Come on, all you Monroes. Let's get horses saddled and ride." She led them to the barn and pointed out which horses she was pairing them with.

"Nags," Bo proclaimed as he looked at the horse she'd chosen for him to ride. "I'm from Texas. I can handle a horse born in the last decade."

"I'll stick with the slower, older, economy model." Jonah gestured toward Davey's mustang, Yoda. "Since I haven't ridden in years, it'll get me where we're going and back again."

Bo moved over to Dastardly's stall. "I'll take this one."

The big black gelding had been sired by the same stallion as Franny's horse. He'd been Kyle's and bore a scar on his chest where he'd been gored the day Kyle had been killed.

"I don't think so." Franny came over to stroke Dastardly's velvety nose. "Only Emily rides him anymore." And who knew if he'd be skittish when he smelled cattle.

"I'll be fine." Bo thumbed his chest. "Texan, remember. Show me where his tack is."

"Hey, Texan." Shane appeared at Franny's shoulder, so close she could feel his warmth. "Have you ever ridden a bull?"

Bo crossed his arms over his broad chest and gave Shane a look that said, *Duh*.

"You'll do." Shane squeezed Franny's shoulder and whispered, "Logistics."

"I don't like the sound of this," Jonah said. "Bull riding?"

"It's typical Shane." Unconcerned, Bo headed for the tack room. "You always get more than you bargained for."

"That's because no one in the family ever makes me spell out the bargain," Shane whispered in Franny's ear. And then, louder, he said, "Which horse am I riding?"

"How about Daisy?" she replied. The older, dappled gray Bo had turned down.

Shane was standing too close to Pandora's stall. She was Zeke's horse and a bit of a character. Pandora reached over the stall door and nibbled the hair on the back of Shane's head. He swatted her away. "Hey, hey! Don't do that!"

Franny bit back a smile. "Looks like Pandora wants you to take her for a ride again." He'd ridden her yesterday morning with Davey.

Shane eyed the mare dubiously. "As long as she won't take me for a ride."

"You'll be fine. Horses tend to stick with the herd." Franny got down to business, saddling the horses. She added a lariat to her rig, plus the shotgun, and then gave Jonah a refresher course in riding. "Because it's been a long time since you've been on board."

Finally, the foursome set out, pausing so Shane could show his cousins the old photo of Gertie and Percy in the tree.

He, Jonah and Bo all waved to Gertie, who stood in the doorway of the ranch house, fully dressed and hair properly combed. Franny took that as a good omen.

As they entered the trees, Jonah called to Franny, "Do you have a plan for us to round up the cattle? Seeing as how we can't rope."

She did. "Think of yourself as part of a fishing net. Most of our stock will go out of *their* way to stay out of *our* way. They know the spring pasture has green grass this time of year and they'll head there, and then, if we point them in the right direction, toward an open gate."

"And the other cattle?" Shane asked, picking up on what she hadn't said. "The wild ones?"

"They don't often show themselves to a large group of riders." The joy Franny had felt when they'd arrived began to wane. She couldn't guarantee the Monroes' safety.

"So, we aren't going to go after anything without the Bucking Bull brand?" Shane rode behind her and spoke at a low volume the others might not catch.

He hasn't warned them about the danger, either.

Guilt knifed Franny's shoulder blades. "Not unless the rare opportunity presents itself."

Franny was reassured to hear birds chirping happily and hoped they'd continue. She turned in the saddle so she could see all three Monroes. "Here's how it's going to go, gentlemen. For your safety, you need to do everything I say, when I say it."

Shane frowned. "But what about—?"

"No *buts*," she interrupted, patting the shotgun holster strapped to her saddle. "We'll always ride single file, follow the leader. And when we get to the upper pasture, we'll spread out and head back this way."

"All right, little lady," Bo said with a twang, doing a bad impression of John Wayne.

"No problem with this merry-go-ride." Jonah looked pleased with his pun.

Franny rode to the point where the trail disappeared into the woods, looking back at her ramshackle crew. Hoping that none of them got hurt. Hoping that they'd be no big deal to the feral bull who presided over the wild herd.

Lost in thought, Franny didn't see a bull lunge out of the trees. Straight at her!

There was no time to scream. Danger leaped out of the way, nimbler than any bull on a good day.

The bull ran toward the open pasture, slowing down after looking back to see if they were following him. He was brown with a big white patch over one eye.

No big deal.

It was no big deal, all right. That bull had the Bucking Bull brand and no horns.

Nevertheless, Franny's hands shook while holding onto the reins. She patted Danger's neck and was effusive in her praise.

Shane bounced in the saddle as Pandora trotted up beside her. "Is that normal? A bull charging you like that?"

Behind Shane, his cousins closed the distance, eyes wide as they scanned the area.

"It's not normal." Shane lowered his voice. "Your hands are shaking."

Franny shushed him, not wanting his cousins to hear. "I'll be fine."

Two yearling bulls rustled through the brush, cast worried glances their way and trotted after the big bull that had tried to run down Franny.

A flash of light in a tree to their left caught her eye. "Look, Shane. It's one of those photos you like so much." Over by a gate bordering federal property.

The diversion worked. The Monroes rode

toward the tree talking about the picture, bull forgotten.

Leaving Franny to collect herself, forgetting nothing.

CHAPTER THIRTEEN

NOT ONLY DID Shane have to worry about angry, horned behemoths emerging from the overgrowth, but now Franny's domesticated stock was also proving they were worry-worthy, too.

Shane cast a glance over at Franny.

"I'm fine." She waved him off.

He knew she was lying. She kept clenching and unclenching her reins.

Shane was the last to reach the tree with the photograph. The bark had grown so that only the faces and shoulders of the people in the picture were showing.

"That's Grandpa Harlan." Bo's horse stood obediently next to the tree. "And his doppel-gänger."

"Identical twins?" Jonah lowered his sunglasses and squinted at the picture. "Or a clone?"

"Spare me the Hollywood explanation." Bo never missed a chance to rib Jonah. "It's got to be a cousin. Grandpa Harlan didn't have brothers."

"We don't know that for sure." Shane leaned forward in the saddle for a closer look. "In fact..." He sat back in the saddle. "I should have remembered this sooner. Last month, two people mentioned what a great person *Hobart* was. I thought they'd misremembered Grandpa Harlan's name. But what if they hadn't?" Shane tapped the plastic. "What if this was his brother?"

"If that man is family, there's a reason no one's ever mentioned him to us." Bo's dark eyebrows lowered. "But why?"

"Maybe Hobart wanted part of Grandpa Harlan's fortune." Jonah stared at Shane. "Maybe Harlan paid him to stay quiet?"

"If that was the case, he'd have been mentioned in the will." Shane glanced up as Franny approached on horseback. "Or Hobart would still be here in Second Chance." That was highly unlikely given Shane had made it a priority to meet everyone in town, although he hadn't checked the cemetery.

"Gentlemen, we need to keep moving." Franny rode up beside Shane, easily guiding her horse next to his. "Those pictures are everywhere out here."

"Really?" Shane gestured toward a narrow trail that had been made behind the tree. "Where does that path lead to?"

Franny followed the direction of his gaze. "Path? That's more like a deer track. And it goes up the mountain to federal land."

"Can we follow it?" Shane asked quickly. "Just for a little while. There's a gate."

"Is that why you offered to help?" Franny used her chin to gesture to the trail. "So you could follow Gertie's bread crumbs?"

"She's onto you." Bo chuckled.

"It's just a detour." Shane forced himself to hold Franny's gaze, to try and look sincere and not think about her kiss. "A few minutes of your time in exchange for a few minutes of ours."

Franny tilted her head, as if listening for birds, and whether they sang overhead. "Okay." She urged her horse forward and opened the gate. She latched it after Bo, who was the last to ride through. "Just this once."

"Thank you." Shane followed her along the trail. Brush swept over his legs, none too gently. He didn't care. "I bet there's a cabin at the end of this trail. Or the boulder that had crushed the infamous Merciless Mike Moody." Their discovery was going to change the fate of Second Chance. It was going to change how Shane's family felt about him.

Franny groaned. "I keep telling you, Merciless Mike's gold is a myth."

"For once—" Jonah ignored their guide "—I'm not going to take your bet, Shane."

"Shane and his hunches," Bo scoffed from the rear.

The trail wound its way up the mountain. Anticipation wound even tighter in Shane's chest. He could feel how close they were to an answer.

"Here's another one." Franny sounded surprised as she stopped near a tree.

"Yes!" Shane was excited now. "We're onto something."

"Maybe," Bo allowed. "The trail is getting steeper. How much longer can we follow it on horseback?"

"No one's going on foot."

Shane had to agree with Franny there.

They continued on. The trail began to switch back and forth, leading them to another photo.

"Same three guys," Jonah said excitedly. "This is weird. Like a good weird. Like multimillion-dollar-script kind of weird."

Franny stared at the ground, and then scanned their surroundings.

"I still hear birds," Shane told her, not wanting to turn back yet. "And I don't see any tracks."

Franny said nothing, but she pressed on.

Shane didn't want to worry, but that seemed to be his stock-in-trade lately. He kept an eye out.

"Why would they put their pictures in trees on federal land?" Bo wondered.

"Back then it was all Clark property." Franny was still focused on the earth beneath her horse's hooves. "My grandfather-in-law sold it to the government fifty years ago, I think."

"Oh, man." Jonah's voice was filled with excitement. "We're going to find something. We're going to find—"

"Merciless Mike Moody's treasure," Shane said, cutting him off.

"Hey, that's my line." Jonah chuckled.

"This is getting a little far-fetched." Franny didn't turn around. "It's a myth."

She could do nothing to crush Shane's spirits. "Come on, Franny. I swear our grandfathers found Merciless Mike's loot."

Franny pulled her horse to a halt. She

turned him sideways, blocking the trail, her face draining of color. "We need to go."

"Yes," Jonah said from behind Shane. "We need to go on. We need to follow this trail."

Franny lifted her gaze to Shane's. There was worry in those gray eyes. Actually, there was more than that. There was outright fear. "There are very large hoofprints here, along with a very large, fresh pile of manure." She pointed to the evidence.

"Bear?" Jonah asked, making Bo chuckle. For whatever reason, they'd been joking about bear traps since they'd arrived.

"Bull." Franny pulled the shotgun free of its holster and then headed down the hill, weaving through bushes to get around the Monroe men. "Come on."

For once, Jonah and Bo were speechless.

"But…" Shane paused to listen.

A bird twittered in the distance. The only branches snapping came from Franny and her horse. And yet, the hair on the back of Shane's neck rose.

"Aren't we looking for bulls?" Jonah asked.

"Not bulls that big," Franny called back to him, already twenty feet away.

"She's right. We have to go." Shane followed her lead, waiting to say more once he caught up to her. "Although at some point we do need to find out where the trail ends."

"I can tell you where it goes next." Franny had the shotgun resting loosely in her arm. She looked like a throwback to a pioneer woman of the Old West. "About a hundred more yards and you'd reach the ridge. There used to be a fire lookout station up there next to the Clark family cemetery, but the station burned last year."

"If we're that close, why can't we just continue to head on up there?" Bo asked.

"Because…" Franny turned in the saddle to face them, lowering her weapon. "There's something out here. Something big and wild and dangerous. I can't guarantee your safety."

"She's joking, right?" Jonah demanded. "I'm the only one allowed to joke about things like that. Me, the soon-to-be writer of horror films."

"She's not joking." Shane swallowed a bitter dose of nerves. He could feel something watching them.

They passed through the gate uneventfully and returned to Clark land. They rode through the upper pasture without incident. As Franny had promised, her cattle moved as if they knew where they were supposed to go—

closer to the ranch house. In a few short hours, all the strays were accounted for.

"Franny." Inside the barn, Shane dismounted. He waited for his contorted legs to go back to where they belonged before he attempted to join her at a stall. "Those tracks… Were they made by the bull we saw yesterday?"

"I told you. That was a smaller feral yesterday." The lines on Franny's face were strained and she was whispering. "I've never seen tracks that large."

Shane wanted to draw her close and forget about feral things altogether. But he couldn't let the mystery of his grandfather's photo trail go unsolved.

"You're talking my language, Franny." Jonah remained sitting on Davey's horse. "Again, the fact that there are clever killer bulls on this mountain is awesome. I'd love to see that cemetery. Maybe spend the night and soak in the atmosphere."

"That wouldn't be wise." Franny took Jonah's reins and tied up his horse to a stall ring.

"The fact that you say that means I have to do it. Don't you see?" Jonah swung his leg around and slid down the side of the horse, hanging onto the saddle as if he might fall to the ground. "I write a movie about possessed bulls with a *based-on-true-events* caption and everybody is going to want to come to Second Chance."

"And drive up the mountain where the daddy of all bulls is?" Franny huffed and moved to Shane's mount. "So now you want to get strangers killed, too? Take a look at Buttercup, will you. He's smaller than whatever's lurking out there."

"Did you say drive up the mountain?" Shane picked up on her slip. "Is there a road to the cemetery?" Of course there was.

Franny winced as she loosened Pandora's girth strap. "Look, I appreciate what you've done for me today. Twenty more head, strays plus ferals, which means I've got bulls with some great potential for rodeo stock. But... I shouldn't tell you this. You're right. There's a road on the other side of the ridge. It's a dirt road on federal land, but we have an easement. If you had permission—which I won't give you—you could take it to the point where the trail reaches the remains of the fire station and the Clark graveyard." Her voice was unsteady. She was scared. Scared of the feral bull that had killed her husband. "I've got to get the horses put up, and then I need to go into town and pick up the boys."

"I need to find the rest of those pictures," Shane said softly.

Franny removed the saddle from Pandora, relinquishing it to Shane when he slid his arms beneath it, hands brushing over her skin. "Shane, you don't understand. There are so many pictures in trees in Second Chance that I don't think about them anymore. They're behind the trading post and in the tree line above the schoolhouse. You could be making this out to be nothing."

Putting yourself at risk for nothing.

That's what she didn't say.

Shane knew he should heed her warning. But he'd had too many months of unknowns to slow down what little momentum he had.

"There are photos in trees in town?" Shane pounced on the alternative. "Can you show them to us?"

"No, I... You know I can't spare the time." She moved to Davey's horse. "I've got to de-horn those feral bulls, not to mention find someone to take a ride on one."

Bo's head shot up. "I thought you were kidding about bull riding."

"I can't ask that of you, even if you are from Texas." Franny spoke in a faraway tone. "Worst case, I'll take a few bull rides myself."

"Franny." Shane glared at everyone and everything in the barn, including Franny. "You will not ride a bucking bull."

Her chin went up. "The buck stops here, Shane. It's got to be done or my kids won't eat."

Something in Shane's chest constricted at the sight of the tightening lines fanning from her eyes and the stiffness of her shoulders. She was taking on the burden of the ranch alone.

Hello, irony.

Because he was alone, too. Alone in the midst of a large family, juggling many of the Monroe interests by himself rather than organizing things by committee. The difference was Shane wasn't risking his life.

"We'll come back tomorrow," Shane promised, picking up a brush and running it over Pandora the way Davey had taught him. "Don't do anything until we return."

His cousins remained silent.

Likewise, Franny had little to say when the trio was ready to go. She offered nothing more than a brief call of thanks.

Gertie would have elbowed someone and said they were too much in their own heads.

Shane wasn't lost in thought. His heart had scaled his throat at the thought of Franny riding one of those bulls.

"Are we giving up on the photo trail?" Bo asked when they were in Shane's Hummer navigating the switchbacks that led to the highway.

Shane shook his head. "No. First off, we need someone to show us where the road on federal land is." That wasn't true. First off, they needed to help Franny prepare the bulls for the stockman.

"I'd say that's it." Jonah shifted in the back seat.

"You're quitting?" Shane slowed, turning to glare at Jonah. "You're done?"

"No." Jonah pointed out the window. "That gate there. It says No Trespassing and there's some legalese that only a government agency would put on a No Trespassing sign."

"There's a lock." Bo put his window down for a better look. "I saw bolt cutters at the general store."

Shane had never noticed bolt cutters. But then again, he'd never ventured very far into the hardware section.

"Might I suggest…" Jonah waited until Shane and Bo turned to look at him. "If Franny has a right of way from the government, she probably has a key."

"She'll never give it to us." Shane let up on the brake and the SUV continued down the hill. And if he and his cousins went up there without Franny's permission, he'd never have the chance to hold her in his arms again.

Jaded Shane thought that was for the best.

Sentimental Shane wasn't so sure.

"If we come back tomorrow to help, we might see the key somewhere." Jonah's voice took on a master-criminal quality as he formulated his plan. "And if that key happens to go missing for a day or two, who's to know?"

Bo and Shane exchanged a quick glance.

"Was Jonah always this evil-minded?" Shane asked. "And we just didn't notice?"

"Yeah." Bo nodded. "It's all that pent-up frustration from writing sugary sweet teenage scripts. It's like a virus that keeps making him worse. Speaking of worse, shouldn't you ask me if I'm willing to ride a bull before offering me up as a sacrificial lamb?"

"Technically," Shane said, "I didn't promise you'd be the one to ride."

"Well, *I'm* not riding," Jonah said staunchly.

"What are you worried about, Bo?" Shane slowed as they approached the narrow highway. "You grew up in Texas. That practically makes you a professional."

"Hardy-har." Bo wasn't amused. "I was twelve and I rode sheep. When I turned thirteen, I rode bulls three, maybe four times one summer before I decided I preferred working on engines to being worked over by six hundred pounds or so of beef."

"But you know how to do it," Shane insisted.

"Baaaaah." Jonah chortled from the back seat.

Bo twisted around and glared at him. "Knowing what to do and being stupid enough to do it are two separate things."

"Okay, if you truly believe Grandpa Harlan would have stood aside and let a woman be in danger when he knew how to do something…"

That silenced his cousins.

"You better hope I don't get myself killed," Bo grumbled.

Shane grinned. "It'll take more than a bull-in-training to take you out."

"Famous last words." Bo grumbled some more.

"I love Second Chance." Jonah clapped his

hands. "It's inspirational gold for a writer. I wish I would've come here sooner."

"Me, too," Shane said.

CHAPTER FOURTEEN

FRANNY WAS LATE picking up the boys from their teacher at the Bent Nickel.

She'd waited for Shane and his cousins to leave the ranch before telling Gertie how well the city slickers had fared. Her grandmother-in-law would be ecstatic to learn Shane was determined to trace his grandfather's history, which she suspected was tied to Merciless Mike's gold.

Shane didn't realize how risky it was to follow those photographs. They could lead nowhere or straight to a large, feral bull.

When she pulled up to the diner, Adam and Charlie tumbled out the door, shouldering backpacks and carrying their sweatshirts with the sleeves dragging on the ground.

"Where's Davey?" Franny asked as they climbed into their seats in the back.

"He's in trouble," Adam said, as if this was an everyday occurrence.

It was not.

"He shoved Jamie and had to write sentences about how bad it is to hit people." Charlie snapped on his seat belt. "But I think Jamie deserved it. Maybe tomorrow when we come back, I'll hit him, too."

"You'll do no such thing." Franny rammed the truck into Park and shut off the engine. "Stay here."

Inside the diner, Davey pressed his face against the glass, looking near tears.

His teacher, Eli Garland, held open the diner door for Franny. Eli ran the independent-study school for the county. He was attractive, of a certain age, but for whatever reason, he hadn't caught Emily's eye. "Thanks for coming in, Franny."

Davey rammed Franny's side, sticking to her like glue.

Eli cleared his throat. "Davey, do you have something to tell your mother?"

"I lost my temper," Davey said in a small voice.

Franny stroked his soft brown hair, tears filling her eyes. There was only one reason Davey ever lost his temper—when someone touched a nerve about his missing hand.

"Jamie made a remark Davey took exception to." Thankfully, Eli didn't repeat it.

"Davey, why don't you get in the truck while your mom and I finish up?"

Davey didn't need the offer of escape repeated. He darted out the door.

There were still some children at the back table of the diner. Jamie wasn't among them.

Their presence made Franny keep her voice down. "I hope Jamie's okay." That was a lie. She hoped Davey had given the kid something to think about the next time he wanted to bully someone.

Franny guiltily shoved aside the thought. Good moms shouldn't condone retribution.

"Jamie's fine." Eli's whisper was designed for privacy. "He got what he deserved. You know how kids can be. They push, looking for a weak spot. I just want Davey to know he shouldn't rise to the bait. Since this won't be the last time someone makes fun of his disability."

"He's not *disabled*." The words tumbled from her stiff lips like ice cubes from the refrigerator dispenser.

"He's not." Eli placed a hand on her shoulder, attempting to soothe. "You're right. But a physical difference will always make him stand out."

Franny jerked her shoulder free, even as she

thought, *Don't upset Eli.* It wasn't his fault. And it was a privilege for her boys to be allowed to be with him and the other local kids every morning. He was only required to give each student one hour a week.

It was just nothing was going her way lately. Disappointments added up like unpaid bills.

But I have Shane.

She didn't have Shane. He had an agenda, one that didn't match her own. He was looking for Merciless Mike's gold, trying to walk in his grandfather's footsteps. A fool's errand.

The cell phone in her jacket pocket began to ring. It was her father-in-law.

She thanked Eli and left the diner to stand outside in the brisk spring air. "Hey, Will. Is everything okay?"

"I was going to ask you the same question." Will Clark's voice was deep and deliberate. "I hate to bring this up, but it's approaching the fifteenth of the month and we haven't received your check."

"Right." Bile rose at the back of her throat. "We've had some weather delays that have kept potential stock buyers away." Not a complete lie. "I hope to send you a check soon. How's Tabitha?"

They exchanged pleasantries as Franny

climbed into the truck on shaky legs. The boys called out greetings to their grandfather—even Davey, who was still looking as if there was a black cloud over his head.

"I'll be looking for that check," Will said before signing off.

"I'll be looking for it, too," Franny murmured. She started the truck and headed for home.

"Is Davey grounded?" Adam asked from the back seat in a woeful voice.

"If he is, I get to use his video-game time." Charlie sounded thrilled. "Maybe he shouldn't go to camp this summer."

"Charlie," Franny warned. "This has nothing to do with Davey's camp."

"Mom." Charlie wasn't giving up on this opportunity to torture his older brother. "You always say we have to watch every dollar."

Davey choked back a sob.

"Charlie, this is your last warning."

Franny wasn't going to take away camp. Davey loved being with kids like himself. And he'd been told there were donor angels that helped regular attendees with the cost of prosthetics.

Huffing while his brothers argued, Davey crossed his arms over his chest.

"What would Dad say?" Adam asked.

It was so hard to keep Kyle's memory alive that Franny had devised a method to keep his presence felt among her sons. "Your dad would say that fighting is a last resort."

Davey huffed again.

"But your dad would also say that you have to defend yourself because bullies won't respect you if you don't."

Davey's scowl slowly morphed into a smile. His arms loosened. He blew out a breath.

"You mean Davey's not getting punished?" Charlie was beside himself. "I should've punched Jamie, too!"

"Not so fast, young man. You know what your dad would say to that." Franny left the statement open ended.

"'Clarks fight their own battles,'" the boys chorused.

There were several Clark-isms in the family arsenal.

Clarks don't quit.

Clarks hang tough.

And Franny's personal favorite: *Clarks know how to survive.*

The only trouble was, Franny was only a Clark by marriage. She wasn't sure she knew how to get them through this rough patch.

Except she did know.

She needed to stop procrastinating and train some bulls.

DAVEY CLARK WAS tired of being the oldest.

His baby brother, Adam, got away with everything.

And Charlie… He had a mouth on him, but never seemed to get in trouble.

No. It was Davey who always got caught, who always got told to stop playing and act like a man.

Sitting in Yoda's stall after school, Davey ground his stubby left wrist into his leg. His arm ached where it ended because he'd slugged Jamie with it.

Not that he hit people often. In fact, hardly ever.

Dad would've been angry. Angrier than Mom.

Davey had been angry, too. If he just had a hand, Jamie wouldn't make fun of him. That strange lady wouldn't have come up to him in front of his friends in the diner a few days ago.

Granny Gertie was always talking about Merciless Mike and his gold. If Davey had Merciless Mike's gold, he could buy a new hand. He could pay for camp with the other missing kids every year. Maybe even buy Mom a new deep freezer, since theirs was always conking out.

Charlie should never have suggested Davey miss out on camp. Charlie had two hands. He didn't understand how important it was for Davey to go to camp with other kids like him.

"UNCLE SHANE, I DON'T want to hike no more." Alex leaned against Shane's leg.

The Monroe men had only just returned to town and collected the twins to relieve Laurel. Intent upon finding more clues about Grandpa Harlan, he and his cousins had taken to the trees behind the trading post, but hadn't found any photographs in the lengthy five minutes they'd been searching.

Shane ruffled Alex's hair. "Is this because your aunt Laurel said she was going to get a milkshake at the diner?"

"No-o-o," Alex said unconvincingly.

"Yes." Andy wasn't interested in playing games.

"We just started hiking." Bo leaned against a tree and frowned at the twins. "Toughen up."

"Have you forgotten what it's like to be a kid?" Jonah still walked stiffly from their ride. "Their four basic food groups are milk-shakes, French fries, pizza and cake."

"I'd expect you to remember all that kid stuff," Bo quipped, rolling his eyes. "Seeing as how you wrote all those kiddie shows."

"It sounds like someone other than the twins needs a milkshake." Shane glanced downhill toward the trading post. And, eureka! "Hey, there's one right there."

Bo perked up. "Where?" He hurried down the hill. "If it is a picture, I'm buying milkshakes."

The twins didn't wait to seek permission. They followed Bo.

"Look. It's Grandpa Harlan and Grandma Ruth." His first wife. Shane rose up on his toes for a closer look. "He's older there than in that other picture we found on the Bucking Bull."

The twins bemoaned being unable to see the photograph.

Shane picked up Alex and pointed out the discovery.

"And there's more of him in the picture." Jonah squinted at it. "Which means it was put here later since the bark hasn't grown over the photograph near as much. What's that behind him?"

"The church." Bo picked up Andy and held him so he could see. "There's the steeple behind Harlan's ear."

"Do you know what we need to do before milkshakes?" Shane asked the twins. "We need a side trip to the church."

The twins groaned.

"Come on, cowpokes." Bo swung Andy around to his back. "It's time for a piggyback ride."

"Piggyback rides," Jonah scoffed, and lifted Alex from Shane's arms onto his shoulders. "Shoulder rides are better. Watch out for tree branches, kid."

It became a race. Jonah versus Bo with the twins giggling and Shane bringing up the rear.

They crossed the highway and hurried farther up the slope behind the church.

"I don't recall Grandpa Harlan being religious," Bo said.

"Maybe he got married here." Shane turned, taking in the view of the valley before continuing uphill. "Like Sophie."

"I am definitely writing a screenplay about this," Jonah muttered. "Only the characters will search for clues during a still, moonlit night."

"If you don't include that bear trap, I'm

going to be disappointed." Bo swung Andy to the ground.

"Look. Right here." Shane stopped in front of a tree on the edge of a narrow rise. "Is that a picture of Grandpa Harlan?"

"Wearing a preacher's suit?" Bo shook his head. "No way was our grandfather ever a preacher."

"What's a pitcher's suit?" Alex asked from atop Jonah's shoulders. "Like in baseball?"

"Prea-cher," Jonah said, enunciating. "Like the man who married your mother and Zeke."

"Oh." Andy craned his neck toward the picture. And then he patted Jonah's head. "I'm ready for my milkshake now. Chocolate, please."

"I need to go see Gertie." Shane rubbed grime from the plastic and peered at the woman Harlan was with. He didn't recognize her. "If I had to guess, I think this is Irene. And the minister is Hobart."

"Who is Irene?" Jonah gaped at him, swinging Andy to the ground. "And why are you holding out on us?"

"I'm just recalling odd bits of information locals have mentioned to me since I arrived. According to Roy, Irene *wasn't* married to

Harlan." Shane blew out a breath. "In a backward twist of logic, it makes sense."

"This is like a game of Clue." Jonah sighed heavily. "I stopped liking that game when Ashley beat me to the library and accused Professor Plum of doing the deed with the rope."

"I'm confused." Bo set Alex on his feet and headed down the path. "And that means only one thing. I need a milkshake."

The twins trailed after Bo, echoing their confusion and thirst.

Shane took a picture of the photograph in the tree. "I'm going to uncover the truth. And I bet the path to the truth begins at the Bucking Bull."

"What do we do now?" Jonah lingered with Shane.

"We're going back to the ranch." He headed after Bo and the twins. "After we treat ourselves to milkshakes."

"THERE WILL BE no homework this afternoon," Franny announced after the boys finished eating their afternoon snacks.

The boys whooped. Granny Gertie lifted her white eyebrows.

Charlie raised his face to the ceiling. "Video-game da-a-a-ay!"

"First dibs!" Davey shouted over his brother.

"No—no." Franny was quick to squelch that idea. "Saddle up. I need you to help me move some stock into the chutes for training."

Everyone looked at her as if she'd lost her mind.

"That's Zeke's job. And Emily's." Charlie scratched his unruly brown locks.

"Before it was their job, it was my job." *Mine and Kyle's.* "It's time you boys began learning how to run the ranch." If the Bucking Bull went under, she wanted her children to experience ranch life while they could.

"Sweet!" Davey ran to the foyer to put on his boots.

Charlie ran after him.

Adam tugged Franny's hand. "Even me?"

It nearly broke Franny's heart as she nodded and said, "Even you." She needed every body, every horseman.

Her youngest galloped to join his brothers.

"Don't." Gertie worked her mouth around the sharp edges of the word. "They're too young."

"Percy and Kyle would disagree." Their

grandfather and father. "The ranch's fortunes have always ridden on the backs of Clarks."

"Bulls, Franny." Danger, she meant.

"I just need them to herd *our stock* into the arena, so we can get some training done." No ferals.

Gertie's head was shaking. "No."

"You can't say no to me." Franny managed to keep her voice even. "I own the ranch."

The old woman pressed her lips into a pale, thin line.

"We'll be all right, Granny." Davey ran over to hug her. "Mom knows what she's doing."

Franny certainly hoped so. She gathered the boys and went to saddle up, lecturing her sons repeatedly the same way she'd lectured the Monroes earlier in the day.

"We get it, Mom," Davey finally told her from atop Yoda. "Do what you say, when you say it."

"Yep." Charlie seconded his brother's words from atop his pony.

"I always follow Charlie, anyway," Adam added. "Don't worry, Mom. We're Clarks."

They rode to the lower pasture.

"The three-year-olds will know what's going on and what to do," Franny explained. "We'll close the gate on either side of the driveway, open the pasture gate and herd them into the chute on the other side." That was the easy part. "There are some heifers out here that were strays. We don't want any in the chute. Davey, if you see heifers heading toward the gate, whoop it up to scare them off, but don't move in their way. If they insist upon following the bulls, let them. Those heifers will learn crossing the road isn't fun and won't be so ready to run next time."

It was a straightforward process. And she was banking on the feral stock to keep their distance in the pasture.

"Mom, I've done this before with Zeke and Emily," Davey said testily. "You don't have to nag."

"Me, too," Charlie said, amending his statement when Davey gave him the stink eye. "It counts no matter which side of the fence you're on, Davey."

Adam pouted. He'd never been allowed near the stock before.

"You okay with this, my littlest man?" Franny asked her youngest. She was a bad mom for making her boys do this. Or she was a good mom and they'd thank her for giving them so much responsibility this early. It was a toss-up. "You can always hang out on the other side of the gate and supervise."

Adam sat up tall in the saddle. "Little men don't hide, Mom."

Franny's heart swelled with pride.

They reached the set of gates. The herd was loosely gathered nearby. Franny dismounted, secured the two driveway gates to create a border crossing and then opened the pasture gate.

She climbed back on Danger. "We can do this." The words were as much for her benefit as her sons'. "Stay away from the ones with long horns."

She heeled Danger forward.

CHAPTER FIFTEEN

EMILY WATCHED THE Monroes traipse around Second Chance from Sophie's trading post.

What were they looking for?

She'd thought if she was in town, she'd have a better opportunity to meet men. Or, since Bo had come to town, she'd assumed she'd have a better opportunity to get to know him.

No such luck.

An older gentleman climbed the steps to the trading post. He stopped at the top and rested his hand on the Edsel's fender, winded. "I'm here to pick up the hand-carved trunk I ordered online."

"Mr. Jolly." She'd been expecting him. "It's in the back room. Come on in."

The trunk was hand-carved teak from Thailand, made in the early 1900s. The craftsmanship was exquisite.

Not surprisingly, it passed Mr. Jolly's inspection. "Do you have someone to help me put it in my truck?" It was listed on the product description as weighing seventy pounds.

Having worked on a ranch all her life, Emily wasn't a wimp. But Mr. Jolly didn't look like he lifted more than an ice-tea glass on a hot day. "I can get help." *Bo!* "Wait here while I have someone call for him." She hurried next door and asked Laurel to contact her cousin. Meanwhile, Emily returned to the trading-post customer and tried to come up with a scintillating topic of conversation that Bo wouldn't consider trying too hard.

Politics? No.

Sophie's inventory? No.

Ranch life? No.

Footsteps sounded on the porch.

Emily turned and smiled, her mind an empty sieve.

Her smile fell.

It wasn't Bo.

"I hear you need some help." Jonah flexed his thin arms, making a muscle. "I've got you covered."

He was as lean as a rake as Granny Gertie would say, not at all convincing in the heavy-lifting department.

"Give it your best shot." She stepped aside and let the two men carry the trunk.

To Jonah's credit, he carried his end without complaint or even straining.

When Mr. Jolly drove off, Emily returned to the trading post, followed by her least favorite Monroe.

"What? I don't get props for being stronger than I look?" Jonah dogged her steps.

"You got me there."

"I suppose there's a story in this."

Emily shuddered to think what that story was. "As long as it has a happy ending."

"Jonah!" Shane called from across the street, where he and Bo stood next to his black Hummer. "Come on. We're headed out to the Bucking Bull."

"Again?" Emily huffed. There was more male action at the ranch than there'd ever been before. Was Franny doing this on purpose?

She rejected the thought almost as soon as it came to mind. Franny wasn't like that. Franny wasn't interested in any man—even Shane, who was clearly smitten with her.

"Yes, we're going to the Bucking Bull again." Jonah lingered, grinning. "See you around, cowgirl."

"Not if I see you first," she retorted, rolling her eyes at her lame remark.

Jonah brought out the worst in her.

It was time to face the truth.

She needed to plan her move to Alaska.

"WHY IS THIS gate blocking the road?" Shane pulled up to the barrier separating them from the ranch house. "It's like a metaphor of my time in Second Chance. Blocked at every turn."

"There's nothing deep about this. I'd say it's closed to move cattle." Bo pointed at a bull that trotted past them toward the pasture. "Park here. We'll walk in."

Jonah hopped out of the back. "If I'd have known Second Chance was filled with one-of-a-kind experiences, myths and spine-chilling eeriness, I would have come with you in January." Jonah had been full of if-I-would-have-known statements ever since they'd left the Bucking Bull this morning.

Shane had a statement of his own: *If I would have known the Bucking Bull was hiding Franny Clark, I would have visited the ranch in January.*

The three men opened each gate in turn and walked up the hill toward the ranch house. Banging metal had them veering toward the arena behind the barn.

"Shane!" Gertie called out. She gestured him closer. "Stop her."

"Who? Franny?"

Something was banging against the metal fencing in the arena. Something big. The barn blocked the arena from sight.

"Yes—Franny." Gertie rattled her walker and scowled at him. "She's in the arena. With bulls and my boys."

A bolt of fear cut through him. Jonah and Bo had disappeared, taking a shortcut through the barn. He was fairly certain they'd make common sense prevail before he got there. The assumption allowed him a few moments for his quest to get answers about Grandpa Harlan.

"Gertie." He faced the old woman, intent upon getting answers. "In town, I found some of those photographs you told me about, like one with Hobart and Irene behind the church."

She nodded, seeming not at all surprised by his use of the names. She didn't try to correct him. But then again, unlike Roy, she hadn't sold property to Harlan or signed a confidentiality agreement.

"Hobart was a minister?" Shane asked.

Gertie nodded again. "We don't have time for questions."

Shane hesitated. "We followed the bread crumbs this morning with Franny, almost to the top of the ridge. Do you think we were close to Merciless Mike's gold?"

More bangs from the arena. Bo shouted something Shane didn't catch.

Gertie paled. "I'll tell you once Franny is safe."

"Shane!" That was Jonah, standing in the breezeway of the barn. "You'd better get over here. Hurry."

Shane ran, slowed only by his cowboy boots.

The brown bull with the white patch over his eye, the one that had tried to run Franny over just that morning, was banging against the chute. Franny leaned over the top railing, cinching a strap around the bull's hips.

"Are you planning to ride that thing?" Shane couldn't contain his horror.

"No." She straddled the bull, balancing one foot on the metal chute railing. She spared Shane a glance. "At least, not if you are."

Shane was surprised that he didn't stop in his tracks. He kept walking. This woman… She needed help. And he… His father would say he needed his head examined, because he hadn't told her he wouldn't get on that bull in her place.

"I'm kidding." Franny grinned. "This is a two-year-old bull. He's been exposed to the flank strap before and also carried some weight. This—" she held up a metal contraption that looked like two triangles with a third triangle missing from the middle "—is a remote-controlled rider. Technically, a weighted box with an ejection button." She bent the straps at the dangerous end of the bull.

Who was Shane kidding? Both ends of the bull were dangerous.

Franny was unfazed. "When he bucks hard or spins quickly, we'll press the release button. The flank strap and the weight will fall off." She straightened and looked around to find her kids. "Ready, boys? Whose turn is it?"

"Mine!" Little Adam stood up. He held a small device in his hand.

"Don't release it early." Charlie made it sound like his little brother had done some early releasing already.

"I'm next," Davey called from the gate at the far end of the arena. "I can't be on release duty all the time. That's not fair."

"I thought you said you trained bulls with cowboy riders." Shane reached Franny's side and stared up at her. She was magnificent, calm and confident, and in control of the beast.

It scared him to death. Where had Bo and Jonah gone?

She settled her cowboy hat more firmly on her head. "Three-year-olds and up get live riders. We don't have many of those. For today, we're just using the remote." She caught Adam's eye. "Ready?"

"Ready." The kindergartner spread his feet and held out the remote.

Franny inched along the railings until she reached a spot with a rope. It was attached to the gate latch, the one holding the bull in the chute. "Come on, baby. Give it your all." She pulled the rope, opening the gate.

Freed, the bull leaped a good six feet forward. And then he began to buck. Small kicks at first, and then higher. The earth shook from his landings.

"Adam!" Franny cried. "Release!"

The boy did as requested. "Ah, Mom. I wanted him to spin."

The strap fell away from the bull's haunches and the metal rider tumbled to the dirt. The bull zigzagged around the arena, finally spotting Davey and the open gate on the far end.

"This stock guy coming to see you." Shane gave Franny a hand getting down. "Is he looking for two-year-olds?"

"He'll buy the twos." Franny waited for Davey to close the gate behind the exiting bull before heading into the arena for her equipment. "He really wants prime athletes that are five and six, but he'll take three- and four-year-olds, too."

"Do you have any older bulls?"

She shook her head. "Just the ferals and I can't let them in the arena until we dehorn them."

"They'll need riders?" Shane asked. "Live ones?" Not metal contraptions with remote-control ejection buttons?

"That's where I come in." Bo appeared, wearing what looked like a bulletproof vest and a crash helmet.

"Bo, ARE YOU sure you know how to do this?" Shane was suddenly struck with worry.

And it wasn't for Franny, who rode that big black horse of hers and gave instructions to Charlie, who was going to operate the exit gate.

"Of course I'm not sure." Bo straddled the bull while standing on the railings. He stared down at the black beast. "Can you at least use my sacrifice to barter for the use of the road?"

"What road?" Davey clung to a railing a safe distance away.

"The road to the cemetery," Bo said before Shane could counsel him to silence.

"Nobody goes up there," Davey said solemnly. "Not even the government. It's part of the woods and the woods are off-limits."

"That's why it's the perfect place to hide Merciless Mike's gold," Bo grumbled. "Under a photograph of your great-grandfather and my grandfather."

"He's joking, Davey." Shane gave Bo the high sign, but his cousin wasn't looking.

"I remember now why I stopped bull riding as a kid." Bo glared at Shane. "But I've suddenly forgotten who I made beneficiary of my life-insurance policy."

"I hope it was me," Jonah said glibly, red hair glinting in the sunlight. "I could use seed money for my film."

"It wasn't you," Bo snapped.

"We're ready down here." Franny positioned her horse near the fence at the middle of the arena. She'd explained she was there to release the straps from the bull and herd him out the exit gate.

"Why don't we strap that metal thing on

him instead?" Shane scanned the area, looking for it.

"Your compassion shows no bounds." Bo was angry. "I'm only doing this if you get the key to that road, Shane."

"I know where the key is," Davey declared. "But I'll want to go with you."

"Your mother will never allow it, kid." Bo drew a deep breath. "On second thought, I don't want the key. I'll take Jonah riding the next bull as payment for this. You always talk about living what you write."

Jonah drew back. "I draw the line at bull riding."

"It'll help your story. That is, if you live, sticks." Bo squeezed the strap again. "Limber up. Stretch. It might make the whiplash a little less painful." He lowered himself onto the bull's back. "Okay. Let's do this."

Jonah released the gate and the bull leaped into the arena. "Shouldn't we have a rodeo clown to rescue Bo if he gets in trouble?"

"Shouldn't you have asked that before you released the gate?" Shane said just as Bo went flying, landing hard in the dirt.

Charlie banged the metal railing on the opposite end of the arena. "Over here, you stupid bull! Over here!"

The bull continued to buck in the vicinity of Bo. Franny galloped closer, whistling sharply and slapping her lasso against her leg.

"Get up, Mr. Bo." Davey had climbed onto the railing, where he was dangerously close to the kicking bull. He hooked his elbow around the rail and leaned toward the passing bull, as if he was going to release the strap that was making the animal buck. Franny wasn't close enough to make a grab for the strap. And now the bull's hooves were landing near Bo's head.

"We need a rodeo clown," Jonah shouted.

Shane jumped into the arena, hit the ground running and yelled, "Get back, Davey." Shane waved his arms in front of the bull, who responded by spinning around and leaping his way.

But first, the bull had to pass by Davey again.

Davey reached down and swiftly released the cinch at the bull's waist. That kid was just like his mother and didn't listen to anyone.

The bull stopped kicking up his heels and huffed, as out of shape as a football player on the first day of training camp. It ran toward Charlie and the open gate.

"I'm okay." Davey straddled the arena fence, strap in hand. "You need to help Mr. Bo."

Shane ran to his cousin. Bo was wheezing

like a balloon with a slow leak. He'd gotten the wind knocked out of him and couldn't catch his breath.

"Bo?" Jonah had scrambled over the arena fence and skidded into the dirt at Bo's side.

"We've got to pound him on the back." Shane dragged Bo to his feet and whacked him for all he was worth.

The wheezing continued. Bo's eyes were wide.

"Darn vest is too thick." On the next try, Shane hit him hard enough that Bo dropped to his knees and gulped in air.

"Oh, no." Jonah yanked Bo's arm, pulling him to his feet. "Run, Bo. Run!"

Shane heard the pounding hooves before he turned.

"Charlie, you were supposed to shut the gate to the chute." Davey's voice was rife with fear. "Look out, everybody! He's coming back."

Jonah and Bo had a head start, tearing the twenty feet or so to the fence.

Shane bolted after them.

In the chute, on the other side of the rail, the bull ran, outpacing Shane.

Jonah reached the fence, pulling Bo along

with him. Together they climbed clumsily to safety.

The Clark boys were shouting. Bo and Jonah were shouting. Shane couldn't make out their words, but he could hear the pounding of hooves as he sprinted.

The bull cleared the chute, spotted Shane and charged toward him.

Shane stumbled and fell.

A rope whirled through the air and landed around the neck of the bull.

Franny and her horse skidded to a stop between Shane and certain death.

CHAPTER SIXTEEN

So MUCH FOR thinking Bo had solved her bull-rider situation when he'd offered to ride.

Franny finished putting away the bull-training equipment and closed the door to the supply room in the barn.

Shane and Bo sat on the narrow bench in the breezeway. Jonah sat on an upside-down bucket nearby.

Franny tried to put on a brave front. "That turned out well, all things considered."

"Yep." Bo got to his feet, as slow as Gertie. "Nobody died."

"Although there was some doubt about that outcome." Jonah grinned. "If only I'd known—"

"We get it." Bo moved toward the open barn doors, followed by Jonah.

"Are you okay?" Shane asked Franny, which was ironic given the fact that he'd nearly been flattened by a freight train of beef.

"I'm fine. How about you?" There was

something different about Shane's expression. His mouth was in a firm, thin line.

"Shane's fine." Bo paused at the door and turned. "Now, me? I feel like I was pulled from the bottom of a pile."

"There's beer in the kitchen," Franny pointed out, not moving to get him any. She wanted a few minutes alone with Shane.

Bo perked up and set his feet in motion. Jonah trailed after him with arms extended, as if ready to catch him if he fell.

That left Franny and Shane alone.

"You don't want a beer?" Suddenly, she wasn't able to look at Shane for fear his ego couldn't handle her saving him in the arena.

Shane took Franny's hands and gave them a squeeze, drawing her gaze to his face and an understanding expression. "That was very nearly a disaster of epic proportions."

"I got to you in time."

"Me?" He laughed mirthlessly. "I'm not worried about me. How are you going to handle this without Bo, much less without Zeke and Emily?" He rested his forehead against hers. "You need trained hands, not inexperienced bodies. And you need them now. I'll call Sophie tomorrow and ask her to cut her honeymoon short. She'll understand. She probably misses the twins like crazy."

"I can't ask you to do that."

"Who said anything about you asking?" He pressed a kiss to her forehead. "If Zeke came back and heard about what had happened today, he'd be furious. At me, not you." He kissed her nose. "Well, maybe a little at you. It's hard to stay mad at you though." He kissed her cheek. "You're just so plucky."

Franny didn't want to be plucky. She suspected plucky women didn't win the hearts of worldly, sophisticated men like Shane. She was falling in love with him. With his pragmatism, his tenderness, his courage. Her heart didn't seem to care that he wasn't staying around.

He was waiting for her to say something.

"I can offer Zeke an extra week of vacation later in the year. Convincing Emily isn't going to be as easy." Franny sighed, relenting. "If Zeke comes back, Sophie comes with him. She won't need anyone to cover at the store." He stared at her, brown eyes warm, just the way she liked them. "Now, you're going to walk into that house and hold your head high. And do you know why?"

"Why?"

His smile was as gentle as his fingers running through her hair. "Because Blackie the Bull is going to make one heck of a rodeo star. He may not have been feral, but he's got that killer instinct, no question." And then he kissed Franny, long and deep and slow, reminding her how wonderful it was to have someone to talk through your problems with, to bolster you when you were down.

"You're good for me," Franny admitted a short time later.

Shane chuckled. "I don't think a woman has ever told me that before."

She felt a stab of jealousy. "You probably don't talk to them about their business or logistics." He certainly didn't help them gather eggs from the henhouse, fix their fences or help train bulls. "Is that how you earned a spot on the town council? Your logistics?"

"I feel like the council wanted to keep an eye on me. You know, hear about my plans for the town." His brow furrowed. "And then block them."

"I'd like to hear about those plans." Especially if it brought back the warmth to his eyes. "I doubt the town council has it out for you."

"That's where you're wrong." His words

became as tense as the lines emanating from his eyes. "I have plans, but the town council won't consider anything I put forth. Everything I put forth is either rejected because it's too much work, or it's too divisive. They can't agree whether to support or kill my ideas." He explained about the Merciless Mike Moody festival.

"Besides raising the idea, what did you propose to do to make it happen?"

"Me? Nothing. I don't know if I'm going to be here next week, much less whenever they decide to hold this festival. *If* they decide to hold the festival."

His words sank in and Franny immediately pulled back. What a timely reminder for her. He was leaving Second Chance some day.

And at the rate she was falling, if she wasn't careful, he'd take her heart with him.

"WHAT ARE YOU guys playing?" Shane walked over to the kitchen table and the card game happening with three Clark boys, two Monroe men and Gertie.

He needed a distraction. The sting of Franny's reality check in the barn had been unexpected and surprised him. It was like being fired all over again in spite of him understanding—and appreciating—Franny stepping back and reinserting space between them.

"We're playing poker," Davey replied.

"They're good," Jonah acknowledged, earning a grin from Davey. His cousin had very few pennies in front of him.

"We play for real money." Charlie rifled a stack of pennies. "Granny Gertie says she can't take the game seriously if we didn't put up the dough."

"And she didn't mean cookie dough." Bo had a stack and a half of nickels in front of him.

"I'm out." Gertie tossed down her cards and gave her stake of pennies to little Adam. "Shane. We need to talk." She led him to the chairs in front of the fireplace.

Shane assumed he was going to receive a set down for not helping Franny properly this afternoon. He had a bruise on his backside that reminded him every second just how dangerous those bulls were. And then there was the fact that he couldn't convince Franny to do anything she didn't want to do. She would always go her own way, and it was usually a more dangerous route.

"You've earned the right—" Gertie drew a brown afghan over her legs, laced her fingers in her lap and then gave him a look that glowed with praise "—to hear Harlan's story."

Finally.

"I fold." Jonah gave his cents to Adam and joined them. He found a seat on the couch and glanced back at Bo. "Don't you want to hear this?"

Bo shook his head. "A Texan never quits a game midhand."

The boys giggled.

"I'd call his bluff, fellas." Jonah winked at Gertie. "I should have brought my laptop."

"Go on." Shane had waited months to hear this story from someone in town.

Gertie leaned forward. "Well—"

The Clark boys hooted, having called Bo's bluff and claimed all the winnings. Gertie twisted around to see what had happened.

"What's going on over here?" Franny had come out of the laundry room with a basket of whites. "Gertie, you look like you're holding a meeting."

"Granny's about to tell a story," Charlie called out. "And Mr. Bo tried to beat Adam with a pair of twos!"

Franny brought the laundry into the living room and sat down near Jonah. She managed not to look at Shane. "Is this about Merciless Mike?"

"No." Gertie's sallow features contorted into a lopsided frown. "It's about Percy, Harlan and Hobart—Harlan's twin."

"Hobart? The preacher?" Jonah asked. "The one married to—"

"Irene." Gertie's expression softened and then saddened. "She was my friend. We were all friends."

"And they found Merciless Mike's gold?" Jonah asked, hot on the trail of an idea for his script.

"Nineteen forty-five," Gertie said with pride. "But they put it back soon after."

"It *is* about Merciless Mike." Franny pressed her lips together and scowled at Gertie, who shoved her hands in her sweater pockets and frowned back.

"Let's hear what she has to say." Shane played the role of peacemaker. "Why didn't they keep the gold?"

Gertie dragged her gaze away from Franny's. "Well…"

With stiff steps, Bo joined them in the living room, sitting on the arm of the couch near Jonah. The boys were quietly listening at the table.

"We all agreed it was bad luck. Blood-tainted money." Gertie sucked in air, then forced out the words. "First, the stage driver. Then, Old Jeb. Finally, Hobart."

Jonah's fingers were flexing in midair, almost as if they were pounding out words on a keyboard. "Did Harlan murder Hobart?"

"No," said Gertie and Shane at the same time.

Shane had reacted on gut instinct. But Gertie…

Bo had moved to the mantel and the nearby built-in shelves that held a picture of Franny accepting a crown in a rodeo queen contest. Bo ignored Franny's crown and peered at Gertie's wedding picture. "Did Percy?"

"No." Gertie scowled.

"You're saying they found the gold and put it right back?" Franny had her arms crossed over her chest—she was closed off to Gertie's story.

"No." Gertie slapped her palms on her thighs. "Harlan made a mistake. He sold the first set of coins to an auction house in Boise. With the money, Percy bought the meanest bull in Idaho—Buttercup. Harlan fixed up the trading post. And Hobart went on a religious mission to Thailand."

"Oh." Shane snapped his fingers. "Hobart and Irene bought an elephant bell over there. Sophie found it in the trading post last month." His honeymooning cousin had felt compelled to donate the piece to the Monroe Art Collection in Philadelphia.

"And then..." Gertie drew a deep breath. "The trading post improvements didn't return Harlan's investment, Hobart showed up having spent all his share and the bull escaped Percy's pasture."

"Here's where the blood comes in," Bo predicted, tilting his head from side to side with a sickening *crack, crack, crack, crack.*

Everyone shushed him. Everyone but Gertie.

She nodded. "Harlan took more gold to the same auction house."

"And someone at the auction house got greedy." Bo's observation earned another group shush.

"Yes." Gertie pointed at him. "The auctioneer followed Harlan to Second Chance and demanded the rest of the gold."

"Did he have a gun?" Adam asked, coming to sit at Gertie's feet.

"Did he shoot somebody?" Charlie joined him.

"He wanted to kill me!" Tears filled Gertie's eyes. "He held me hostage. Me and Irene."

"The things people do for money." Shane thought about the dissenting eight. At least, no guns had been drawn in their family feud.

"What happened next, Granny?" Davey stared at Gertie as if hypnotized.

"The men rushed the auctioneer." Gertie gripped Davey's hand, staring at the boy although she seemed to see something else. "There was a scuffle. A gunshot." She jolted. "And then another."

"Where did this happen?" Bo scanned the floor as if searching for bloodstains.

"Who shot who?" Jonah demanded, sitting on the edge of his seat.

Gertie blinked back to the present, taking inventory of her audience, which included impressionable children. "I shouldn't say."

The room erupted with protests. Gertie looked at her great-grandsons as if she feared her story had ruined them for life.

"Boys, you have to go to your room." Franny wasn't using her indoor voice. *"Now."*

They protested. They pleaded. But eventually they stomped upstairs and were much too silent. Most likely, they'd be pressing their ears to the floorboards to listen.

"What happened, Gertie?" Shane took hold of her hand.

"Hobart. He was shot twice in the gut." She swallowed thickly, blinking back tears. She had a handkerchief fisted in her hand. She pressed it to her stomach. "It was painful. Almost worse to watch."

"But…" Jonah was at a loss. "Did they rush Hobart to the hospital? Did they overpower the thief?"

"Jonah, this isn't one of your movies with a neatly wrapped happily-ever-after," Bo snapped.

"The auctioneer took the gold, but he got his," Gertie said in a cold voice Shane had never heard her use before. "On the trail down the mountain. It was all Clark land back then."

And federal land now, Shane surmised.

"A bull," Franny guessed. "The original Buttercup."

"Buttercup, indeed." Gertie's tone was colder than a January wind in the mountains. "The meanest bull in Idaho."

"How horrible," Franny murmured, no doubt thinking about her husband.

Shane came to sit next to her, wrapping an arm around her.

A lone tear spilled down Gertie's cheek.

"And what about Hobart?" But Shane had a sinking suspicion he knew how this had ended. He'd never heard a word about Grandpa Harlan's brother.

Gertie's gaze was hollow, as if she was seeing it all play out again. "We didn't have a town doctor. Not back then." And they were an hour's drive to the nearest hospital.

No one said anything for a time.

"That auctioneer. They buried that loser in the woods, I hope," Bo said.

"He got what he wanted." Gertie's expression hardened to match the chill of her words. "In the end."

"They buried him with the gold?" Jonah covered his mouth, but it didn't stop anyone from hearing him. "That is Old-West justice."

"And the bull?" Shane asked, although he thought he knew.

"We never caught Buttercup." Gertie's face crumpled. "We should've. Over the years, he created his own herd, one that terrorized this ranch."

Her features pinched, Franny sniffed and leaned into Shane's shoulder.

"But what about the gold?" Shane drew Franny close, offering what comfort he could. "Is it still out there? Harlan didn't take it to buy an oil field?"

"No." Gertie shook her handkerchief at

Shane. "We decided it was bad luck. Harlan sold his family's property here and left for Texas."

There wasn't a huge mystery surrounding Harlan's original stake, after all. Shane was kind of disappointed.

"I see it all," Jonah said absently. "Like a movie playing in my head."

Bo slugged his shoulder and shushed him.

"Ow." Jonah rubbed his arm. "What happened to Irene?"

"She left town and returned to her family in Denver, I think." Gertie rubbed her shoulder with her fist.

"I want to talk to her." There was excitement in Jonah's eyes, and it wasn't from gold.

"Don't get your hopes up," Bo whispered. "She might not be alive."

"I don't think the gold is still there," Shane said slowly. "Not in the cemetery. Or at least, not all of it."

"Would you listen to yourselves?" Franny scooted out from under Shane's arm. "Whatever happened with Merciless Mike's gold is in the past and that's where it should stay. For everyone's sake, especially Gertie's."

Shane shook his head. "Then why did Harlan and Percy leave a trail of pictures? They wouldn't have done that if they didn't want to return to take the gold someday."

"It's in the cemetery," Gertie insisted. "In the northwest corner."

Bo began talking about needing gloves, shovels and a wheelbarrow. Jonah started talking about wanting a decent camera to capture the expedition for behind-the-scenes footage.

"You can't just go digging in the cemetery." Franny was nearly beside herself. "For one thing, it's probably illegal, not to mention immoral, to disturb the dead. And for another, that is right in the heart of feral territory."

"I'm certain the gold is out there, but I'm not convinced it's in the cemetery." Shane let Franny's arguments slide. "Why would they leave their photos in the trees if it was in a cemetery?"

"It's in the cemetery." Gertie was adamant. "Percy told me so. And that's where I told Kyle to look."

Everyone stilled.

"You…" Franny swallowed, blood draining from her face. "You told Kyle about the gold? You sent him up there…alone? And he…" Her voice cracked. "How could you? He died because…"

Gertie swallowed thickly, plucking at the handkerchief. "I wanted the ranch to carry on. The Monroes are fine. They don't need their cut. But *we* need a boost, Franny. Kyle understood that."

And in that one statement, Shane understood Franny's husband. He'd been willing to risk everything to save his family and provide for the woman he loved.

Franny shook her head and dashed away her tears. "I'm sorry, Gertie, but you haven't been remembering things clearly lately. If there ever was a Merciless Mike—" she captured Shane's gaze with her tear-filled one "—no one found his gold. You've been telling this story for years." She dashed at her tears again. "You just... You just had to make up a new ending, one where the gold was found by you and your friends. And then you told Kyle." She pressed a hand on her throat. "And then he... *For nothing.*"

Shane went to put his arm around Franny, but she shrugged him off. "You're no better than Gertie. You want to go up there and risk your life for *nothing.*"

"*You...*" Gertie's hand, the one clutching the handkerchief, shook. Her face was red and streaked with tears. "You think I'm old and dotty? You think something in here isn't right?" She tapped her temple. "You think I'd send Kyle on a fool's mission? My own grandson?"

"Yes," Franny whispered.

"I am *not* delusional," Gertie said through a throat choked with tears. "I'm *not* a liar."

And then she opened the handkerchief and held out her hand, revealing a gold coin.

CHAPTER SEVENTEEN

FRANNY SAT ON the couch, wrapped in an afghan, unable to get warm.

The Monroe men bounced plans back and forth about retracing their grandfather's steps and following the picture trail.

I used to love Gertie's stories.

Kyle had loved Gertie's stories.

Kyle.

She'd lost him over a quest for gold. She held Gertie's gold coin pressed between her palms. Holding the thing her husband had coveted didn't make her feel better.

Kyle, why didn't you tell me?

She kept the gold tight in her hand as she clutched her aching stomach.

I used to have faith in happy endings.

In justice being served. In the sense of rightness that came with tales of the Old West.

My father was right.

It didn't pay to believe in fairy tales. It didn't pay to cut corners. To dream of a different way of life. This was karma circling back around and taking its due.

The Monroes wanted to dig up the northwest corner of the cemetery, as did Gertie. The last time Franny had been up there, she'd laid her husband to rest. Her father had kept watch with a rifle. Back then, shock and disbelief had bent Franny nearly to the breaking point. She couldn't go through that again.

"No one's going after that gold," Franny said in a hard voice that even she didn't recognize.

Shane sat next to her and drew her close. "That money will make things easier on you and the boys. It could save your ranch."

I bet Kyle believed that, too.

"No one else is going to die for money they didn't earn." The words felt hard and sharp in Franny's mouth.

"What if we round up all the feral bulls in the woods first?" Bo suggested.

"What if you die trying?" Franny stood. The room seemed to be spinning. She tossed the gold coin onto the coffee table and immediately felt better, steadier, lighter.

"We have to find the truth," Shane said. "I don't care about the gold, if there's any left.

But if this legend has merit, it could help the town stay afloat."

"Please don't try and turn this into a charitable expedition." Franny still couldn't bear to look at Gertie. "If you choose to believe there's more gold where this came from, then I choose to believe it's blood money and going after it will only bring more heartache."

Jonah knelt beside Gertie. "Why did you wait so long to tell your story?"

"Percy died." Gertie shifted awkwardly in her seat. There would be no comfort found anywhere today. "I thought it would help Kyle, and then he died. I had a stroke, and then Harlan died. I wanted someone to know before it was too late. And I wanted the chance to tell Franny that I'm sorry about Kyle."

Franny stiffened her spine. She knew she needed to accept Gertie's apology, but it was too soon.

It might always be too soon.

No one talked as Shane drove himself and his cousins back to the inn.

They passed sweeping vistas, but Shane didn't see anything.

Was there gold? Wasn't there gold? Was it in the cemetery or somewhere else?

Should they respect Franny's wishes and stay away, despite what it might mean to the town and Shane's status with his family? Should he respect Franny's wishes and keep his distance, despite wanting to comfort her?

Shane didn't have an answer to anything.

"There's a new car in the lot." Jonah pointed to an expensive sedan parked in front of the Lodgepole Inn.

Bo groaned. "Please don't tell me a new visitor is one of your horror-story plots."

"I've never heard of that," Jonah said. "But it sounds like an idea for consideration."

The trio traipsed inside the inn. Dusty, dirty and dejected.

A blonde with thick, black-rimmed glasses sat near the fireplace talking to Laurel and Odette. "Ah, you're back."

"Dr. Carlisle." Shane didn't know how he should react to her presence. The last time they'd been in the same room together, she'd threatened to report him to the authorities.

Introductions were made and then the doctor asked Shane to share a meal with her at the diner.

They took opposite sides of a booth and sized up one another.

Dr. Carlisle adjusted her glasses and cleared

her throat. "I suppose you're wondering why I'm here."

Shane nodded, not that he thought she was here to accept the position of town physician.

A smile passed fleetingly over her features. "Holden told me you'd ask me to reconsider the job up here. He said you'd come up with an excuse to try and get me to visit one more time."

"Ah, the consultant gig regarding the clinic." Shane wondered at the audacity of his cousin. "Technically, I didn't ask you about it. I asked for a recommendation."

She cleared her throat. "Holden told me not to come, regardless."

"So why are you here?"

"Because he told me not to come," she said again, gaining steam. "He told me so many times that I wanted to know why."

Shane knew why. His cousin didn't want the town to get a doctor, to succeed, especially if Shane was involved.

"Holden is somewhat competitive," Shane allowed diplomatically. "But still, I wouldn't have expected him to focus conversation on Second Chance the few nights you saw each other." Here and in Ketchum last weekend.

Her slender eyebrows disappeared behind

the top rim of her black glasses. "I've seen him several times."

A cold feeling came over Shane. But it wasn't the cold of slow-falling snow on a winter's night. Instead, it was a skittering anger, like freshly sharpened blades on ice.

"Holden sent me flowers after we first met." Dr. Carlisle's cheeks pinkened. She adjusted her black glasses and studied the photo of loggers on the wall.

Shane decided to make it easy on her. "Of course he did. And then there'd be lunch."

Her gaze flew to his. "How did you—?"

Shane held up a hand. "Lunch is less threatening than dinner. And Holden can be larger than life." Shane thought that was his cousin's appeal. Women saw him as a powerful man, a challenge to bring to heel. "And then there'd be an outing somewhere classy, like a museum, a sail on a harbor, or a ski trip." Shane would bet on the latter given they were surrounded by several ski resorts. "Finally, there'd be dinner. White tablecloth. Candle-light."

Dr. Carlisle's mouth dropped open.

"Holden has a method of operation." Shane tried to break it to her gently, tried not to touch the scar on his chin.

She gathered her big black purse to her side. "It wasn't a game." But something in her eyes recognized the truth.

"Of course not. I'm sure he cares about you. I have to believe he has a heart since he was married once before." That might be a bit cruel, but it was honest. Shane was willing to wager Holden hadn't told her about his previous marriage.

It meant she wouldn't just be mad at Shane. She'd be mad at Holden too.

Her hands fisted around the supple leather of her bag. "I hadn't heard about an ex."

"I didn't tell you to hurt you." Shane leaned forward. "I told you because this town needs a doctor and he's interfering with my search. And in the meantime, an old man had a heart attack last month and nearly died. I was out at a ranch today where my cousin got thrown by a bull and I was nearly run over by the same animal. This town *needs* a doctor." He slumped back in his seat.

"I don't want to work here. Not with—"

"I'm not asking you to be our doctor." He knew that ship had sailed. "But if you can help us update the clinic so we can entice a doctor to take the job, I'd appreciate it."

Her grip loosened on her purse. "Do they serve alcohol here?"

"No. And frankly, the food isn't as pleasurable as wherever Holden took you to dinner."

Ivy chose that moment to appear at their table with her ordering pad and a frown.

"But the burgers are good," Shane said, hoping for a quick recovery. "And if you help with the clinic update, I'm buying."

"WHY DID SHANE say Merciless Mike's gold would save our ranch?" Davey asked Franny at dinner.

The bowl of green beans clattered on the table, having slipped through Franny's fingers.

"Are we going to lose the ranch?" Charlie asked, wide-eyed.

"But…" Adam's eyes teared up. "This is where we live."

"What nonsense," Emily said, a reply that went unnoticed.

"Pfft." Gertie couldn't quite remain silent, although she hadn't said a word to Franny since Shane had left.

"We're fine, boys. The bulls are in the pasture. The heifers are dropping calves. We're going to be fine." Franny gave Gertie a hard stare. "Everything will be fine without tales of Merciless Mike's gold." Franny had hidden the gold coin in a jar that she used to save all of her spare change.

Davey stared at his wrist. "I don't need to go to camp this summer." His lower lip trembled. "It's just kids and sleeping bags. I can skip rocks and ride horses at home."

Franny felt awful. Davey loved that camp. "You're going to camp, Davey."

"But, Mom. It's so expensive." Her oldest sounded like he might cry.

"It's worth every penny." Franny sat down hard, trying not to look at anyone or she might cry, too. "Why is no one eating?"

"Because we need to get the gold." Davey pounded the end of his fork on the table. "Then you won't have to worry and Aunt Em won't have to work in town and I can go to camp."

Charlie and Adam joined the raucous chorus.

"Do you see what you've started?" Franny said to Gertie. "Now they want to risk their lives like Kyle did."

Gertie pressed her lips together, but her brow was furrowed.

"Hey, little man." Emily tapped Davey's

shoulder. "I'm not working in town because I need the money."

"Are you working for free?" Adam asked.

"No, I…" Emily squared her shoulders and blew out a breath. "I'm looking for a husband."

"But you're so old!" Charlie's mouth dropped open.

"Ha-ha, squirt." Emily served him string beans. "I'll remember that remark."

"Are husbands hard to find?" Adam stole a green bean with his fingers and took a bite. "Mom doesn't have one, either."

"She could go anywhere in the world and find one if we had that gold," Davey mumbled.

"Enough." Franny stabbed a pork chop with her fork. "Gertie, the least you could do is give them the gold-is-cursed speech." Although, that hadn't worked on the Monroes. Franny took out her aggression on the pork chop, hacking at it with a dull knife.

"Will I have to sell Yoda when we move?" Davey's lower lip trembled.

"We're not moving." Franny's head pounded.

"But you asked Zeke to come home early because of an emergency."

"I need him and Emily to help train the bulls."

"But we did so good today with training." Charlie nodded vigorously. "Except for Mr. Bo. He probably has an *owie* somewhere." He paused to join his brothers in the giggle department. "But he should be better next time."

"You let Bo Monroe ride a bull?" Emily laid down her utensils with a clatter. "Was he hurt? Franny, what were you thinking?"

"He offered. He said he'd done it before… in Texas. How was I to know it was when he was a kid?" And that he'd suck at it.

Emily pushed away her plate. "You should have called me. I should have been here."

"To take his place?" Gertie asked, grinning.

"To tend to his wounds." Franny grinned right back, disputes over myths, gold and Kyle temporarily on the back burner. "Bo had the wind knocked out of him is all."

"He stopped breathing?" Emily lowered her voice and scowled. "Did he need CPR?"

"No." Franny made sure that was clear.

"Is Mr. Bo your future husband?" Adam picked up another green bean with his fingers. Butter dripped into his lap. "I like him. He doesn't know how to play poker."

"He played poker?" Emily looked heartsick. "You should have told me, Franny." She dumped her untouched green beans back into the bowl and excused herself.

"Hey," Franny called after her. "I didn't plan their visit, any more than I planned on Gertie sharing that fable about Merciless Mike Moody." She narrowed her eyes, hoping to cast doubt on Gertie's story. "It was a very tall tale."

Gertie harrumphed. "Except for that gold coin."

The boys gasped.

It was all downhill from there.

CHAPTER EIGHTEEN

JONAH POUNDED AWAY on his keyboard.

Bo paced.

Laurel's knitting needles clacked.

Even Mitch, sitting at the check-in desk, wasn't silent. He kept staring at his fiancée and heaving heavy sighs.

Shane wanted peace and quiet. His head hurt. And his brain was muddled.

He'd blown it with Franny. And maybe it was for the best.

His heart ached, refuting that thought.

He felt like he was blowing his chance to save the town.

His head pounded harder.

"Is there more I should be doing for our side of things. I mean, about keeping the town?" Shane asked Laurel, because she was the one family member present who'd come with him to Second Chance in January.

"That depends, doesn't it?" Laurel lowered her knitting. "On what's needed."

"He should be doing more around town," Mitch said, taking a break from heavy sighs.

"Dude, you almost got trampled by a bull." Bo stopped pacing and shook his head. "Seriously, Shane. That's enough volunteering for you."

"Likewise," Shane murmured, turning to Jonah.

His goateed cousin didn't stop pounding on the keyboard. "I can't answer, or I'll lose my train of thought." His fingers stilled. "I lost my train of thought. What was the question?"

"Shane volunteering," Laurel prompted.

"Clearly, he's not doing enough," Jonah teased. "Or the inn would be full and there would be a line of folks clamoring to eat at the diner." He had the most annoying grin. It got under Shane's skin. "But never fear. Once my movie is made, the town will be filled with people searching for the elusive and unlucky gold. In the meantime, keep stepping up to the plate, buddy."

"But not when it comes to ranches or ranching because you're not good at it." Bo resumed pacing. "You should leave that serious stuff to the professional cowboys."

"Like you." Shane snorted.

Bo twisted his neck to the side and back, filling the room with cracks. "You know, I could be out on an oil rig in the Gulf Coast making good money right now. Instead, I came here to *contribute*. If we find that gold—and we will, with or without Franny's permission—that's my contribution."

"And if we don't find it?" Shane played devil's advocate. "I've seen one of those feral bulls in the wild. He was huge."

"How huge?" Jonah asked. "Purely for research purposes."

"As-long-as-a-minivan huge." Shane blew out a breath, making a decision. "I don't care if we don't have confirmation if Merciless Mike Moody existed or not. I'm taking the idea of a festival to celebrate the Old West and running with it."

"Is that because you want to stay in town longer and get to know a certain rancher?" Bo waggled his dark eyebrows.

Shane let that question go unanswered. He wasn't about to tell Bo he was staying because he wanted to prove to his father and his generation of Monroes that he could make lemonade out of any lemons someone threw his way.

Because that would be lying to himself.

"EMILY?" FRANNY CALLED to her from downstairs. "Shouldn't you be leaving for the trading post soon?"

The front door banged open and closed. Emily figured Franny was taking refuge in the barn.

Her sister-in-law was in a mood. It had something to do with Gertie and her love affair with Merciless Mike. The tension was thicker at the Bucking Bull than any time before, even when Emily had first put forth the idea of working in town.

"I should have left five minutes ago," Emily muttered, as she gritted her teeth and continued wrestling her hair with the flat iron. She'd run out of her special conditioner a week ago and with everything going on, she hadn't had time to drive to Ketchum to buy a new bottle.

Her hair refused to be tamed.

"I have feral hair," she mumbled.

But at least she had on her favorite black blouse. If Bo came by the trading post today, she'd toss her hair over her shoulders—because it looked halfway decent that way—and let the blouse do the talking.

I'll have more things to say to him today.

Things like "I hear my grandmother told you about Merciless Mike's gold."

Emily had years of experience with that tale. She could recite it over and over, if need be.

She checked her appearance in the mirror, turning from side to side. Everyone said they had one good side, their prettiest side. Emily decided her good side was the left. There was a stubborn lock of hair over her right ear that kept frizzing.

She had no more time to fiddle with it. Besides, if she put the flat iron on a higher setting, she might burn the hair off her head. That would be worse.

Emily grabbed her purse and hurried down the stairs. "I'll be home in time for dinner." She ran out to her truck, where she'd left the keys in the ignition.

This was her last day working in town. Surely, something would go her way today.

She could tell Bo "I know where one of my grandfather's tree photos is. We can take a ride if you like."

There was a photo in a tree bordering the pasture behind the barn. The one where the heifers were tucked far away from the bulls, in case any of them went into heat. It was near a stream and would be the perfect place for a romantic picnic.

Emily came around a bend in the road and slammed on the brakes.

A huge bull stood in the road staring at her, as if trying to decide if it should charge or not.

Her heart raced.

The bull was bigger than Buttercup, its horns a massive spread. Maybe five feet wide. He had scars across his powerful chest from pushing over barbed-wire fences.

He slowly trotted down the ditch and into the trees. An I'm-not-worried-about-you trot.

Emily was worried. More accurately, Emily was afraid. She could believe this was the bull that had done in Kyle.

She picked up her cell phone and called Franny. The call went to voice mail. And again…

Franny was horrible when it came to keeping her phone handy.

It wasn't until Emily was braking in front of the Lodgepole Inn that Franny picked up.

Quickly, she told Franny about the bull. "Are the boys inside? I should have turned around."

"He's going after the heifers." Franny's voice had a distant quality to it, the way it'd been in the months after Kyle died. "One of them could have gone into heat early."

"Get the shotgun." They'd be eating grass-fed beef through Christmas. That bull was that big.

"We've finally caught him." It was like Franny wasn't hearing Emily. "I'll check the fence line and see where he's knocked it down."

"Wait. What? Capture him?" Emily rammed the truck in Park. "No. Stay inside. Don't you do anything without me." She'd ask Laurel to cover for her at the trading post. Or Mitch's daughter, Gabby. She didn't expect much store traffic today.

Just then, Bo stepped out on the porch of the inn, leaned on the railing and stared down at her. He flapped his hand in a weak wave.

It was a sign!

And look. Jonah was nowhere in sight.

"Don't do anything rash, Franny. We'll talk strategy at dinner." All thoughts fled of immediately returning to the ranch. After all, Franny knew what to do. It was like the time they'd seen a mountain lion near the ridge line. Everyone remained on the lookout and no kids or animals were allowed outside by themselves until he'd been killed.

Without realizing Franny hadn't answered, Emily tossed her hair over her shoulder and got out of the truck.

"WE'RE NOT SUPPOSED to have town-council meetings more than once a week." Roy sat at the woodstove in the Bent Nickel in protest, refusing to come to the table.

"I'm presenting ideas for the Merciless Mike Moody Festival," Shane said, frustrated already. "You know, to revitalize the town to protect your way of life."

"You'll probably want me to volunteer for something," Roy griped.

"Nope. This is all on me." Already seated, Shane pulled out a chair at the table where they normally met and patted the cushion to entice Roy.

With a put-upon sigh, Roy ambled over, shoving up the sleeves of his blue coveralls. He'd been sulky since his doctor had told him he'd had a panic attack the other day, not a heart attack.

Mitch was already in his seat, bent over his cell phone. Ivy was bringing a plate of cookies.

Luck was with Shane. Mack had just arrived. "What's all the fuss?" she asked, a bit breathless.

"Big plans," Mitch said sarcastically. "Game-changing plans."

"Thank you for your support, future cousin-in-law," Shane said, heavy on the sarcasm. "Here's what I think it will take. We'll rent a cast of actors to reenact the robbing of the stage, the fight with Old Jeb and the chase by the posse. We'll need all shops open along the main drag in town, plus, another restaurant or two to handle the influx of tourists."

"Another restaurant?" Ivy shook her head, her brown hair uncharacteristically loose.

"What are these new stores going to sell?" Mack frowned fiercely, no doubt, at the idea of competition.

"Are you planning to do this before the end of the year?" Mitch asked.

"Yes," Shane said with certainty. Because he needed to make an impact before January rolled around again.

Roy shook his head. "Do you want to know what I think?"

"Of course. Isn't that why I'm here?" Smiling in the face of people who could care less about Merciless Mike or Shane.

Roy stifled a belch. "I think we should fire you."

Stunned, Shane fell back in his chair. "You can't fire an honorary council member." Could they? The roiling in his gut said yes.

"None of us like your ideas," Roy continued.

"At least, I have ideas." That came out more defensively than was wise.

"And your ideas stress Ivy out," Roy explained. "Not to mention Mack."

Shane rolled his eyes. And he wasn't an eye-roller. "I'm glad you got that off your chest."

"I think we should fire you, too." Ivy was well-versed in giving the stink-eye. She hit Shane with one now. "Last night, you told the doctor you wouldn't hire her. We need an advocate who is seriously committed to making this town safe. That's not you."

"Whatever you heard was out of context, Ivy, I assure you. She didn't want the job, anyway." Shane turned to Mack. "I suppose you want me off the council, too."

Mack narrowed her eyes. "Were you serious about other stores opening here?"

"Yes."

"Fired." Mack slapped her palms on the table. "Meeting adjourned."

"Hang on. We haven't heard from the mayor." Shane gave Mitch a stern stare. "Are you going to make it a quorum and fire me?"

Mitch took them in, one by one. And then his steady gaze settled on Shane. "I abstain since I've got a conflict of interest. I'm going to marry your cousin."

Oh, brother. Shane stood. "All right. Fire me. But mark my words, you'll regret it." He stomped out the door.

Fired. Again!

Shane battled the warring emotions inside him. Gut-eating shame. Breath-stealing betrayal. He'd thought Mitch was his friend. He'd thought the two of them wanted the same things. He'd thought playing nice with the council was the way to get things done.

I thought wrong on all counts.

"Hey, Shane!" Emily waved from the trading post as he walked toward the inn. "Do you have a minute?"

He had the rest of the day. The rest of the year. The rest of his life.

Emily met him on the trading-post porch. "Have you heard from Franny this afternoon?"

"No."

"Huh." She hesitated, polishing a silver trophy. She started to speak. Stopped. And then said, "I haven't, either."

Fear rapidly settled in his gut. "Should we worry?" Had Franny decided to go after the gold?

"No." But Emily sure looked worried. "Yes. I saw a bull on the drive into town and I think Franny wanted to capture it. Alone."

Now Shane had something to do.

CHAPTER NINETEEN

A STAIR CREAKED, which wasn't unusual in the old farmhouse.

Franny was making lasagna and removing noodles from the pot. As soon as her lasagna was assembled, she was heading out in the ATV to find where the bull had knocked down a fence before he paid the heifers a visit and then disappeared into the mountains again.

Three ferals. Bradley Holliday would be beside himself.

Granny Gertie sat in her chair by the fire, snoring lightly. The boys were supposed to be upstairs getting their schoolwork done.

A stair creaked again.

Unable to see the foyer, Franny paused, a wide floppy noodle hanging from her fork. "Where are you going?" Because at least one of her boys was trying to go somewhere.

Little-boy groans filled the air.

"I told you Mom has eyes in the back of her head," Charlie said.

All three boys traipsed through the living room and filed into the kitchen, waking Gertie.

"There will be no hunting for gold," Franny said firmly. She hadn't told them Emily had spotted the feral bull on the driveway. "It's a myth."

"Mom." Davey held up the gold coin, laying to rest the idea she'd put forth about myths and Merciless Mike. "I know we can find more gold. Charlie and I have seen those old photos plenty of times in the woods."

Franny tamped down a shiver of fear. "And what's my rule about the woods?" The one she'd made after Kyle died.

"We can't go in the woods." Adam hugged her leg. "Are you going to make cookies? I'll help."

"He just wants to eat the chocolate chips," Charlie said, ratting out his brother.

"Same as you." Adam jutted his lower lip.

"We don't want cookies." Davey was uncharacteristically adamant. "We want gold."

"You'll have to share that gold coin because no matter what Granny Gertie says, there's no more gold." Franny let her irritation seep into her words. "Now, if you've finished your schoolwork you can play video games, but only for an hour."

Charlie and Adam ran to the television. Davey frowned, but followed his brothers. The video games were enough of a distraction that the boys were guaranteed not to think about treasure hunts until after dinner. And then it'd be too dark to sneak out.

"Can I help?" Gertie turned around her walker and sat on the seat.

"No," Franny said automatically, still nursing hurt over Gertie's duplicity.

"I was wrong." Gertie's voice was thick with regret. "I should have told all three of you—you, Kyle and Emily. And afterward... I should have admitted I was the reason Kyle went up the mountain. But I... I was ashamed." Her voice cracked.

Franny's heart clenched, not because of her grief, but for Gertie, who'd born her guilt for more than two years.

"I know I don't deserve your forgiveness... But I'm going to try and make it up to you every day until I die."

Franny couldn't get the words out to absolve Gertie. But she could tell Gertie without words that fences were being mended. She gave her a fierce hug. It lasted long enough for the two women to spill tears.

"Go on." Gertie blew her nose in her handkerchief. "I can finish the lasagna and make cookies. I'm sure there's something that needs doing outside."

"Always." Franny gave her another, drier hug. "But promise me there'll be no tales of gold while I'm gone." That was the last thing she needed.

"Pfft. Video games and cookies. Those boys find that more fun than gold."

Franny hurried toward the door but detoured to her bedroom on the second floor. She removed the shotgun from the gun case, made sure both barrels were loaded and made it out of the house undetected.

She loaded the carriage of the ATV with fence-repair supplies and equipment, and then headed down the drive. She reached the highway without finding any fence down in the northern pasture. The fencing on the southern side was trickier to see since it was twenty or more feet back in the trees.

Franny drove slowly back up the drive, peering into the trees. She was going to have to search the rest of the ranch yard to find the breach.

She slowed as she rounded a hairpin turn.

That's when the bull struck.

He leaped out of the overgrown brush in the

ditch and T-boned the ATV, knocking it over. Luckily, he hit the back end. Luckily, Franny jumped clear. But she did so without finesse.

Her hat flew off and she skidded and tumbled a few feet on the road. Gravel bit into her skin and jabbed through denim.

The bull trotted away and half turned, staring her down as she got to her feet. He was a king among bulls. Truly humongous. His cold eyes said he'd fought his way to the top of the herd by trampling anything that got in his path. Like Kyle.

The fight seeped out of her.

He was a king, and she was...

No big deal. No big deal. No big deal.

That kind of thinking had gotten Kyle killed.

Franny's life flashed before her eyes, just not how she'd expected. The false freedom she'd felt as a kid, riding her family's spread on Sunny, her bright palomino. Her ranch made safe because Dad kept only tame stock and invested time and money in quality cutting horses.

Dad's insistence that she learn how to take care of tasks on a ranch and herself.

Kyle's insistence that he take care of her. That he shield her from the danger of the

Bucking Bull. The regular spots where the fencing went down. The regular presence of straggler bulls in spring. At least stragglers had been regular until Kyle died and Zeke came on board and the fences became harder to breach. Until the bull in front of her matured and the fire had limited his range or his harem.

The daddy of all bulls shifted forward and back, growing weary of her standing in place.

The ATV was still idling, the engine noise as annoying to the bull as the hornets' nest she'd disturbed last July had been to her.

Franny was bent down, frozen in fear. But her revelations changed all that. She stood, determined to make it out of this encounter alive.

Stick to the facts. That was Shane's voice.

Fact. Big Daddy Buttercup didn't like her moving. He aligned himself to her and pawed the gravel. He was a dangerously magnificent beast, who made no bones about wanting to kill her.

The smiling faces of her sons flickered in her mind's eye. Then Kyle's comforting smile. Gertie's lopsided expression of love. Emily's scowl right before she launched a lariat. Shane's gentle touch in her hair.

If Franny wanted to see any of them again, she had to find cover. Or take aim.

The ATV was immediately to her left. The shotgun on the ground six feet to her right.

It'd take both barrels to bring him down. If she was lucky.

It'd take more than barbed wire to hold him. If she was lucky enough to fence him in.

Franny couldn't afford to be lucky. She had to be smart.

She gripped the cargo cage and the footrest and gave the ATV a big heave. The daily grind of tossing hay bales combined with the adrenaline rush of fear had her shoving the ATV upright.

Big Daddy Buttercup bore down on her barricade. He rammed the front end with no finesse, pushing Franny and her machine backward in a screech of metal. One of his horns tangled in the handlebars as he reached for her. Time slowed. His breath was hot and angry. His eyes wild, but oddly familiar. The eyes of a bull in the chute, trapped, but waiting for his chance, knowing it would come.

He huffed and retreated, dragging the ATV back a few feet—dragging her back across the gravel on her knees. When that didn't free him, he bucked. Spun, breaking his horn free.

He trotted back to the bend in the road and glared at her.

Heart pounding, Franny hid behind the ATV. She tugged her cell phone out of her pocket but was struck with a dilemma: whom to call.

Emily was a twenty-minute drive away. No one at the house could help her. She didn't have Shane's number.

She tried not to recall Kyle's broken body, his trampled face. But she couldn't unsee, just as she couldn't survive this onslaught for twenty minutes.

Big Daddy Buttercup stomped his feet and gave her a coldhearted stare, most likely calculating the situation and the odds.

Her ears buzzed. Or maybe the ATV idle increased. Or...

That was a car engine.

Franny's hopes lifted.

Someone was coming up the drive.

Big Daddy Buttercup lifted his head and sniffed the air, then turned to face this new threat.

A big black SUV came into view and accelerated up the hill.

"Shane!" She hadn't realized she'd shouted

his name until the bull swung his head around to look at her.

Shane blew his horn.

Big Daddy Buttercup may have realized the odds had shifted in her favor. He trotted off into the trees.

Franny collapsed behind the ATV, holding onto one handlebar and the cargo cage. Her body ached and stung. She was shaking, but alive. *Alive.*

"Franny." Shane hopped out of his vehicle. "Are you okay?" He was by her side in what seemed like an instant, hauling her to her feet, wrapping his arms around her.

What had they fought about yesterday?

She couldn't remember, not when he was raining kisses on her face and confessing how scared he'd been.

"How did you know?" Franny asked, immediately feeling silly, because he had no way of knowing she was in trouble. "Why did you come?"

"Emily mentioned something to me about a bull and I just knew you wouldn't wait for reinforcements to get out here."

He didn't let go for her to answer, and in that moment, Franny realized she loved him. Not only did he know what she'd do, but he'd also known what she needed. He didn't lecture. He held on. Not protectively, as Kyle had done, but with equality. It didn't matter that he had lots of money and she had next to none. It didn't matter that she had a lifetime of knowledge in ranching and he had next to none. His embrace wasn't there to lock her behind doors and cattle guards. His embrace was supportive, helping her to stand on her own two feet, ready to shore her up if need be. And she loved him for it.

She'd loved Kyle. She'd needed to feel safe while she was pregnant. She'd needed to feel her babies were protected. But now she needed a different kind of love. Shane's love. If only until Bradley Holliday showed up. She'd lean on Shane and love him, and then she'd accept that he would go back to his life of loafers and expensive cars.

"Thank you." She pressed a kiss to Shane's lips and clung to him while her heart and knees returned to business as usual. "Thank you to Emily. But we've got to get out of here now."

"What you've got to do is put that bull down." Shane released her and grabbed the shotgun, handing it to her without a moment's hesitation. "I don't know how to shoot, or I'd do it."

"No." She took the gun from him and shoved it into the cargo cage, loving that Shane knew action needed to be taken, but was wise enough to admit he lacked the skill to do so.

"No?" Shane looked like he wanted to argue. His eyes were a stormy brown. The wind ruffled his hair the way the bull had ruffled his calm.

"We can talk about this when we get back to the house." Because she needed to talk, to plan, to be smart. She got on the ATV, which was scraped up but still running. "Follow me."

She gunned it all the way back home, over the cattle guard and into the ranch yard.

"Do you want me to put the ATV away?" Shane asked when he parked.

"Not yet." She cupped his cheek, needing to touch him while she explained about the Clark way of letting bulls in and her theory about the fire and Big Daddy Buttercup's reduced range.

Scowling, Shane turned protective. "Fact—a bull that size can go wherever he wants, whenever he wants. Shoring up fence posts with rocks won't stop him."

"Fixing the fence line is a short-term solution, a gamble to make him stay in the area until I can organize help to pen him up." Her hand drifted to Shane's chest. She was comforted by his strong heartbeat and his lack of argument. "I need to train that bull for the circuit. Once folks see him, they'll see his value as a breeder. Old Buttercup isn't going to last another winter. That bull will keep us going long after Old Buttercup is gone."

Shane's scowl faded. He stared into her eyes. "You need my help."

"Yes."

"Fact—ranching has an element of physical risk." He covered her hand with one of his. "I can't protect you."

"I'm not asking you to." Her voice was steady, even if inside she wasn't. "I'm asking you to help me while you can. To be with me while you can. No strings. No expectations."

"Franny." Her name was gruff on his lips. He lowered his forehead to hers. "I'm not sure how to take on this responsibility."

She'd lived in fear of wild bulls for two years. But this… "But you do want to…"

"Yes. Franny, yes." He kissed her forehead, and then turned to look back the way they'd come. "There are cattle guards at the highway entrance and one up here. Where can he go besides where the heifers are? Here?"

"No. There are fences that would keep him away from the barn."

"Are you sure?" Shane's gaze traveled over the ranch yard. "The other night when I was stuck here, I thought I saw him by the barn."

My babies.

The ball of fear she'd had when the bull had charged her ATV returned. "That's not possible," she said weakly, knowing instantly it wasn't true. "He'd have to have knocked over fences in multiple places. The federal road, for one, or he wouldn't be able to get in. The secondary fence behind the barn, too."

"Not to mention he'd have to be smart enough not to be seen." Worry lined Shane's eyes. "Until today. Something bothered him today."

"Heifers don't usually come into heat this early, but it's not unheard of." She dragged Shane up the porch steps, perusing the yard, listening to birdsong. "We have to be careful."

"You need to move your family into town. We can come back with reinforcements when things are safe."

She shook her head. "That's not how I was raised."

"Mom? What are you doing with the gun?" Charlie opened the front door and scratched his unruly brown locks. "Did you have to put something down?"

Normalcy intruded. "No, honey. I didn't shoot a thing."

"Darn it." Charlie made a silly face. "I love steak and Granny Gertie says there's not a lot left in the freezer."

"Charlie, there's a bull roaming in the yard." Franny checked to make sure the shotgun was loaded properly. "Tell everyone to stay inside."

"Okay." Shrugging, he shut the door.

"I can't leave." Franny faced Shane. "There's stock to care for."

"And train," he said absently. "But the kids—"

"They're ranch kids. They know the rules to keep them safe."

He was worried.

She touched his cheek again. "If I don't catch that bull in a day or two, I'll send the boys to my dad's ranch." She left him on the porch to retrieve her tranquilizer gun, stopping to reiterate to the family that there was a bull on the loose and they were to stay inside.

She didn't get any arguments, possibly because she told them they could play video games for another hour.

When she returned to the porch, Shane was loading fence-mending supplies from the ATV into his vehicle.

"What are you doing?" She loaded the tranquilizer gun with a dart.

"We're checking fence line on a road." His smile was grim. "And it just so happens that my Hummer is made for driving on roads."

"I love the way you think." She helped him load, and then they were off.

CHAPTER TWENTY

"YOU LOOK GOOD in blue jeans and boots."

Shane spared Franny a look of disbelief, not that she noticed. She was too busy staring out the window at the fence and any possible breaks. She hadn't been too busy earlier to give him a kiss or to touch him tenderly.

After the morning he'd had—*fired once again*—he cherished a little tenderness.

"You're just complimenting me because I'm helping you." Shane was exactly where he wanted to be right now—on the federal road leading to the Clark cemetery. And yet, he'd do anything not to be there under these circumstances. "I'm having second thoughts about the timing. We shouldn't be doing this now."

"Now is the perfect time, trust me." Clutching the door handle, Franny remained stoic and with her eyes on the fence line. "He got some of his anger out of his system."

"The bull?"

"Yep." She nodded. "Big Daddy Buttercup."

"You named him?" Jonah would be thrilled. "You know what they say about animals."

"I do." She spared Shane a quick grin. "Never name them unless you plan to keep them. He's perfect."

"He nearly killed you!"

"That's why he's perfect."

"But…" Shane didn't want to ask the obvious question, but he couldn't stop myself. "If this was the bull that killed Kyle, how can you not want to put a bullet in his head?"

She kept her face averted, but her fingers curled tighter around the door handle. "A bull like that— Kyle would see the justice in catching him." She sat up. "Stop."

Two fence posts had been pushed over.

Neither one of them said anything as they scanned the undergrowth and the shadows between the trees, which stood so close together it was hard to imagine the big bull charging through and trampling them.

"We'll be fine," Franny pronounced, hopping out of the SUV and heading for the downed fence. "Big Daddy Buttercup might be hurting from bashing the ATV. He'll have second thoughts about engaging us so soon."

"He doesn't look like the kind of animal

to have regrets." Shane got out and joined Franny at the rear bumper. "A dog who chews your slippers shows remorse. He hides in the corner and hangs his head. This thing..." He opened the back of the Hummer and tried to ignore the way dread raked his insides. If Franny needed him to be strong, he'd be strong, even if he recognized the veneer of courage for what it was—a thin coat.

Franny handed him the shovel. "If he's got a hangover, he'll most likely be mooning after my heifers."

"You're too cavalier."

"And you're too cautious. Listen to those birds singing." She slid down into the ditch. "Shoot. He snapped the wire. Even if I strung seven wires instead of four, he'd come through."

Shane strained his eyes looking for movement in the brush. "I don't suppose there's room in the barn for your heifers. If he couldn't reach them, he might wander off." He could only hope.

"Nope. Even if there was room for my female stock, bulls have been known to come through wood walls for a chance at love." Franny sounded happy, chipper even.

Shane joined her, examining the soil around

the fence post. It was more compact than the other downed poles they'd come across the other day. He supposed the snapped wire was a mixed blessing. "Can anything hold him back?"

"Metal fencing like we've got around the arena. A couple ropes around his neck from some sturdy cowboys." She clipped a broken wire near the fence post and set it aside. "That's how we'll catch him. Either drive him into the arena or get a few ropes around him."

Both options sounded risky to Shane. "Suddenly, the problems of hosting a fifty-thousand-member convention in Las Vegas seem very small. We should rethink the benefits and rewards of this endeavor."

"Gertie was making cookies when I left." Franny gave him that sweet-as-molasses smile again and touched his cheek.

"Cookies don't seem like proper combat pay." And they were definitely in a war zone. But he was honored to be the one she wanted by her side.

"Play your cards right, cowboy, and you might get a cookie and a kiss." Her fingers drifted to his chin. "Where did you get that scar?"

He hesitated too long, then admitted, "I fell."

She hesitated too long before she said, "I don't think you've ever lied to me before."

Shane captured her hand and gave it a squeeze. "I was pushed." By Cousin Holden at a campground in Tennessee. "Some might say I asked for it." He'd always had a smart mouth and Holden made him itch to let off steam. "Others might say I was bullied." Not the Monroes, but someone like Franny.

"And?" She arched her eyebrows.

"Are you asking if I got up swinging?" Shane decided shoring up the fence post was safer than looking in her eyes. "I did not. That's not the Monroe way."

"But you did seek retribution?" Oh, she was on to him, all right.

"Continuously." By choosing the best Christmas gifts for his grandparents. By running the more profitable arm of the Monroe Holding Company. By figuring out Grandpa Harlan's connections to Second Chance and then leading the charge to protect and grow the small town. "Although that was made a little harder today when I was dismissed from the town council."

A branch snapped in the brush.

Franny immediately raised the shotgun.

A coyote poked his head between leaves, and then disappeared.

Franny lowered her weapon. "Why did they fire you?"

"I'm not sure." He returned his attention to the pole. "But I suspect it had something to do with Ivy and Mack not wanting competition. And the idea of change scares Roy."

"Then it's their loss." Franny said it with such conviction that Shane stopped messing with his shovel, leaned forward and kissed her.

Much as Shane wanted the kiss to last, there were pressing matters at hand. He straightened and gave her a smile. "I'd like to kiss you without feeling the need to listen to your early warning system." He'd like to kiss her long and leisurely in front of a roaring fire.

Who was he kidding? He'd like to kiss her whenever he felt like it. Franny Clark was high on his scale of kissability.

But she was more than kissable. He enjoyed being in her company, discussing facts and options, calming her down and having her do the same for him. It wasn't that she was a cowgirl, the likes of which he'd never dated before. Franny would be successful at anything she set her mind to. And she didn't need a man by her side to do it.

The exception being fence repair and bull training.

The point was she wasn't his responsibility, although he'd promised to watch out for her. She'd been managing on her own before he came to town and she'd most likely do just fine after he left. He actually loved that about her. Because…

I love her.

Shane nearly took off his toe with a wayward slice of the shovel into the earth. He paused, ostensibly to take a breather. Reality was, he needed a moment to take in Franny. She knelt at the next post, wrangling wire patiently. Her jeans were dirty and torn. Her boots as scuffed as the secondhand pair he'd purchased. Her hat tilted back, framing her light brown hair.

He tested the words once more: *I love Franny.*

She glanced up at him, rubbing her nose with her forearm. "What?"

"I was just thinking about what you said earlier. About being together."

Her gray eyes widened. "I've scared you away."

"No. It's… It's refreshing. I'm not sure I told you I agree. With it all. Your terms. Us together."

Franny chuckled.

"What's so funny?"

"Terms? It's not like we're dating." Her eyes sparkled beneath the brim of her hat. "And I'm not going to stalk you when you leave. My life is here."

Shane was filled with regret that his life wasn't here, too.

"I'm going to roll out the wire now." She stood, still smiling. "My offer of cookies and kisses later still stands."

"Sounds like a plan." And the sad part was they didn't have plans beyond those cookies and kisses.

SHANE AND FRANNY mended the fence in two spots and drove to the top of the ridge to make sure there weren't any other breaches.

Shane shut off the SUV in front of the lookout station. "I want to search around, if that's all right."

"I'm hoping Big Daddy is trapped on Bucking Bull property right now, so have at it." Franny exited the vehicle with him and brought the shotgun.

"I hear birds." Shane never thought he'd say those words with the same confidence, as if he'd seen highly armed security guards nearby. He searched the trees in the vicinity for Grandpa Harlan's bread crumbs. He found one at the rear of the cemetery, which was located at the bottom of a rise and surrounded by several large boulders. "Didn't the legend mention Merciless Mike was crushed by a boulder?"

"Yes." Franny stared at her husband's gravestone.

"Don't a lot of Westerns feature bandit hideouts in caves?" Shane bent and peered into a slim crevasse between two pieces of rock that looked like praying hands.

"Shane." Franny rested the gun barrel in her arms. "It could never be that easy. Besides, there's no way a grown man could fit between those rocks."

"The earth moves." Shane shrugged.

"And birds stop singing." Franny immediately went on alert. "Let's get out of here."

Shane didn't need to be told twice. He followed her back to his SUV. "Do you think Big Daddy pushed his way through another section of fence?"

"Maybe." Franny stood on the Hummer's

running board, looking for horns, no doubt. "Or he might have a brother out here somewhere."

Shane started the SUV's engine. "Relatives are an annoyance."

"ZEKE IS BACK in town," Emily announced when she arrived home after a day spent working in the trading post. "He and Sophie are staying in her cabin, but he said he'd be out here first thing in the morning to work the bulls with me."

"We'll all work the bulls," Franny called back from what sounded like the kitchen.

"Me, too," Davey said.

"No," Franny said firmly.

"I'm going to miss working in town." Emily rounded the corner of the living room to find Shane there. "I didn't achieve anything I set out to do."

Shane was eating a chocolate-chip cookie. "Like what?"

"Um…" Emily wasn't going to admit her man search to a Monroe.

"She's looking for a husband." Adam set down his milk. He had a milk mustache and swiped at it with the back of his hand.

"Napkin." Gertie handed him a paper one

and then glanced up at Emily. "What's wrong with your hair?"

Emily's cheeks heated. She finger-combed her hair over her shoulders away from her left side. "I had the window down on the way home." A lie. It was that dratted lock of hair she couldn't straighten this morning. She'd talked to Bo for a good fifteen minutes before opening the trading post. No wonder he'd looked at her funny.

"Shane was telling us about Merciless Mike's cave." Davey crumpled his napkin. "Up at the lookout. He's supersmart and figured out where the gold is."

"I never said anything about there actually being a cave." Shane held up his hands. "Only that there was a pile of boulders and there might be a cave."

"If it is a cave, you'd have to be a hobbit to crawl through the opening and get inside," Shane continued.

"Not even hobbits could get in there," Franny said decisively, clearly sending a cease-and-desist order to Shane and a discouraging message to the boys.

"You could use a loader." Emily decided the attention was off her and swiped a cookie.

They were still warm. "Franny's dad has one and so does Sheriff Connelly."

"The sheriff used to work for the state highway department." Shane took another cookie.

Franny looked at him sideways. "How do you know that?"

"I know everyone in town." He grinned at Franny the way Emily wanted Bo to grin at her. "I used to be on the town council."

"Past tense," Emily said in a thorny voice. How had Franny nabbed a man without leaving the ranch? At Franny's sideways glance, she added, "Roy told me."

"Then it must be true," Shane murmured.

"Cookie eating will now stop because the lasagna should be ready soon," Franny announced with firm looks at her children. "Hopefully someone will be hungry for dinner. I'll do the barn chores if you can make a salad, Em."

"But…" Emily looked at the boys. They were in charge of feeding the stock at night and closing up the barn.

"We're on lockdown," Davey explained.

"Yeah," Charlie added. "Mom trapped a feral in the ranch yard, so we're on house arrest."

With all the talk about husbands, chocolate-chip cookies and Merciless Mike's hideout, Emily had forgotten about the bull. "You trapped him?" The biggest side of beef she'd seen in a long time?

"I'm not sure where he is," Franny admitted in a guarded voice. Clearly, she hadn't told the boys just how large the bull was. "We fixed the fences lining the federal road. You, Zeke and I can do a sweep in the morning. If he's still on the property, we'll move him to one of the arena pens."

Franny made it sound so easy, as if the bull wasn't larger than Buttercup and years younger.

"I'll come out in the morning to give you a hand," Shane said, like any good boyfriend would.

Franny had all the luck.

"Maybe Bo would want to help, too." Emily had no pride when suggesting it.

No pride at all.

CHAPTER TWENTY-ONE

"Wake up," Davey whispered, shaking first Charlie's shoulder and then Adam's.

"What time is it?" Charlie grumbled, rolling over. "I don't smell bacon."

Davey tugged his brother back to face him. "It's four. We need to go now."

"Where?" Adam sat up and rubbed his eyes.

"To the lookout." He tossed the clothes to them that they had taken off the night before. "You heard Shane yesterday. Only someone as small as a hobbit could get in Merciless Mike's cave."

Adam blinked. "I'm the size of a hobbit. Charlie always says so."

"We can't go." Charlie squeezed his eyes shut. "We're on lockdown."

"We're taking the truck." Davey had thought it all through. "We take the truck to school when we're on lockdown. We'll be fine."

Adam rolled out of bed and reached for

his jeans. "Come on, Charlie. Maybe when it comes to Merciless Mike's hideout you're a hobbit, too."

"Mom will worry." Charlie yawned.

"And if we get the gold, Mom won't worry anymore." Davey shook his brother's shoulder. Gold meant money for trips down to Ketchum to see a movie. It meant Grandpa Clark wouldn't call to ask Mom for money that she owed him. It meant Davey could go to camp with the missing kids this year and every year until he was eighteen. Maybe they'd have enough left over to buy new stuff for the ranch, too.

"But it's dark outside." Charlie yanked the covers over his head.

"If we get the gold, you can buy a new video game," Davey said, sweetening the pot. "I'll let you play my turn the first day."

Charlie thrust the quilt down to his waist. "Promise?"

"I swear." Davey offered his hand for a shake because that's what grown men did when they made a deal.

Adam was nearly dressed. "Did you ask Mom?"

"No, stupid." Davey rolled his eyes. "This is a surprise. A hobbit surprise." He'd already taken the keys to both the old ranch truck and the federal gate. They just needed to sneak out without being discovered.

They made it downstairs before they met with trouble.

"What are you doing?" Granny Gertie wheeled her walker up to them. She always slept in sweatpants and a sweatshirt. Her hair looked like a white haystack. "Up to no good, I bet."

The way Davey figured it, he had two choices. Make a run for it and hope Mom and Aunt Em were slow getting out of bed and chasing after them. Or he could enlist Granny on their quest.

"We're going for the gold," Davey whispered. "You know it's up on lookout point, don't you?"

Gertie stared at them in silence for a moment before asking for her coat and boots.

They were so loud getting out the door with Granny's walker, Davey thought for sure Mom or Aunt Em would come downstairs.

Then Charlie slammed the old truck door and Davey figured they were caught this time.

But no one came.

Davey released the parking brake and coasted down the hill and over the cattle guard before starting the engine.

CHAPTER TWENTY-TWO

"WHERE ARE THE BOYS?" Emily opened Franny's bedroom door at zero-dark-hundred.

"Sleeping?" Franny sat up groggily. It was the first good night's sleep she'd had since Bradley Holliday had told her he didn't like the quality of their bulls. Her alarm wasn't set to go off for another ten minutes.

"Their bedroom door is open, and no one is in bed. They aren't downstairs, either." There was fear in Emily's voice.

"That darn gold." Franny launched herself out of bed, stumbling on the hall rug and catching herself on the door frame of the boys' room. Their bed covers looked as if they'd been thrown aside as if the boys had had no time to lose. "It would be just like them to set out early to try and find it."

She ran down the stairs, calling out their names.

"Granny Gertie isn't here, either." Emily followed her. "Her boots are gone."

The rumble of an engine approaching had them running out the front door.

It was Shane in his Hummer with Zeke in the passenger seat. He parked the SUV in the old ranch truck's spot. Bo and Jonah got out of the back.

Franny sprinted upstairs to get dressed, leaving Emily to ask if they'd seen the old truck on their way up the drive.

The sun was just rising. The stock would be hungry. They had water. They could wait.

Soon enough, Franny was outside with Kyle's shotgun and the tranquilizer gun. "Someone needs to stay here in case they return."

"Bo and Jonah." Shane delegated without hesitation while he gave Franny's shoulder an encouraging quick rub. "I got them out here early because I didn't want you heading out without backup."

"You never should have told my boys about those boulders and hobbits," Franny snapped.

Shane drew back. "I'm sorry. We'll find them safe and sound. I promise."

"Don't make promises you can't keep," Franny snapped again, overcome with concern.

"I have to go," Jonah protested. "It's my story."

"I'll stay with Bo." Emily fussed with her hair, which she had yet to comb. "I put a couple lariats in the back of Shane's SUV, along with the first-aid kit. A sleeping bag in case someone's in shock. Water. A couple of energy bars, including the chocolate kind Adam likes."

"Perfect." Franny had been too flustered to think so far ahead. She hugged Em. "Thanks."

Jonah was scowling at Emily and mumbling something about women who didn't play hard to get.

"If you're coming, Jonah, get in." Shane climbed behind the steering wheel.

Franny hopped in the back with Jonah. "Thanks for cutting your honeymoon short, Zeke."

"Hey, that's real job security, right?" But Zeke didn't say it with his usual good humor. He'd come to work for them after Kyle had died and was fond of the boys.

The sky was getting lighter. It was going to be a clear, sunny day. Franny hoped it would make finding the boys easier.

"The gate's latched, but not locked." Shane pulled up to the federal gate. "We locked it yesterday."

They had indeed.

Zeke opened the gate, then closed and latched it behind them. And then Shane gunned the Hummer up the mountain.

Franny held back a sob of relief when they reached the top. "There's the truck." It was on the other side of the lookout's concrete foundation near the cemetery and the pile of boulders. "That's where we found Kyle."

Kyle.

Panic rose up in her throat, threatening to cut off air.

"Where are the boys?" Jonah craned his neck.

A flash of black, a crunch of metal and then the SUV jerked to a halt.

"A bull just rammed us." Jonah couldn't believe it. "What the heck?"

"So much for fence mending," Shane muttered, leaning forward to look down the hill, where the bull had disappeared.

"It's him. It's Big Daddy Buttercup." Franny gasped and pressed a hand over her heart. "Where are my kids?" From this distance, she couldn't see any heads in the ranch truck window, not even Gertie's.

"That thing doesn't deserve the name *Buttercup.*" Jonah unbuckled his seat belt and twisted around for a better look. "You should call him Killer."

"Here he comes again," Zeke said in a voice that was too calm. "Hold on."

Franny gripped the door handle and the seat belt across her chest while Shane jammed the SUV into Park and put both feet on the brake pedal.

The bull rammed the Hummer head-on in a clash of metal that seemed to press on Franny's chest. The SUV rocked but didn't move. Franny sucked in air as Big Daddy spread his legs and shook himself.

"That's right, numbskull." Shane shook his fist toward the bull. "Military grade."

"I've got to get to my family." Franny opened her door. "That old truck isn't made for a war zone."

"Franny, don't!" Shane spun around in his seat.

Jonah reached over and closed her door. "Haven't you ever seen a *Jaws* movie? Stay in the boat."

"Jonah's right, Franny. Stay inside." Zeke took command. "Shane, drive. We've got to get closer to that truck."

Shane honked the horn, startling the still-groggy bull, who trotted out of the way.

They drove around the lookout-tower foundation, the SUV tilting at an awkward angle. One strike from the bull and they'd slide down the slope.

Franny's fingers knotted in her lap, but the bull left them alone.

The sun cleared the Sawtooth Mountains and the ranch truck came fully into view. Its fenders were pulverized, and it listed to one side.

Three heads popped up in the rearview window.

Sucking in air, Franny dialed 911, but she had no service. "Where's Gertie?"

"I think I see her hair above the passenger headrest." Shane reached back and gave Franny's hand a reassuring squeeze.

A crash rocked the SUV from Jonah's side, crumpling the doors inward.

Big Daddy Buttercup had followed them. He trotted around the SUV, scraping the metal with his long horns.

Franny covered her ears. "I have to get to my kids."

"Let me and Jonah go." Shane couldn't get his door open. He rolled down his window.

"What? Why?" Franny held on to the door

latch and looked around for the bull, ready to make a run for it.

"Because you and Zeke are going to climb to the roof and rope that beast," Shane explained. "Didn't you say you needed at least two people to rope him? You can tie Big Daddy to the roof rack while Jonah and I jump into the truck bed and protect the others."

Shane at his logistical best.

"You're assuming he won't knock us off the roof." Franny rooted in the back until she found Zeke's coiled lasso and her own.

"Or the hood," Jonah pointed out. "We shouldn't get off the boat."

Zeke half turned to stare down Jonah. "Haven't you ever been on a boat in rough waters?"

"No." Jonah was not amused. "Hollywood is landlocked."

"That makes Big Daddy a land-shark," Shane pointed out, easing the SUV forward until he bumped the ranch truck tailgate with his grill.

"Very funny." Jonah wasn't laughing.

"If there's one thing Grandpa Harlan taught me, it was to stay *calm* in a crisis. He didn't say to stay *serious* in a crisis." Shane climbed out of the window and leaned back in to speak to Franny. "You trust me to protect the boys, don't you?"

"She loves you, so of course she does." Jonah scrambled out of his window and onto the roof, joined by Shane. "Any fool can see it, except you two, obviously."

Franny sputtered. Yes…she loved Shane, but she hadn't told him and hadn't planned to, either. Confessions of love were for people committed to living in the same county.

The bull rammed her door, shattering the glass window. Jonah and Shane stumbled on the roof, but didn't fall off. Gasping, Franny punched the remaining glass out of the window with her elbow as the bull backed up and sniffed the air.

"This is a big deal," Franny murmured, staring into Big Daddy's eyes. "You, my friend, are gonna pay for that." Literally. When she put him on the rodeo circuit.

Shane and Jonah leaped safely from the hood of the Hummer to the ranch truck's bed.

The bull trotted around the vehicles, looking for a target.

"Shane!" Her boys pounded the rearview window. "Help! Shane!"

Gertie peered over the seat and gave a little wave.

Franny wanted to go to her children. She wanted to reassure them everything was going to be all right. But she had a job to do. She climbed out the window onto the Hummer's hood.

"Just one problem," Zeke said when he was standing on the Hummer's roof beside her. "If we both tie off on the Hummer, we have no leverage to guide him back to the ranch."

They could catch him, but they couldn't keep him. He'd just ram them until the metal gave or he popped a tire.

"There's got to be a way." Other than hitting him with a tranquilizer dart, which would only make him dead weight.

SHANE HAD LEARNED many things in business school.

Evading feral beasts and rescuing families from them hadn't been on the curriculum.

"Shane!" The boys pounded on the rear windshield, fear in their eyes. "Help! Shane!"

Shane willed his courage to hold out. If anything happened to those little guys, he'd play chicken with that bull and the Hummer's grill, and win or lose, those kids would be safe.

Davey leaned out the driver-side window

and waved. The door itself was caved in. Who knew if the old, thin metal would hold up?

"Stay where you are!" Shane commanded, reaching for Davey's hand to give it a reassuring squeeze. "Back in the cab. We'll get you out of there."

"Is he gone?" Zeke held the rope with a big loop at the end and surveyed the area.

"Do you hear that?" Standing on the hood, Franny clung to the luggage rack above the front windshield of the Hummer. She had a similar rope in her hand but wasn't ready to throw.

"I don't hear anything." Jonah's gaze darted around.

"Exactly." Franny peered into the brush. "You'd hear birds if he'd left."

"Birds. Don't forget to put that in your script, Jonah." Emergency humor. Shane swallowed thickly, wondering if he could kick in the ranch truck's rear window without hurting anyone inside. He feared the bull would ram the truck if they tried taking the boys out the side windows. And then there was Gertie. Her walker was in the truck bed.

A heavy snort. A crack of brush. The giant devil struck the Hummer again, knocking Zeke to his knees. Big Daddy was quick.

Shane would've thought they'd have more warning than that.

The bull disappeared down the slope on the other side of them.

Someone had a hold of Shane's shirt back. Someone was screaming.

"It's okay. You're okay," Shane repeated and glanced over his shoulder at Jonah. "Stop. You're scaring the boys."

Jonah snapped his mouth shut. "Sorry. That just sorta…came out. Don't tell Emily. I mean, Bo. I mean, Emily or Bo."

Shane had no time to figure out what was going on in his cousin's head.

"Keep down." Zeke twirled the lariat above his head. "Come on, Buttercup. Come out, come out, wherever you are."

The air was still. Even the boys were quiet. *Snort. Crack.*

They all looked left.

The bull emerged from the trees ten feet away and charged the rear of the SUV.

Zeke flung the rope. It glanced off the bull, having missed one of his long horns.

The bull put on the brakes and slammed sideways into the tailgate.

Franny fell to her knees.

Everyone in or on the ranch truck screamed.

The bull shook his head, then spun around, kicked at the rear bumper and bucked toward the brush.

"Let me try." Franny got to her feet and twirled the lasso over her head while Zeke coiled his rope, kneeling at her feet.

"Hey," Shane called. "If you need to tie him to a second anchor, you should use this hitch in the truck bed. It's for a fifth-wheel trailer, isn't it?" He'd seen them on the highway before.

"Great idea." Zeke slid down the Hummer's windshield and across the hood, jumping to join them in the truck bed. "Get down so I can give this another try."

"Let me throw first." Franny scanned the tree line.

"I don't want to be a hobbit no more," Adam wailed.

Snap. Crack. Hooves pounded, shaking the earth as the bull broke through the brush and charged.

Franny tossed her rope. The loop cleared both horns and his muzzle. She yanked it tight around his neck and then fell to her knees, tying the rope to the roof rack. Zeke sent his rope hissing through the air. It encircled one horn and his head. Zeke pulled his rope tight and shouldered Shane and Jonah aside, shoving the length of rope through the center hole of the big round hitch and tying it off quickly.

And just like that, Big Daddy realized he was caught. He tried to back up. He bucked. And when that failed, he rammed the Hummer again. Denting the entire passenger side.

Shane didn't wait to see if the rope held. He jumped to the ground on the driver's side and yanked open the back door. Quickly, he and Jonah transferred the boys to the Hummer on the driver's side. It took him longer to open the driver's door, which looked to have crumpled around Big Daddy's head. Gertie had scooted to his side. He scooped her up and deposited her in the Hummer's back seat with the boys.

Shane climbed back in the truck bed. "What now? Wait until Big Daddy passes out from a concussion?"

"His skull is too thick for that." Franny was still kneeling on top of the SUV. "At least, I hope."

"Only if he's part bighorn sheep." Zeke kept both hands on the rope as if afraid his knots wouldn't hold.

Jonah held his cell phone skyward. "I have

no signal. Do we make a run for it? We can fireman-carry Gertie."

"No. We need to lead this guy down the hill." Zeke looked grim. "Or he's going to pound the life out of both vehicles and then we'll have to start all over again."

The SUV was rocking, tugged back by the bull and then absorbing the shock of his charges.

"I'll drive the truck." Shane hopped down once more and got behind the wheel while Jonah prepared to drive the Hummer.

Franny sat on top of the SUV and Zeke knelt in the truck bed. Both held on tight.

A flash of sunlight reflected on something near the truck's front bumper. The glint came from the sliver of space between the two boulders.

In a day of breath-stealing moments, Shane held his breath.

Rocks in crevices didn't mirror sunlight. He'd bet there was a photograph behind those boulders. A photograph of three men holding shovels and smiling as if they'd found the mother lode.

This was where Merciless Mike hid his money. This was where Harlan, Hobart and Percy found it. And somewhere on this ridge was where the antiquities auctioneer had died. Where Hobart had been shot. This was where Franny's husband had met his end.

And very nearly where Shane and the people he loved and trusted had met theirs.

As soon as it was possible, Shane was returning to pay homage to the men whose lives had changed or ended here. But most especially, he wanted to honor the man who'd forced him to explore a life free of corporate responsibilities. His grandfather.

It was slow going. Two vehicles backing down the hill.

Big Daddy Buttercup was resigned to his fate before they reached the federal gate.

Shane wasn't sure what the future held—not when it came to Second Chance, stolen gold, or Franny Clark. But he knew one thing for certain. He'd never felt as alive as he did when he was around Franny and the Bucking Bull ranch.

It was too bad that the most satisfying experience of his life couldn't last forever.

CHAPTER TWENTY-THREE

"THAT WAS QUITE a morning for my first day back." Zeke pushed up his cowboy hat and grinned at Franny.

"It was quite a morning regardless." Franny nudged Zeke's shoulder with her own. "Thanks for cutting your honeymoon short."

"Are you kidding?" Zeke pointed to Big Daddy with both hands spread out, like a fisherman describing the size of his catch. "I wouldn't have missed getting this guy for the world."

They sat on the tailgate of the nearly dead old ranch truck near a small metal holding pen containing the fearsome bull. There were many good things to be thankful for today. First and foremost, the safety of her family.

Franny glanced over her shoulder. Shane and his cousins were making plans to search for gold, with Emily and the Clark boys a safe distance away. Gertie had retired to her bedroom, chastised for encouraging the boys and praised for going with them. The ranch gleamed in the sunlight and the promise of more sunny days ahead.

Zeke looked back at the boisterous group. "You really think Merciless Mike's gold is up there?"

"I think I'm going to have to let them look." The idea filled her with trepidation, not just for everyone's safety, but because she suspected Shane would be leaving as soon as the gold was found. She returned her attention to Big Daddy, who had his back turned to them like a sullen child. "But they can only search if they take precautions."

"There must be more to the herd out there." Zeke grinned. "It'd be fun to go rope a few. Thin them out."

And line the Bucking Bull's pockets. A few weeks ago, Franny would have cringed at the idea. But today... Today she felt as if she could handle anything.

"Why don't we put in a few gates and leave feed in the upper pasture." Franny couldn't believe she was brave enough to suggest such an option. "They're used to coming in over knocked-down fence. Why not make it easier for them?"

Big Daddy snorted his disapproval of fencing in any of his herd.

Shane appeared next to her and put his palm on the back of her neck. "That bull is taller than I am. How are you going to tame him?"

Zeke snorted as lustily as Big Daddy. "He'll decide how well he wants to tolerate us, not the other way around."

"For a start, the vet will swing by this afternoon." Franny tilted her head until her cheek touched Shane's arm. Things might have ended differently on the mountain if he hadn't have been there. If they all hadn't have been there. They made quite a team. "He'll make sure the ferals are healthy, dewormed and get their shots. And that we dehorn them safely." She, Zeke and Emily would inoculate the rest of the herd.

"We should call your dad and ask him to bring his loader." Shane's tone was casual, but the look in his eyes was not. "We could use it to move those boulders."

It was Franny's turn to huff. "My father wants nothing to do with this ranch or Merciless Mike Moody." He didn't understand... He couldn't know...

"It's just that I..." Shane's gaze softened.

He straightened her cowboy hat. "I was thinking a lot about my grandfather today and how he went to drastic measures to implement a do-over with his grandchildren, as if…" His eyebrows dropped for just a moment, but it was long enough for Franny to realize how deeply he felt for the subject. "As if he'd given up on having a close relationship with his own kids, which is sad."

"Shane, I—"

"What happened today should be a reminder to us all that life can change in an instant." Shane turned. "And things should be settled if they do."

She watched him walk away, acutely aware that nothing was settled between them.

"MR. BOUCHARD?" SHANE stood at the front door of the Silver Spur Ranch, holding his sunglasses and staring at Franny's father.

Rich looked over Shane's shoulder to the crumpled mess that was his SUV.

"It took a beating from one of those bulls you refused to help Franny with," Shane explained.

Franny would say he was meddling. Grandpa Harlan would say he was watching out for the people he cared for.

The woman I love.

Not that he was going to act on that emotion. Although he wasn't about to stop helping her.

Rich chewed on his cheek. "I'm surprised it still runs."

Shane shrugged, although he agreed. "I'm here because Franny needs your help." Not just for the use of his loader, but for the wisdom and a shoulder she could rely on when times got tough.

When I'm not around.

"And where is *Francis*?"

"Comforting your grandchildren. Their truck didn't fare as well."

Humanity flashed behind Rich's gray eyes. "Are they…?"

"They're okay." They'd be more than okay if they had Merciless Mike's nest egg. "You know, times are changing everywhere, including in the cattle industry. Franny is changing, too." She'd gained confidence since Sophie's wedding. "But that doesn't mean she couldn't use her father's help and advice now and then."

Rich's expression closed. "You're butting in where you shouldn't, son."

Son.

No one had called him that in a long time, certainly not with any affection.

"Don't let her go." Shane slid on his sunglasses, wishing they hid his eyes completely. "She's too strong to admit she needs anyone. You or me."

Rich shifted his weight, stamping his foot. "Anyone can help her move cattle."

"But not anyone can be a part of her life." Shane turned away. It was a move he was going to have to repeat with Franny in a few days.

"You're just like him."

Shane paused and turned. "Who?"

"Harlan. He never could mind his own business. Telling people what to do and how to do it."

"My grandfather..." Shane choked up, but he faced Rich head-on. "My grandfather cared for people enough to speak his mind. Not just for his friends, but for strangers, too. He donated millions to good causes because he considered himself a global citizen."

"A citizen?" Rich leaned against his door frame. "He gave up being a citizen when people here refused to heed his advice. If he couldn't control you, he wouldn't help you."

Shane stomped off.

But he couldn't put distance between himself and the idea that Rich was right. The terms of his grandfather's will meant Grandpa Harlan could control his family from the afterlife.

Thirty minutes later, Shane entered the Lodgepole Inn, still in a foul mood.

Mitch sat at the check-in desk, laptop open. He drew back in mock horror. "Whoever upset you is not in this building."

"Uh-oh." Jonah closed his laptop. "I've only seen you look like that a few times in my life. Is Holden back?"

"No." Shane tried to collect himself. He really did. But the truth had a way of working free. "My grandfather was an honorary council member."

"Is there a question in there?" Having been an attorney in a previous life, Mitch was naturally cagey.

Shane shifted his weight and stomped his booted foot, the same way Rich had earlier. "My grandfather sat on the town council after he bought this town and you fired him." The same way they'd fired him.

"Dang, he's good." Roy came out of his room, looking at Shane with admiration.

Shane wasn't calmed by the old man's observation. "I know my grandfather. He'd never be able to sit around here and not suggest changes. He couldn't even stand to ride in the back seat of a car."

"True that," Jonah agreed with a half smile.

"So, he visited Second Chance, because he had roots here and he loved people." And the people in Second Chance were friendly. "But he couldn't have lived here because he recognized you were all your own worst enemies."

Your own worst enemies.

Shane felt cold. That's what he'd been when he'd run the family's hotels. He'd been trying to be just like his father, a man who'd rejected him, who continued to reject him. He'd been trying to be a coldhearted businessman. That wasn't how his grandfather had earned his fortune. He'd built teams, makeshift families to replace the one he lost here.

And the money...

Could it have been that Harlan was earning money and donating big chunks of it to make amends for what happened to his twin?

"Shane?" Jonah stood before him.

Shane hadn't seen him get up. "It's not about money, you know."

His cousin studied him, took hold of Shane's arm and led him to the couch. "Nothing's ever about the money."

"It's about doing what you love," Shane said as he sat down. "And leaving your mark."

"And Grandpa Harlan did that," Jonah reassured him.

Shane raised his gaze to Jonah's. "But we didn't."

Jonah sat down next to Shane, understanding dawning.

Roy pressed a glass of water into Shane's hands. "Maybe we should take his blood pressure. He don't look so good."

Jonah leaned forward and looped his arms around his knees. "I don't feel so good, either."

"I can't stand not being in the thick of things," Shane admitted. "I can't stand by and let an opportunity pass." It drove him nuts. "I can't stay here."

"It took you months to see that." Roy chuckled, rubbing his palms together. "I saw that the first day you came to town."

"That's it, then." This time he knew it for a fact. He was leaving Second Chance.

And leaving the love of his life behind.

CHAPTER TWENTY-FOUR

"So, THIS IS IT?" Franny's father had his hands on his hips and a dubious expression on his face two days after they'd caught a new Buttercup. He surveyed the two oblong boulders leaning together at a bump on the ridge. "Merciless Mike Moody's hideout, undiscovered for over a hundred years."

"Yep," Jonah said. "It's either here or buried with a dead man over there." He pointed to the northwest corner of the Clark cemetery.

"Dad." Franny sent apologetic glances to the crowd gathered, including Shane, who took her hand.

"I don't believe in myths." Dad swung his dubious gaze from the large rocks to Shane and their clasped hands. "Or Monroes."

"But, Dad…" Surely, he wasn't going to head back down the hill without doing anything? Franny squared her shoulders and tried not to sound as if not knowing what was behind a ton of rocks was driving everyone assembled bonkers. "Dad, it's a safety issue. I don't want the boys to come up here and get hurt."

Emily stood guard nearby with a shotgun. Zeke wore a pistol and carried his lariat.

"Sounds like a discipline problem to me." But her father walked to his trailer and began loosening the tie-down straps. He even laughed. "That Davey. He drove all the way up here in the dark? And in a stick shift, too."

Franny breathed a sigh of relief.

Branches snapped. Hooves pounded. They all turned.

A horse burst through the trees. It was Yoda and Davey.

"Am I too late?" Davey asked. "Did you find anything?"

"Davey!" Shane marched over to Yoda and grabbed his reins. "Your mother told you to stay at the ranch."

"I know, but—"

"There are still wild bulls in these woods," Shane continued at a high volume.

Davey's forehead crinkled. "I know, but—"

"Not to mention Emily and Zeke could have mistaken you for a bull."

"I know," Davey said in a much smaller voice. "But...I wanted to see."

No one said a word.

Until Franny's father spoke up. "The thing about parenting is... Your words only go so far. Then you have to trust that the rest of what you teach them keeps them safe."

Franny's breath caught in her throat. Her father had taught her how to stay safe. He couldn't have given her a better gift. It was one she'd passed down to her son. "He's here, Shane. It's not like I'm going to send him home alone."

Shane scowled, looking like he wanted to.

A few minutes later, the boulders were pushed aside, revealing a narrow, deep cave.

Her father hopped out of the loader and knelt next to one of the large stones. "It's like this was where these rocks were before."

Jonah dropped down with him. "Could you use a burro and a pulley system to set them up like gates?"

Her father took in Jonah's bright red hair and form-fitting T-shirt. He sighed. "A donkey, maybe." He glanced at the twenty-foot cliff above them. "There's probably something up there you could use for leverage."

Jonah blew out a contented breath and mumbled something about his affection for Second Chance.

Inside the cave, there was a framed photograph on a ledge of three men—Percy, Harlan and Hobart. They leaned on shovels and mugged for the camera.

Shane picked up the photo and stared at it, stroking his thumb over the glass.

They found a small wooden chest in the back of the cave. Its edges were banded with tin. The tin was stamped with a name.

"R.H. Goody Bank and Express." Jonah was near as excited as Davey, who flipped open the lid.

"It's gold." Davey looked over his shoulder at Franny, a wide grin splitting his cheeks. "It's gold."

"I thought there'd be more of it." Bo peered inside the chest over Davey's head.

"It's a small box, but it's still filled," Jonah said defensively.

"Well, I'll be." Franny's father stood behind her.

She went to give him a hug. "I guess you'll have to become a believer in myths."

"And Monroes," Bo murmured with a sly sideways glance at Shane.

"Only those who stick around," Shane said cryptically and without looking at Franny.

Her heart clenched.

But before she could ask Shane for clarification, Davey ran to the cave's opening and pointed to the cemetery. "Are we going to dig up the man who shot Hobart?"

Every adult answered similarly. *"No."*

"WHY DO YOU have your suitcase?"

It was Mitch who asked the question, but the common room was filled with Monroes and they all turned toward Shane.

"I'm leaving." Shane had arrived at a place of peace with his grandfather. He knew the discovery of Merciless Mike's gold would pique the curiosity of the Monroe family. The rest of the dissenting eight would want to come and see for themselves.

His news about leaving gave rise to a cacophony of objections, which made Shane feel good. But not good enough to stay.

"I can't stay any longer." Shane needed challenges. He craved working in a business that mattered to him. And perhaps selfishly, he wanted to be appreciated wherever he was.

"But…" Jonah reached him first. "What if you remember something about Harlan or Hobart that helps my script?"

"I'll call," Shane reassured him with a hearty hug.

"But…" Laurel used her baby bump to get close enough to sling an arm around Shane's neck. "You're going to miss my babies."

"You can send pictures." He gave her a gentle squeeze.

Bo crossed his arms over his chest. "You're giving up on Franny."

"I'm not giving up." But Shane's gaze slid to the floor. "I'm stepping aside for someone more suitable." A man who fit into a place like Second Chance.

"Sounds like—" Mitch shook his hand "—you're giving up on you."

Shane swallowed past the lump in his throat. "Actually, I'm giving myself a second chance. Pun intended."

Mitch's daughter, Gabby, ran out of their apartment and threw herself into his arms. "You're the only person who ever wanted to learn about which of the boards on the inn's stairs were silent and which ones make a noise."

Because Shane liked the freedom of no one monitoring his movements and knew it made Mitch jittery. He bent to the preteen's level, ruffling her strawberry-blond hair. "Someday, you're going to find a guy your age to teach all the inn's secrets to. And then your father better watch out."

Mitch frowned.

They clustered around him as he carried his suitcase out the door and to his mutilated SUV.

"Are you going to get rid of this thing?" Jonah ran a hand over a crumpled fender. "I'm kind of fond of it."

"If I do, I'll give you first crack at it," Shane promised.

There was another round of hugs.

A familiar truck rumbled down the highway and turned into a parking space at the Bent Nickel. Three familiar boys tumbled out, calling greetings to Shane before disappearing inside the diner. A woman wearing a cowboy hat sat behind the wheel, staring in Shane's direction.

The pack of friends and family surrounding him dissipated. Shane stowed his suitcase in the rear compartment and closed the hatch.

His heart felt heavy.

The time had come to say goodbye.

CHAPTER TWENTY-FIVE

FRANNY HAD KNOWN this day would come.

She just hadn't expected it to be today.

Shane walked toward her, every step a crushing blow to her heart.

Willing herself not to cry, Franny hopped out of the truck and went to meet him on the sidewalk in front of the general store. Mack was in the window organizing a display of gold-panning equipment. Not that there was gold in the Salmon River, but that was probably the only gold-related merchandise she had on hand.

Franny reached past the heartache for a smile.

Shane reached past her smile to clasp her hand. "I suppose every good story has a fitting end."

"This one was a doozy." She catalogued every beloved angle of his face, every wave in his hair.

"It wouldn't have been as sweet if I hadn't

met Franny Clark, rodeo queen and winner of Best Mom in the West."

He always said the right things to lift her spirits. "What am I going to do when you're gone?" The words were wrenched out of her.

Shane startled, like Bolt did when surprised by a sudden plop of rain from the porch eaves. To his credit, he recovered quickly. "You don't want me to hang around. I'd annoy you with facts and logistics." His hand fell away from hers, along with his gaze and the strength in his voice. "No one ever wants me to stay."

"That's not true. That was your dad. And only your dad." She wanted to fight for him to find a home in Second Chance, but not if it would make him unhappy. And if he was leaving, she wanted him to know he had worth. To his family. To her.

She expected Shane's expression to harden, to close off, and the look in his eyes to turn jaded. She expected him to pull himself up tall and shield himself behind that mantle of Monroe pride.

He touched the back of his head instead. "Nobody wants me to stay here," he amended, almost absently.

"Then they're stupid." He was caring and clever. He was brave and honorable. She

was going to have words with those council members.

"I'm too intense. I push and push to get
things done." He wouldn't look at her.

She wanted him to look at her. To stare into
her eyes with that warm gaze that said he saw
the woman beneath the hat, not the rancher,
not the mom. "I like getting things done," she
said quietly.

"I wear people down. They want to relax.
They want to play. They want to ski in Aspen
or, worse, lie on the beach in St. Tropez and
do nothing." He ran his hand up the back of
his head, rubbing the wavy locks on top of
his crown.

He didn't know how to unwind.

She almost smiled. "You don't have anything to prove to me."

"Don't I?" He pointed north, in the direction of the Bucking Bull. "What good am I
here?"

What good am I to you?

That's what he didn't say. "You're everything that's good."

He shook his head. "I hurt Davey's feelings
yesterday. I almost got my cousin killed riding
one of your bulls. And…" His gaze landed on

her. "I needed you to rescue me. Twice. With your rope."

She'd been prepared to argue, since all of his other statements required an argument. He'd hurt Davey's feelings, but with words her son had needed to hear about being careful and staying safe. And it wasn't as if Franny wasn't partially to blame for Bo riding that bull. She'd wanted a miracle and she'd thought a volunteer would be able to provide what she needed.

"I rescued you," she said simply. But it was anything but simple. "It's what the rider in the ring does when a bull turns deadly. I did my job." That didn't mean her heart hadn't raced and her body hadn't been flooded with adrenaline. That's what the owner of a ranch did. They protected people. How she wished she could protect him every day. "I did my job, Shane."

"And that's just it." His gaze finally landed on her, but there was no warmth to it. There was only frustration. "I don't have a job here. I can't ride like you. I can't rope like you. I can't look at an animal and see whether or not they need medical attention. I don't know how to dehorn or deworm farm animals." He eyed Mack, who was still in the window and pretending to pan for gold. "You want me to stay?"

She hadn't asked, but her heart leaped that he'd considered it.

Shane shook his head. "I'd just be another burden for you to carry."

"That's not true." But Franny couldn't think of an argument to prove it.

"The truth is that I like being in charge. I *love* being in charge. There is nothing in this world I'd rather do than run my family's empire. Make decisions about how much to invest in oil this year. Have the final say about what advertising to run for the hotels. Lead the acquisitions team to expand our holdings. But this… I don't know how to run a ranch."

That got her back up. "I'm not asking you to."

He drew back slightly, as shocked by her outburst as she was.

Franny spared a glance to Mack, who wasn't even pretending not to listen. Her hands were pressed to the glass.

"Shane, *I* run the Bucking Bull. And except for the lack of trained bulls these past few years, I do a pretty good job."

"Well, you were grieving." Shane tried to make an excuse for her.

She scowled. "I know I can do better. Zeke is back and Emily might have gotten the town out of her system."

"You've got a good team."

A team that didn't include Shane. Exasperation flooded her system. She darted to the general store, opened the door and shouted at Mack, "If you don't mind your own business right now, Mackenzie, I'm going to do all my grocery shopping online!"

Mack blinked, and then climbed out of her display window.

Franny turned back to Shane, forcing a smile on her face, although it felt weak and watery. "The fact of the matter is…"

He'd said he couldn't help her on the ranch, but from the day he'd been stranded by the rain he'd given her advice on how to run a business, how to break overwhelming things down into manageable chunks, how forgiving she should be of past mistakes made by herself and others. He needed to hear that he'd made an impact on her life. He needed to contribute. And neither she, nor the town, had let him do that.

"The *fact* is, Shane." She gentled her voice. "You want to be a CEO, but that position at the Bucking Bull is already taken. I decide what happens at the ranch. How many animals to have. How much feed to buy. Which vendors to use. I don't need another man in charge…"

I need the man I love by my side.

Words escaped her, the same way the air had escaped her moments before.

I need Shane by my side.

But, Shane…

He took a step back. Perhaps he saw the helpless longing in her eyes. Perhaps he knew his limits better than she knew them.

"The fact is…" Franny wasn't sure what the fact was any longer, but her mouth didn't seem to know that. Her mouth kept moving. Ahead of her brain. Maybe even ahead of her heart. "Shane, I like running the ranch. I know I was still grieving, and things got to be too much, what with the decision to send Davey to an expensive camp, Gertie's stroke and my lackluster training efforts. I put family first, but I know what I have to do now. I know the steps I need to take."

"Good," he said gruffly. Softly. Without looking her in her eye.

"The fact is…" She wanted to be touching him. She wanted him to touch her. But now, in this moment, she needed to stand alone and say her piece, if only to give voice to the thoughts and feelings she'd kept inside herself for too long. "Nobody thought I could do this after Kyle died. Not really. Nobody... Except for you."

"So..." The warmth returned to his gaze. "Where does that leave us?" Ever the pragmatist.

"I don't know. I want to run things here. You need to run things..." She waved a helpless hand.

"We're back to where we started," he said softly.

Those gentle eyes. They were going to be her undoing. She worked hard to swallow back her tears, knowing they wouldn't change anything Shane chose to do.

"We agreed—several times—that we weren't right for each other." He turned away.

She grabbed his arm. "Just because I don't need you to balance my checkbook or help train a bull for the rodeo doesn't mean I don't *need* you."

That I don't love you.

He frowned. "To do what? Walk a step behind you? Be there to pat you on the back and say 'good job'? Warm your bed at night?" He gently pulled his arm free. "I can't not have a goal, a purpose…"

"A what?" Why didn't she understand? It was for the best that he was leaving, after all.

His frown deepened into a category-five scowl. "I can't not be in charge of something of value. Of something important. Like my family's holdings." And then he faced her and took her hands. "I can't *not* be Shane Monroe. This town has been eating me up inside since I arrived because the people here don't want me to change anything, not even if it means they'll be happier in the long run with a more stable income and a better quality of life."

And him staying would just be the same. He could learn how to ranch. He could go through the motions of ranch life. But it would never satisfy him deep down inside. No matter how much he loved her.

If he loved her.

"I understand." She stretched up on her toes and kissed him one last time. "It's got to tear you up inside owning a place and having no say." She traced the scar on his chin with her thumb. It was the one thing about him that wasn't perfect. And yet, it fit who he was. "Go out and conquer something. Let those bullies know they can't get anything past you."

"I'm sorry."

"Shh." Franny pressed her fingers over his lips even as she stepped back into her own space, her own life. "Go out and do something grand, Shane. Earn the respect of your family. Let them see who you really are inside." The way he'd let her see. The way he'd won her heart. "There is no better Monroe to run the world." There couldn't be.

"I'm sorry," he said again, lingering.

Franny tried to smile. "I've got to feed the chickens and you've got to do whatever future CEOs do."

He nodded but didn't move away. His gaze was full of love and longing and regret.

They hadn't exchanged pretty words. They hadn't allowed themselves to make promises. But there was love between them. It was there. In his eyes.

"You need to leave," she said, firmly this time, hoping that persistence would keep her heart from breaking in front of him.

"Go!" Anger rose up like a wave. "Go!" Or she wouldn't have the heart to set him free.

He did turn away then, making her regret her anger.

But it was the only thing that had severed the ties between them for good. The only thing that propelled him to a place where he could move forward and be happy.

Her knight got into his SUV, that battle-scarred, noble black steed, and drove away.

She repeated the question she'd asked him earlier, only this time she asked it of the wind. "What am I going to do when you're gone?"

She had the rest of her life to find out.

SHANE DROVE AWAY from Second Chance feeling as if his heart had been ripped out of his chest.

Who needs a heart when you have a business to run? A legacy to uphold?

None of that seemed important now. He would be the businessman his grandfather had been.

Shane stopped at the overlook on top of the mountain pass. From here, the Sawtooth Mountains rose up across the valley in their forbidding grandeur. In the meadow across the river, a pair of coyotes ran toward cover. He wouldn't wake listening to their song anymore.

From here, Second Chance looked small, just a piece of roof breaking the tree line here or there. Just a thin curl of smoke from a chimney. The biggest structure, the Lodgepole Inn, stood next to the river and Sled Hill. It was Tuesday. Mitch would have chili on the stove and a small fire in the fireplace. Mack would be rearranging her store window to attract customers. Ivy would be wiping down counters at the Bent Nickel Diner, talking to Roy while he finished his coffee and stared out at the near empty highway.

From here, he could see it all. He could feel the memories closing up, ready to be stored away. Another chapter in his life was over. Another set of friends left behind as he moved on.

From here, he could imagine Franny's truck driving along the river toward home later this afternoon.

Adam would be humming in the back seat. Charlie would be talking nonstop about video games. Davey would be staring out the window and dreaming about what he'd do one day when the ranch was his, what he'd do with all that gold. And Franny…

She'd be smiling tightly because she wouldn't want the boys to catch on to her upset. She'd have a firm grip on the wheel and a schedule in her head regarding what needed to be done in the next few hours, the next few days, the rest of her life.

A life without him.

Grandpa Harlan's words came back to him. The sentiment that people often forgot to say they care.

I never told Franny I love her.

Grandpa Harlan had been a wealthy man. He'd married strong women who'd pursued their own individual careers—the actress, the pilot, the politician and the oil heiress who ran a national charity. And he'd fostered their dreams while pursuing his own.

Had his grandfather made mistakes? Yes.

He'd lost a brother and left behind a friend. But he'd returned sixty years later and made amends. Or tried to.

Sixty years was a long time to carry guilt and regret.

Sixty years…

By that time, Franny's hair would be white. She'd still be as lean as a string bean and just as tough. She'd have her family around her at the Bucking Bull. There'd be a new Buttercup in the barn and a new set of boys running around the ranch yard. Davey would run the show and she'd push him, the same way Gertie pushed Franny now. She'd sit by the fire in Gertie's chair, alone. She'd sit by the fire and think of Shane. There might be a business magazine in the rack, tattered from repeated reading. She'd pick it up and stroke a hand over the picture of Shane's face on the cover, touch the gray at his temples. She'd ignore the headline about his latest corporate takeover and stare into his eyes.

But she wouldn't be staring into his real eyes.

She wouldn't be holding his real body close.

She wouldn't have someone to bring her coffee in the morning, to make sure she ate, to make sure she remembered to take care of herself in the midst of caring for everyone else and running a successful ranch.

Because Shane had chosen glory over love.

Grandpa Harlan would never have done that. He'd been driven by a need to replace the gold his brother had wanted so badly, gold that—had Hobart lived—he would have shared with many. Harlan had been a man with a big heart. He'd left Second Chance a lost, broken man. And it had taken him six decades, four marriages and twelve unruly grandchildren to discover what was most important to him.

Not his reputation.

Not his wealth.

But the love and happiness of his grandchildren. And this small town hidden in a mountain, where life wasn't always easy, but the people who chose to stay knew it, accepted it and embraced it.

His grandfather had found a way to have it all.

Shane turned the SUV around.

CHAPTER TWENTY-SIX

FRANNY COULDN'T BELIEVE her eyes. But yes, there it was—Shane's large black Hummer was parked at the Bucking Bull's gate as she made her way down the mountain to pick up the boys from school.

Shane was skipping rocks nearby at the camp shore.

Franny's heart beat faster at the sight of him. She turned off the truck and walked through the green, knee-high grass to reach him. "Hey."

He slanted her a sideways look. "I was thinking what a shame this camp is. No one swims here anymore. Or skips rocks. Or sings around the campfire at night."

"Stories," Franny corrected. "They used to tell stories here around the campfire." She and Emily had listened in a time or two, creeping close like desperados spying on wagon train settlers.

"Stories about Merciless Mike?"

"Among others." She smiled, still standing a good ten feet away from him. "That story has grown proportionally, hasn't it? Too bad the town council wouldn't approve of your festival."

"Do you know what?" He laughed, turning to her. "I own this town. Or, at least a share of it, which means I can choose my own board of directors."

Franny paused to process that information. "You want to be the CEO of Second Chance? Is that legal?"

"I'm staging my own coup." He closed the distance between them. "Mitch was relieved to be…relieved."

"Really." Franny couldn't find more words because her heart was beating faster than Danger's hooves at a gallop.

Shane found his CEO job. Here. In Second Chance.

"I have lots of changes in mind." His smile slanted wickedly. "Reopening this camp and making it available for a few weeks to kids like Davey."

"Davey would love that." Franny would love it, too.

"And there's the Merciless Mike Moody festival, of course."

That wicked grin set her heart fluttering. "Of course."

He took her hands, intertwining their fingers. "My grandfather had a really good attorney. I asked Daniel to look into obtaining an easement on federal land to operate tours. I figure by the time all the paperwork is done, you'll have caught all the stray bulls."

"Are you telling me what to do?" She arched her eyebrows.

"Never." He cleared his throat. "Or, if I do make *suggestions*, I hope you'll take them under consideration."

"You make it all sound so simple."

"And you see many complications where there are few."

It's no big deal.

Kyle's words took on a new meaning. What worries should she have about life as long as Shane was happily challenged and by her side?

"Do you know what my grandfather used to say?" He moved closer then, brushing the hair out of her eyes. "He used to say that nothing was impossible. And if you look at his life, nothing was. He was always reaching higher and then reaching back for the rest of us."

His touch was riveting. It made Franny forget about emptiness. It made birdsong a sound of joy, not a warning.

"Do you know what Granny Gertie used to say?" She moved closer to him, too, resting her hands on his hips. "She used to say that money didn't grow in the woods. She kept her feet on the ground all these years. She kept my grandfather's feet on the ground, too. They could have returned for that gold at any time, but she was happy with the ranch the way it was."

She and Shane were so close now that they should be kissing.

"Remind me. When are you leaving?" Franny forced herself to take a step back and tease.

Shane drew her to him, encircling her with his arms. "Who said anything about leaving?"

"We had that long talk in town just this morning."

"I was an idiot." And then he was kissing her.

The boys needed to be picked up. She needed to make a casserole and drop it off at her dad's house. It wasn't only the Bucking Bull's fences that had been mended in the past few weeks. A family had mended as well. There were bulls to train and cowboys to call. None of it mattered.

When she'd first seen Shane, she'd wondered how it would feel to kiss him. Would she feel like she was betraying Kyle? Would another man's kiss be unable to compare to her husband's?

There was no comparison. They were different things.

Shane held her differently. Shane kissed her differently. His touch was more urgent, more possessive, more worldly. She held on. She held on to strong shoulders and a strong heart. She'd had no one to lean on—no man to lean on—for more than two years. And now him. Maybe for forever?

Did that make her weak?

Shane drew back. He tapped her temple gently. "What's going on in that head of yours? I'm kissing someone, but it doesn't seem to be you."

He'd noticed?

Her cheeks flushed with heat. She stepped out of his embrace. "I got distracted."

"I was kissing you." He didn't look happy.

News flash. She wasn't happy, either. "I was thinking…" She traced the scar on his chin and stared up at Shane. She hoped he wouldn't see the longing in her eyes. Longing for another kiss, another embrace, another person to lean on. Not just at this sunset, but for the rest of her life. She wanted to say the words first. "It's been a busy week and a half and I never got the chance to thank you."

"Thank me?"

She nodded, allowing herself a small smile. "Thank you for loving me without ties or promises."

"That was before," he said in a gruff voice, tugging her closer.

She placed her palms on his chest, pressing back so that she could see his eyes. "And everything that comes now is the after. After we caught Big Daddy. After you tried to leave town."

"After I realized I loved you so much I couldn't let you go." He dropped down on one knee. "I love you, Franny. I wasn't looking for it. I wasn't expecting to find it. But here I am. Taking over a town. Maybe starting a charity for kids like Davey. And planning on settling down in a rambling farmhouse. Will you marry me?"

"I want to say yes, because I love you, Shane." She drew him to his feet. "But I want to ask my boys if they're okay with it."

"I'll be happy to do that." He grabbed her hand and they headed for their vehicles. "I should stop at the general store first."

"To buy them a video game?" Franny firmed her voice. "Shane, I won't let you bribe them."

He stopped walking, turned and kissed her soundly. "Franny, love of my heart, I was going to buy you a bouquet of flowers."

"Oh." She let herself be escorted to the truck, let him drive them into town and stood with a grin on her face and a bunch of daisies in her hand as Shane asked her children for her hand in marriage.

They said yes.

* * * * *

More great romances in
The Mountain Monroes series
by Melinda Curtis are available at
www.Harlequin.com!

Get 4 FREE REWARDS!

We'll send you 2 FREE Books <u>plus</u> 2 FREE Mystery Gifts.

Love Inspired® books feature contemporary inspirational romances with Christian characters facing the challenges of life and love.

FREE
Value Over
$20

YES! Please send me 2 FREE Love Inspired® Romance novels and my 2 FREE mystery gifts (gifts are worth about $10 retail). After receiving them, if I don't wish to receive any more books, I can return the shipping statement marked "cancel." If I don't cancel, I will receive 6 brand-new novels every month and be billed just $5.24 for the regular-print edition or $5.99 each for the larger-print edition in the U.S., or $5.74 each for the regular-print edition or $6.24 each for the larger-print edition in Canada. That's a savings of at least 13% off the cover price. It's quite a bargain! Shipping and handling is just 50¢ per book in the U.S. and $1.25 per book in Canada.* I understand that accepting the 2 free books and gifts places me under no obligation to buy anything. I can always return a shipment and cancel at any time. The free books and gifts are mine to keep no matter what I decide.

Choose one: ☐ **Love Inspired® Romance**
Regular-Print
(105/305 IDN GNWC)

☐ **Love Inspired® Romance**
Larger-Print
(122/322 IDN GNWC)

Name (please print)

Address
Apt. #

City
State/Province
Zip/Postal Code

Mail to the **Reader Service:**
IN U.S.A.: P.O. Box 1341, Buffalo, NY 14240-8531
IN CANADA: P.O. Box 603, Fort Erie, Ontario L2A 5X3

Want to try 2 free books from another series? Call 1-800-873-8635 or visit www.ReaderService.com.

*Terms and prices subject to change without notice. Prices do not include sales taxes, which will be charged (if applicable) based on your state or country of residence. Canadian residents will be charged applicable taxes. Offer not valid in Quebec. This offer is limited to one order per household. Books received may not be as shown. Not valid for current subscribers to Love Inspired Romance books. All orders subject to approval. Credit or debit balances in a customer's account(s) may be offset by any other outstanding balance owed by or to the customer. Please allow 4 to 6 weeks for delivery. Offer available while quantities last.

Your Privacy—The Reader Service is committed to protecting your privacy. Our Privacy Policy is available online at www.ReaderService.com or upon request from the Reader Service. We make a portion of our mailing list available to reputable third parties that offer products we believe may interest you. If you prefer that we not exchange your name with third parties, or if you wish to clarify or modify your communication preferences, please visit us at www.ReaderService.com/consumerchoice or write to us at Reader Service Preference Service, P.O. Box 9062, Buffalo, NY 14240-9062. Include your complete name and address.

LI20

Get 4 FREE REWARDS!

We'll send you 2 FREE Books plus 2 FREE Mystery Gifts.

TRAIL OF DANGER — VALERIE HANSEN

FATAL MEMORIES — TANYA STOWE

Love Inspired® Suspense books feature Christian characters facing challenges to their faith... and lives.

FREE Value Over $20

THE FORTUNES OF TEXAS COLLECTION!

18 FREE BOOKS in all!

Treat yourself to the rich legacy of the Fortune and Mendoza clans in this remarkable 50-book collection. This collection is packed with cowboys, tycoons and Texas-sized romances!

YES! Please send me **The Fortunes of Texas Collection** in Larger Print. This collection begins with 3 FREE books and 2 FREE gifts in the first shipment. Along with my 3 free books, I'll also get the next 4 books from The Fortunes of Texas Collection, in LARGER PRINT, which I may either return and owe nothing, or keep for the low price of $5.24 U.S./$5.89 CDN each plus $2.99 for shipping and handling per shipment*. If I decide to continue, about once a month for 8 months I will get 6 or 7 more books but will only need to pay for 4. That means 2 or 3 books in every shipment will be FREE! If I decide to keep the entire collection, I'll have paid for only 32 books because 18 books are FREE! I understand that accepting the 3 free books and gifts places me under no obligation to buy anything. I can always return a shipment and cancel at any time. My free books and gifts are mine to keep no matter what I decide.

☐ 269 HCN 4622　　　　　☐ 469 HCN 4622

Name (please print)

Address　　　　　　　　　　　　　　　　　　　　　Apt. #

City　　　　　　　　　State/Province　　　　　　　Zip/Postal Code

Mail to the Reader Service:
IN U.S.A.: P.O. Box 1341, Buffalo, N.Y. 14240-8531
IN CANADA: P.O. Box 603, Fort Erie, Ontario L2A 5X3

Get 4 FREE REWARDS!

We'll send you 2 FREE Books plus 2 FREE Mystery Gifts.

JUDE DEVERAUX
As You Wish

SUSAN MALLERY
Sisters Like Us

WHAT DOESN'T KILL
CHRISTINA DODD

LISA UNGER

FREE
Value Over
$20

Both the **Romance** and **Suspense** collections feature compelling novels written by many of today's bestselling authors.

YES! Please send me 2 FREE novels from the Essential Romance or Essential Suspense Collection and my 2 FREE gifts (gifts are worth about $10 retail). After receiving them, if I don't wish to receive any more books, I can return the shipping statement marked "cancel." If I don't cancel, I will receive 4 brand-new novels every month and be billed just $6.99 each in the U.S. or $7.24 each in Canada. That's a savings of at least 13% off the cover price. It's quite a bargain! Shipping and handling is just 50¢ per book in the U.S. and $1.25 per book in Canada.* I understand that accepting the 2 free books and gifts places me under no obligation to buy anything. I can always return a shipment and cancel at any time. The free books and gifts are mine to keep no matter what I decide.

Choose one: ☐ **Essential Romance** (194/394 MDN GNNP)   ☐ **Essential Suspense** (191/391 MDN GNNP)

Name (please print)

Address   Apt. #

City   State/Province   Zip/Postal Code

Mail to the **Reader Service:**
IN U.S.A.: P.O. Box 1341, Buffalo, NY 14240-8531
IN CANADA: P.O. Box 603, Fort Erie, Ontario L2A 5X3

Want to try 2 free books from another series! Call 1-800-873-8635 or visit www.ReaderService.com.

---

*Terms and prices subject to change without notice. Prices do not include sales taxes, which will be charged (if applicable) based on your state or country of residence. Canadian residents will be charged applicable taxes. Offer not valid in Quebec. This offer is limited to one order per household. Books received may not be as shown. Not valid for current subscribers to the Essential Romance or Essential Suspense Collection. All orders subject to approval. Credit or debit balances in a customer's account(s) may be offset by any other outstanding balance owed by or to the customer. Please allow 4 to 6 weeks for delivery. Offer available while quantities last.

Your Privacy—The Reader Service is committed to protecting your privacy. Our Privacy Policy is available online at www.ReaderService.com or upon request from the Reader Service. We make a portion of our mailing list available to reputable third parties that offer products we believe may interest you. If you prefer that we not exchange your name with third parties, or if you wish to clarify or modify your communication preferences, please visit us at www.ReaderService.com/consumerschoice or write to us at Reader Service Preference Service, P.O. Box 9062, Buffalo, NY 14240-9082. Include your complete name and address.

STRS20

ReaderService.com has a new look!

We have refreshed our website and we want to share our new look with you. Head over to ReaderService.com and check it out!

On ReaderService.com, you can:

- Try 2 free books from any series
- Access risk-free special offers
- View your account history & manage payments
- Browse the latest Bonus Bucks catalog

Don't miss out!

If you want to stay up-to-date on the latest at the Reader Service and enjoy more Harlequin content, make sure you've signed up for our monthly News & Notes email newsletter. Sign up online at ReaderService.com.

INTRODUCING OUR
FABULOUS NEW COVER LOOK!
COMING FEBRUARY 2020

Find your favorite series in-store, online or subscribe to the Reader Service!